ANGELA M. SANDERS

The *Lanvin* *Murders*

WK

WIDOW'S KISS

This book is a work of fiction. The names, characters, places, and incidents are either products of the author's imagination or are used fictitiously.

Copyright © 2014 by Angela M. Sanders

All rights reserved. This book or any portion thereof may not be reproduced or used in any manner whatsoever without the express written permission of the publisher except for the use of brief quotations in a book review.

Printed in the United States of America

First Printing, 2014

ISBN 978-0-9904133-0-1 (pbk.)
ISBN 978-0-9904133-1-8 (e-book)

Widow's Kiss
P.O. Box 82488
Portland, OR 97282

www.WidowsKiss.com

Book design: Eric Lancaster

For everyone who hazards the bins at thrift shops and flips lovingly through the racks at vintage clothing stores to find that one-in-a-million chiffon cocktail dress or pair of patent leather mules: You look fabulous, darlings.

The Lanvin Murders

Chapter 1

Joanna Hayworth's fingers dipped into silver-brown fur. She eased the heavy coat out of its plastic bag and laid it over the bench in the middle of her vintage clothing store.

Her eyes widened. It couldn't be, could it?

She lifted her gaze to the elderly woman standing across from her. "Where did you get this?"

"Oh, I've had it for a while," Marnie said in a voice roughened by cigarettes.

Red leather barely a palm's width encircled the fur coat's low waist and cuffs. Definitely 1930s. Joanna's heart began to beat faster. She pulled the coat open. Not the original lining, but nicely done. Holding her breath, she opened the garment further, showing the label sewn inside the collar. Yes, there it was. The words "Jeanne Lanvin" and the tiny image of a mother and child dancing. A real pre-war Lanvin coat, here in her store. Amazing.

"You've never brought in something like this to sell before. The truth, Marnie. Where did you get it?"

"What? An old boyfriend gave it to me. I never wore it much — it didn't fit me that great. Doesn't matter now anyway, he's dead." Marnie lost focus for a moment, then returned her attention to the business at hand. "So, do you think it's worth anything?"

"It's a little beat up, or I'd say you should try to sell it at auction. You could probably get more online than I can pay you."

"I don't care about that, I just need the cash."

Typical. As far as Joanna could tell, Marnie's retirement consisted of a house an old lover bought for her back in her heyday as a show-girl—more than fifty years ago—and her wardrobe, which she was selling to Tallulah's Closet by the bag load.

"I've got more things by the door. I—" The older woman started coughing, a deep cough that wracked her small body.

"Oh Marnie, sit down. You really should see a doctor. Want a drink of water?"

Marnie took deep breaths and put a hand to her chest.

"Just sit there. I'll get the bag."

"I'm fine," she said when she could finally speak. "Doctor. Ha. Anyway, you're the one who should be seeing someone, and I'm not talking about any doctor, either."

Marnie would change the subject, and she would have to get personal about it. But Joanna had long figured out how to navigate her crankier moods. If she wasn't telling Joanna to get out more, she was putting down the store's decor, telling her the tiki bar she repur-posed as a cashier's stand was tacky, or that the chipped chandeliers, lovingly gathered at estate sales, should match.

"I know. I read too much, am too set in my ways, all I care about is old clothes, blah blah blah." Joanna pulled open the new bag of clothes. "What else did you bring?"

After the Lanvin coat, visions of wasp-waisted dinner suits and Schiaparelli gowns filled Joanna's head. Her eye caught a corner of pink chiffon that looked promising. She pulled a peony-colored cocktail dress from the bag, shaking it by the shoulders to smooth its wrinkles. Definitely a keeper. Doris Day might have worn a dress like this on the town with Rock Hudson. Doris would have carried a white patent leather clutch and worn matching kitten heels — not too high, she was tall — with a bow at the toes. The rest of the clothes in the bag were 1960s day wear: cotton blouses in pastels and flower-patterned shifts.

She wasn't going to get rich running a vintage clothing store, but the excitement of sorting through a rack of dresses at an estate sale or digging into a bin of clothes at a thrift store made it all worth it. She loved laying a cotton sundress over a chair and imagining its original life on a woman who rode in fin-tailed convertibles. A suit with padded shoulders and wool the color of a sunset brought to mind courthouse weddings during the war, when the bride would have pinned a gardenia on her suit jacket. She marveled at the stacks of gloves, still white and so small, that people brought in from their grandmother's closets. There was so much grace in the past. So much elegance.

"Wake up. I'm talking to you." Marnie nodded at the box. "Well, what do you think?"

Joanna did a quick calculation. The dry cleaning bills would be high. "I can give you a hundred dollars for the lot, including the coat."

"Great." Marnie stood, stone-faced.

"I'll write you a check — "

"No. Cash. Please."

That figures, Joanna thought. Marnie seemed to live on a strictly cash basis, but so many people used credit cards that she'd be lucky if there were fifteen dollars in the till. "Could you come back tomorrow? I have to be at the store all day today, but I'll go to the bank in the morning."

"All right. Tomorrow, then." She fished in her shoulder bag, drawing out a pack of cigarettes. "You like that coat, don't you?"

"It's gorgeous." Nineteen-thirties Lanvin. Joanna still couldn't believe her luck.

Marnie's expression softened. "It means a lot to me, too. The man who gave it to me, he was special. Not like the rest."

"I wonder where he got it?" He couldn't have bought it for Marnie new. She would have been a baby when Lanvin showed the coat.

"Don't know. He didn't have a lot of money—at least, not then. The coat belonged to someone in his family." She touched the red elbow patch with reverence. "See that? He told me it's antelope."

Marnie had never been sentimental about the clothes she'd sold before. "Are you sure you're ready to give it up? Maybe you'd like to keep it." Joanna drew a finger down the coat's fox sleeve. Even owning the Lanvin for a few minutes was something.

Marnie shook her head. "No, no. I've kept it a good long time. Now I want you to have it. Make it earn a little for the store."

"I'm doing all right. But thank you, that's so sweet."

Marnie turned toward the front window. "The neighborhood's picking up, anyway. I see that the theater is for rent."

Portland's Clinton Street neighborhood had taken a decided turn for the better in the few years Joanna had owned Tallulah's Closet. The aluminum awning place had become a video store renting cult movies, and a restaurant touting local, organic food had replaced the dictaphone repair shop.

Marnie lay a dry hand on Joanna's. "You stick with it, honey. I just want to see you do well, you know." She leaned forward and whispered, "You're family."

Surprise—and warmth—washed over Joanna. Hugging Marnie

was like embracing a sack of bird bones. "That means a lot to me. Thank you."

The older woman stepped away, looking down. "Someday I'll tell you more about him, the man who gave me the coat."

"I'd like that."

Marnie paused as if to say something else, then seemed to change her mind. "Tomorrow, then." She stepped to the sidewalk and lit her cigarette.

Joanna returned to the Lanvin coat and touched its collar. It was going to need a good airing out to shed the cigarette smoke. Despite the August heat, she decided to display it in the shop's front window. Before dressing the mannequin, she went to the stereo and put on Mel Tormé. People kept telling her she should subscribe to some kind of streaming music service, but she didn't see the point when she had stacks of records and a perfectly good turntable. She wasn't planning to give up her rotary phone or handwritten receipts, either.

While Tormé sang "It's Too Darned Hot," she pulled a pale blue satin 1930s nightgown from the racks and slid it over the mannequin's body, then clipped a quadruple strand of Czech crystals around its neck. Finally she draped the Lanvin coat over the mannequin's shoulders.

She boosted the mannequin onto the platform at the front window, then went outside to survey her work. Not bad, she thought. If I were Jean Harlow, I'd be intrigued. She couldn't picture Marnie wearing the coat—it would dwarf her. Marnie seemed to have shrunk even in the past year.

The coat sat slightly crooked on the mannequin's shoulders. She stepped back up on the platform and adjusted the hem, straightening the fox trim. As she tugged, she heard a soft "plink." A small brass key had fallen through the coat's frayed lining onto the floor.

She turned the key in her palm. "U. S. Bank" was engraved on it. Probably a safe deposit box key. Funny, Marnie seemed more the type to hide things under her mattress. Joanna went to the door and looked up the street, hoping to catch her smoking one last cigarette, but Marnie was nowhere to be seen.

When the phone rang later that afternoon, Joanna was helping a customer try on a daisy-sprigged 1940s dress. She was out of breath when she answered. "Hello, Tallulah's Closet."

"I need the coat back." Marnie didn't introduce herself, but there was no need. Her ragged voice gave her away.

Joanna's heart sank. "I thought you said…"

"I need it. Can you bring it to me now?"

It was barely three in the afternoon. "Now? No. I have customers. The store doesn't close for three more hours."

"But I—"

Joanna gave an exasperated sigh. "Look, I won't sell it. I promise. It's not going anywhere." She'd keep it on display, though. No harm in that. Maybe it would lure in a few more customers. "Aren't you coming in tomorrow? I won't have your money for the rest of things until then, anyway."

"Yes, but I need the coat now."

What had got into her? Joanna was used to a little orneriness, but this was ridiculous. "I'm sorry, but I really can't. Tonight's the twilight rummage sale at the Eagles Lodge, but I could stop by afterward, say about eight o'clock?" At the last rummage sale she'd scored a pile of

Vera silk scarves in 1970s colors. They practically flew out of the store.

"Today. I said today." Marnie coughed.

Joanna held the phone away from her ear until the coughing subsided. "I'm telling you it won't work," she said sharply. Too sharply. Her voice softened. "Oh Marnie, if I could, I'd bring it back right away. But it will be here first thing in the morning, and I'll see you then. Right?"

No reply.

"Right? Marnie?"

She'd hung up.

Chapter 2

"That's it, you've almost got it," Joanna said to the teenage girl wobbling across the carpet in a pair of black patent stilettos. "Step on the ball of your feet and loosen your hips. Right. Like that. See, it's not so hard."

"These shoes are awesome." The girl stopped in front of the gilt mirror in the back of the store. She posed, hips turned to the side, one leg bent, and examined herself. Mid-thigh down she was Betty Grable, but the rest was straight from the mall.

Joanna never ceased to be amazed at how a flattering dress, or, in this case, a sculpted shoe, could transform a person. Without knowing it, the wearer stood straighter and a new seductiveness emerged. The girl in the stilettos was just discovering her power. "Ten minutes of practice a night, and you'll walk like you were born in them."

As she rang up the shoes, the bell at the door jangled. Joanna glanced up. Not Marnie. "Hi, Apple," she said. "Hey, why don't you leave the door open? Maybe it will cool it down in here a little."

Rain drummed steadily on the aluminum awning, a rare late-summer shower that filled the air with the scent of humid ozone. Apple's bangles clinked as she lodged the doorstop, a rock-filled Beatles boot, in front of the door.

Joanna handed the stilettos, now wrapped in pink tissue and

tucked into a zebra-print bag, to the girl. "Goodbye, and remember, walk from your hips."

Apple dropped her fringed leather tote behind the cash register and went straight for the front window. "Where did you get that coat?" She lifted the mannequin from the window platform to the ground. "This is fabulous. A little worn, kind of smelly, but outrageous. No wonder — a Lanvin." She peeled the coat off the mannequin. "Hmm. Weird energy."

"You always say that." She had been having "feelings" about things since they were girls together and Apple's name was Daphne.

"Not like this. Not good." She draped the coat over her shoulders for only a moment before shrugging it off. "Definitely weird energy."

Joanna took the coat from Apple. "Marnie brought it yesterday. Said it belonged to an old beau. It was too good not to put in the window, even with the heat." She ran her fingers through the sleeve's fox cuff. "A moujik-style — that's Russian peasant — coat. I found a photo in one of my old *Harper's Bazaars*. See the red patches? Practically Courrèges. Or Fendi."

Apple shook her head. "There's something off about this coat, gorgeous as it is."

Joanna wasn't going to let Apple's intuition mar the glory of vintage Lanvin. She put the coat back on the mannequin and posed it in the window. "Her beau must have come from money." She rested her hands on her hips and admired the coat from its rear. "Listen to this — she called me yesterday afternoon and demanded the coat back. Wanted me to bring it to her right away. I told her it would have to wait until this morning, but she hasn't shown up."

"She sold it to you then demanded it back? Strange."

"Oh, I don't blame her. I'd have a hard time giving up the coat, too.

But she insisted that she get it back stat, that I bring it to her. And now she doesn't even care enough to show up for it or the money I owe her."

"It's only been a day."

"I know. But you should have heard her. I've tried calling, and she doesn't answer."

"Give her a week and keep trying to call. Who knows? Maybe she's out of town or on a bender or something."

"I worry about her. You should see her. Skin and bones." Joanna returned to the tiki bar and filed the receipt for the stilettos in a cigar box. "Anyway, what brings you in? Your shift isn't until Friday."

"Gavin has a friend with a band playing at the Doug Fir at nine. Come with me?"

"Standing in a crowded room for three hours listening to some skinny, bearded guy whining about his love life?" A good dinner, hot bath, and early to bed sounded so much better. Besides, she had just started reading a biography of Cleopatra, and her *Gilda* rental was due back at the video store tomorrow.

"I knew you'd say that." She folded her arms. "Come on, Jo. What are you going to do? Sit home alone all your life? You're such a hermit."

"Listen, I'm with people all day at the store, and I like some time to myself in the evenings." Apple had touched a nerve. Joanna knew some people might say she was in a rut, but if so it was a contented rut with good food, engrossing novels, and the occasional icy Martini.

"Fine. No need to get so defensive."

"I'm not." Joanna changed tactics. "I would go, but I think I'd better check on Marnie."

"Really?" Apple looked her straight in the eyes. "Do you even know where she lives?"

Strangely, she didn't. All their interactions had happened at the store. Come to think of it, there wasn't a lot she did know about Marnie. "Maybe she fell and can't get to the phone. I should look in on her." Although if her address wasn't in the phone book, she didn't know how she'd track her down.

As she spoke, Joanna fidgeted with the worn pearl ring on her middle finger. Tiny rubies flanked the pearl. Her grandmother's ring. It wasn't worth much, but Joanna wouldn't leave the house without it.

The doorbell rang again and what looked to be a mother and daughter came in, probably planning ahead for a homecoming dance. The mother lagged back, clutching her sensible handbag, while the daughter strode confidently toward a rack of tulle-skirted prom dresses.

Apple smiled at the customers, then turned toward Joanna. "All right. Can't blame me for trying. If you change your mind, give me a call. Don't worry too much about Marnie. I'm sure she's fine."

As Joanna pulled a lemon-yellow Emma Domb crinolined gown from the rack, her thoughts stayed with Marnie. She had been so determined to get the coat back, and Joanna had never known her to wait around when someone owed her cash.

"What size shoes do you wear?" Joanna asked the daughter. "You really should try the dress with heels, see where the hem hits your calf."

"An eight," said the daughter.

"Not too high, though," the mother said.

Joanna grabbed a pair of silver evening sandals by their ankle straps. Maybe Apple was right. Marnie was probably fine, and Joanna was making too big a deal about it. She helped the daughter zip up her dress. Yellow was a trying color, but it suited the girl's porcelain complexion and crow-black hair.

She'd try calling Marnie again tonight, from home. Yes, that's what she'd do. Maybe this time she'd answer.

.

The next morning, Joanna prepared for work. When exactly four minutes were up, she plunged the handle on the French press and poured her morning coffee into a thermos. She wrapped a Spode teacup in a linen napkin embroidered with bees and tucked both the cup and thermos into a tote bag. The opera length black gloves from *Gilda* stuck in her mind. If she could get her hands on a few pairs, they'd sell like hotcakes.

The tote bounced gently against her hips as Joanna walked the scant five minutes to Tallulah's Closet. She needed the extra boost of caffeine. After watching the movie, she'd stayed up past midnight reading. Marnie hadn't answered her calls. Joanna had toyed with the idea of somehow finding her house and visiting her in person, but Marnie was a private person and wouldn't appreciate an unannounced drop in, anyway. Or so Joanna had convinced herself.

The morning was dim, and it was still raining off and on. People ducked in and out of the corner café, but the other businesses along Clinton Street wouldn't open for another hour, when the lunch trade began. Joanna rounded the corner, raised her head to take in the view of Tallulah's Closet's front window, and halted in her tracks.

Where was the Lanvin coat?

The front window's mannequin stood slightly turned, the bottom half of its silk slip reflecting light from the street. Surely she'd left the coat on the mannequin at the end of the day. She was a stickler for making sure the window always looked good. But maybe a customer had tried it on and left it near the dressing rooms. Maybe.

Frowning, Joanna unlocked the door and flicked on the front light switches. She set her tote on the store's center bench and glanced toward the dressing rooms at the rear. No coat there. Panic rose. Could it have been stolen? She rushed to the tiki bar to look for the cash box and let out a sigh of relief. The Lanvin coat lay heaped on the floor. She must have forgotten that she'd put it on the rack behind the counter, and at some point during the night it slipped off its hanger. She grasped the heavy coat by its shoulders to fold over her arm then instantly let it fall to the ground behind her.

Under the coat lay Marnie, face up, eyes open. Dead.

Chapter 3

Joanna grabbed the edge of the jewelry counter for support. Breathe deeply, she told herself. Stay calm. She took a shuddering breath and stepped again behind the tiki bar. Her heart clutched. Yes, definitely Marnie.

The skin on the older woman's face was clean and translucent white, and her open eyes, glassy, stared to the left. Thin wisps of hair clung to her scalp. She hadn't ever seen Marnie without a wig or makeup. She looked so small, vulnerable. Hands trembling, Joanna stepped away. She didn't have a lot of experience with death. Once on a high school choir trip the school bus passed an accident, and she had seen a man's body hanging out the driver's side of a car. Then, of course, there was her grandmother. Naturally, they didn't have an open casket. Couldn't.

Joanna couldn't force herself to reach across Marnie's body for the phone under the tiki bar. She ran next door to Dot's Cafe and banged on the door. Maybe someone was setting up for lunch. The prep cook greeted her with a smile, but Joanna shoved past him and ran towards the phone. She returned to Tallulah's Closet a few minutes later and sank on the bench, gaze firmly averted from Marnie's body.

A rapping on the door jolted her to her feet. A uniformed policeman and policewoman stood outside the door. "Back there." Joanna gestured toward the tiki bar. They pushed past her.

An unmarked Crown Victoria pulled up behind the cruiser. A tall man wearing a bolo tie and cowboy boots got out. He dropped his cell phone in his pocket and slammed the car door behind him.

In the store, he extended a hand. "Detective Foster Crisp." He approached the tiki bar and stopped short of the Lanvin coat, a pile of fur and wool now pushed to the side. "What's that?"

"A coat. It was covering her." Joanna reached to pick it up, but the detective stepped in front of her.

"Please, don't touch it. We'll need to check it for evidence." The police behind the tiki bar parted as the detective knelt beside the body. After a few minutes, he rose. He placed a hand in the small of Joanna's back and directed her back to the red velvet bench.

"You know the victim?" he asked.

"Yes, Marnie. Marnie Evans." Joanna didn't want to leave her, but at the same time she was glad to be distracted. "How did she die?"

"Crowley?" Crisp asked one of the policemen.

"Can't say until the autopsy. Nothing obvious."

"Sit," the detective said and patted the bench. A chunk of turquoise anchored his bolo tie. Its silver-tipped ends dangled as he leaned forward. "This is your store, is it?"

She nodded, still casting anxious glances behind the tiki bar.

"Tell me what happened. Start from the beginning."

Joanna recounted the last quarter hour, from noticing the Lanvin coat missing to trembling over the phone at Dot's.

"Did —" Detective Crisp looked at his notebook " — Ms. Evans have a key to the store?"

"No. I don't know how she got in. The door was locked when I got here."

"Only a handle lock. Easy enough to pick. I'm surprised you don't have better security, actually. But there's no reason she would be at the store?"

"Closed? No." She bit her lip. "That coat, the one that covered her. She sold it to me the day before yesterday. That same day she called to say she wanted it back. I told her she could come by yesterday morning to get it, but she never did." She wouldn't have come back to get it by herself, would she?

The detective made a few notes. "Tell me about Ms. Evans."

While a policeman stepped away from Marnie and punched numbers in his cell phone, Detective Crisp kept his attention on Joanna. From where Joanna sat she could only see one of Marnie's slipper-clad feet.

"I've known her not quite a year. She sells—sold me—some of her old clothes."

"Tell me about it," the detective said.

The day Marnie first appeared the fall before, the store had been quiet. Joanna had looked up from a skirt she was mending to find Marnie standing at the door with a cardboard box at her feet.

"Do you buy old clothes?" she'd asked.

"Yes, I do." Although Marnie's appearance—baggy pants, water-proof jacket—didn't suggest a glamour puss, Joanna had enough experience to know the box could contain anything from 1930s silk nighties to an old wedding gown to a stack of batik hippie skirts.

"Got a few things I don't need anymore." Marnie had pulled a dress from the box and held it up by its shoulders. It was Nile green and covered with an intricate pattern of bugle beads that gleamed in the dim morning light. From its length and strong nylon lining, Joanna guessed it was from the mid-1960s. She could imagine a guest wearing it on the Merv Griffin Show. Maybe Nancy Sinatra.

While Joanna was trying to figure out how to flush the cigarette smoke out of the dress, Marnie had commented on her grandmother's ring. She took Joanna's hand in her dry palm and touched the ring's pearl. Then she mentioned she had a few other things she could bring in, as well.

Early on she had dreaded when Marnie came to the store because she was so difficult to talk to. But as they got to know each other, their relationship eased. Marnie might sit on the red velvet bench in the center of the store, the bench Joanna sat on now, and recount her days dancing at Mary's Club. She described her dresses, the nightclubs she visited, and laughed about some of the people she used to know. One snowy afternoon when the store was deserted, she'd even brought Martinis from the bar next door to sip while they sorted through some Ship 'N Shore capris and blouses. Joanna had come to look forward to Marnie's visits.

How could she explain to the detective the friendship that had sprung up between them? She tried to think of a polite way to put it. "We had a sort of understanding, but I'm not sure Marnie was the type to have a lot of close friends."

"Maybe the type to have enemies?" The detective looked alert again.

"I didn't say that." Was he trying to confuse her? "Why, do you think someone killed her?"

"Is there a reason she'd be murdered?"

"No, I mean, not that I know of." She grabbed a scarf on a nearby display and began folding it meticulously, willing her hands to be calm. "But I don't know why she'd go out in house shoes."

The detective glanced at Marnie's feet. "Getting a little confused, was she?"

Joanna shook her head. "She had a bad cough and could be curt, but she was still sharp. Nothing wrong there."

"I see." Detective Crisp's tone was indifferent. "Anything else?" he prompted. The policeman who had been on the phone was engrossed in figuring out the latch on a lizard handbag.

"No. Nothing."

"You're sure?"

"Yes." His gaze unnerved her.

He jotted a few things in his notebook. Joanna couldn't read his upside down, scratchy writing. "You don't have any plans to leave town right away, do you?" he asked.

"No. I'll be here." The detective couldn't possibly think she killed Marnie. Could he?

The policeman had abandoned the lizard clutch and was examining a marabou boa. Detective Crisp had to tap him on the shoulder to get his attention. "Sorry. The medical examiner will be here in a few minutes, and you can get back to business."

"Crisp, look at this." The policewoman held the Lanvin coat open with latex-gloved hands. A foot-long cut sliced the lining cleanly a few inches above the hem.

Joanna's jaw dropped. "That wasn't there yesterday. I'm sure of it."

"The lining looks old. Could have frayed. Maybe one of your customers got her heel stuck in it. That happened to my wife once," Detective Crisp said.

"Sure, but not against the grain of the fabric like that. I've seen enough old silk to know shredding from a clean cut. That lining was definitely slit."

Chapter 4

The Lanvin coat hung lifeless from the mannequin's shoulders. Each time it caught Joanna's eye later that day, she remembered Marnie. Remembered the gurney trundling past a rack of skirts. Remembered Marnie's frail shape under the white cover.

A man the landlord had sent to replace the lock on the front door worked quietly. He was tall with sandy brown hair and long, tapered fingers. He wore a tee shirt with an old wool shirt open over it, its sleeves rolled up to the elbows. The odor of raw wood and oil drifted from the front of the store.

She picked up the steamer and ran it under the skirt of a 1940s peach slip, releasing the scent of lavender sachets. She'd shut off the stereo. No music suited her mood. June Christie was too sad, Sarah Vaughn too yearning, Tom Jones too Tom Jones.

The bell jangled as a tall blond man in a business suit entered the store. Her ex. "Hey Jo, I brought you a poster for Chick's rally. Think you could put it in the window?" He set his umbrella near the door. His words rattled the emotion-laden silence. He glanced at the workman. "Am I interrupting something?"

With her foot Joanna clicked off the steamer at its base. "Hi Andrew. No, I just —" She thought about telling him about Marnie, but she didn't want to get into it. Not with him. " —I'm getting a new lock."

Despite the rain, Andrew looked cool and unruffled, more like a tennis pro on his day off than a congressional aide in the heat of a contentious campaign.

"It's stuffy in here," Andrew said. "You should get air conditioning."

"You know how I feel about that. No thanks. Stand by the fan." People were slaves to climate control these days. Why architects began making office buildings with windows that couldn't open was beyond her.

Andrew ignored her advice and stared at the man at the door. Responding to Andrew's attention, the workman stepped forward. "Hi, I'm Paul." He wiped his palm on his jeans and shook Andrew's hand. "A little bit of a mess." He nodded at the pieces of brass at his feet and then glanced at Joanna.

"Is he going to be here long?" Andrew sized up the workman.

What was his deal? He had no reason — or right — to be jealous. He was married now.

Paul unflinchingly returned his gaze. She took a second look at the workman. Not movie star handsome, but there was something about him.

"I don't know. As long as it takes, I guess," Joanna said. She noted Andrew's expression and changed the subject. "Why are you delivering posters, anyway? Don't you have volunteers to do that?"

"Sure, but I was in the area and thought I'd drop by. Chick asked, actually. He said this is an up-and-coming neighborhood." He set the poster on the bench at the center of the store and sat down. "I left you a message the other day, but you never called back."

"It's been busy." She clicked the steamer on again. If Andrew was going to stick around, she might as well get some work done. "How's the campaign going?"

He grimaced. "The polls are close. Mayer is arguing that Chick's too old, that he's too much of an insider, all the standard bull. In the Senate, though, he'll be far from the oldest. And he's definitely the best candidate, policy-wise."

"You don't have to convince me."

"He's a little freaked out, actually. We've stepped up the campaigning. It's been a lot of running around. I think last night was the only night we've had off for weeks." He picked a piece of lint from his pants. "You're coming to the rally on Tuesday, aren't you?"

"I don't know. Apple has the day off and I'd have to close the store."

"Only for a few hours. You have to come. Tell Apple and Gavin to come, too. It's a big deal." His cell phone buzzed, and he glanced at its screen. "Got to go. But I'll see you at the rally." He rose from the bench and gave Joanna a quick peck on the cheek as if the matter were settled. "Arpège, right? Smells nice."

"Thanks." She'd chosen the Lanvin perfume in honor of the coat. Now she didn't think she'd ever wear it again.

He picked up his umbrella by the door. He turned and smiled again, but his smile dropped off when he caught sight of the workman. Andrew had so many good qualities. He could be so engaging, so charming. If only he weren't so self-absorbed. She had spent three years thinking "if only" before deciding to pull the plug.

The workman put down his screwdriver as Andrew left. "The lock works now, but I need to get longer bolts to replace the ones I put in today. I'll be back tomorrow, if that's all right with you."

As he came closer, she smelled the soap he'd used to shower that morning. She opened her mouth, but no words came out. Must be lack of sleep. "Your shirt looks like an old Pendleton," was all she could think to say.

He slipped off the shirt to look at the label. The tee shirt he wore underneath showed strong shoulders and a tiny scar on his upper arm. She saw half-dressed women all day at the store, but this felt distinctly — different. Apple would have a heyday if she knew he was here. Paul slung the shirt over an arm. "Yeah, you're right. It was my uncle's." He smiled, revealing a gap between his front teeth. "Well, until later then."

Her gaze followed him out the door and past the front window. Where it landed, again, on the Lanvin coat.

Joanna closed the store an hour early. True to the twists of weather that make up a Portland summer, the rain had stopped, and the sky shone brilliant blue. She lived in what a real estate agent might have once called a "G. I. dream house": two tiny bedrooms, a bathroom barely larger than something found on a train, but a comfortable kitchen and a living room with a fireplace.

"I'm home. Godfrey, prepare my Martini," she commanded the imaginary butler. "And make it snappy. I've had one hell of a day."

She tossed her purse on the down cushions of the chaise longue near the front window and piled the mail on the end table next to a stack of Depression-era *Vogues*. She kicked one shoe, then the next, across the faded oriental carpet, and saluted the mishmash of amateur portraits on one wall. "Hello, Aunt Vanderburgh," she said to a pastel of a tight-lipped woman.

In the bedroom, Joanna slid off her dress and hung it on a satin-padded hanger. She pulled a loose 1940s housedress over her head. Its cotton skirt swished about her legs as she made her way to the kitchen.

She took a hefty ribeye steak from the freezer. With a pile of mashed potatoes and a handful of green beans from the garden, her dinner would be as close as she could get to Valium on a plate. No pre-fab meal here. People were always surprised when they found out she refused to have a microwave or even a cell phone. If Carole Lombard didn't need them, why should she? Joanna laid the steak out to thaw.

Her hand paused over a salt shaker that had belonged to her grandmother. On the face of it they couldn't be more different, but her grandmother was a lot like Marnie. Like Marnie, her grandmother knew how to take care of herself. When Joanna was six years old, after her grandparents had taken her in, she had heard the saying that "dogs are a man's best friend," but also that "diamonds are a girl's best friend." She complained to her grandmother she understood how dogs could be a friend, but wasn't claiming diamonds as a friend going too far?

Her grandmother had put down her dish towel and laughed. "Honey," she'd told her, "If you've got a diamond you can buy all the dogs you want." Could have come straight from Marnie's mouth.

Joanna's smile faded. The accident. After her grandmother's death, her grandfather had sunk into a depression. She would sit for hours reading in their closet with the comfort of brightly colored house dresses hanging around her, still redolent of Moondrops perfume. She'd tamped down the memory of the accident for years. Now, after this morning at the store, it was back. Without thinking, her fingers sought her grandmother's pearl ring.

Joanna pulled a saucepan from the row of well-used pans hanging above the stove and filled it with water. She carried a porcelain bowl to the backyard and pinched green beans from vines covering a bamboo teepee. Back inside, while the potatoes boiled she poured a glass of Languedoc and set the table with a linen napkin and a plate painted with buttercups.

Why did Marnie come to the store after hours? Yes, she was frail, but would she really have pulled the Lanvin coat over herself and died? She'd wanted the coat back desperately, but had to have been unhinged to break into the store to get it. At least, that's what the detective seemed to think.

Maybe if Joanna had given back the Lanvin coat when Marnie asked, she'd still be alive. Or if she'd only checked in on Marnie when she told Apple she would. With a pang she remembered their last, sharp words. She wished her last interaction with Marnie could have been that morning when she had sold her the coat. She'd been so sweet. "You're family," she'd said.

Now Marnie was dead.

The detective had warned her not to leave town. Her stomach churned, but she suppressed the thought of the autopsy until no emotion, not even curiosity, was left.

As a girl, she hadn't cried at her grandmother's funeral, either. After the service, a handful of relatives, including her father who had driven all night from Colorado, gathered at her uncle's house. Joanna had sat in the living room and read a book her father brought for her while the adults talked quietly in the kitchen. It had been years since she'd thought about that day.

Joanna wandered to the stereo and slid an LP of Schubert lieder from its sleeve. "For you, Aunt Vanderburgh." She nodded at the portrait. The tenor's voice wound through the accompanying piano.

That night, Joanna, full of beef and red wine, slept without dreaming.

Chapter 5

Fridays were Apple's day to work at the store and Joanna's day to find new stock. Estate sales were her favorite part of owning a vintage clothing store, and today they'd be a perfect distraction. This morning she was bound for a sale at a house high on Terwilliger Boulevard. She folded a few large bags and tucked them under her arm — estate sales never seemed to have enough bags. She filled her travel mug with coffee and was on her way while the sun still rose behind Mount Hood.

The sale wouldn't start for a few hours, but as she expected, a line had already formed at the door of the house. The people closest to the door were arguing about who'd arrived first. She wondered if they would be standing in front of Marnie's house sometime soon. Her throat tightened. She didn't know if Marnie had anyone in her life to take care of her estate. Or even to arrange a funeral.

"Hi Susan, hello," Joanna greeted a few of the estate sale regulars. She spotted Nora's beehive hairdo further up the line and made a mental note to get to the perfume while Nora was waylaid by costume jewelry, otherwise Nora would snag it all for her case at the antiques mall. Ben, an elegantly dressed man with a new Range Rover parked down the block, cased the outside of the house, trampling asters as he peered into the bedroom windows. She didn't have to worry about competition from him since he'd be slapping his "Sold to Ben Cub Interiors" stickers only on furniture.

In fact, except for one rumpled man studying a textbook, she recognized everyone. Just then, a whippet-thin blonde, take-out coffee cup in hand, strolled up to the student.

"Eve," Joanna said under her breath. Damn.

The student shut his textbook and looked eagerly at the woman, who handed him a twenty-dollar bill and said a few words. He continued to smile at her while she took his place in line and ignored his attention. He slumped off the lawn.

Now Joanna would really have to be on the alert, or Eve would snatch the best clothes for her online shop. Given the chance, Eve would rip them right off the racks in front of her. And that poor student. Obviously infatuated. Like most men Eve came in contact with.

"Bad form, paying a guy to stand in line for her," someone behind Joanna mumbled.

The line began to move. Joanna handed her number to the sentinel at the door. Gold and black flocked wallpaper lined the entry hall. To the right was the living room, which let on to a terrace with a sweeping view of the city. The low-slung couch and swag lamps suggested cocktail parties during the Kennedy administration. The hostess might have worn a chartreuse gown with marabou trim and carried a tray heavy with glasses and a pitcher of Manhattans.

At estate sales, Joanna was always struck by what people left behind when they died. The golf clubs in the garage, piles of cheap satin sheets in linen closets, and chipped champagne glasses outlined a life. The way an armchair sagged told about the man who watched TV in it for years. The pristine burgundy patent pumps and matching purse, tags still attached, hinted at a life aspired to, if not lived.

Marnie's home would tell similar stories, but Joanna didn't want to think of people tramping through her living room, pawing through her kitchen and bedroom. Marnie had never mentioned anyone who might manage her affairs after she died. It didn't seem right. Did she have a will or an attorney to help sort things out? Her gut ached.

The clothing was in the master bedroom, to the left of the entry hall. The estate sale staff had set up racks at the perimeter of the room. Eve was already there, fingers flying through a box of jewelry. Joanna scooped up a Pierre Cardin cocoa silk dress, a Givenchy black moiré evening coat, and some 1960s day dresses, including a few orange and pink jungle prints from one of Joanna's favorite labels, the Vested Gentress. On the dresser she also found an old bottle of Parure eau de toilette. Into her bag they went.

She glanced over her shoulder at Eve and slipped into the guest room. Eureka! Against the wall stood a rack of winter clothes, including several mod Bonnie Cashin dresses and matching coats, each with its distinctive leather trim. Quickly examining them for moth holes and stains, she flung them over her arm. Eve raced to the rack Joanna had just pillaged and shot her a nasty look. Joanna smiled in return.

"Oh well, I suppose you need the clothes more than I do to keep your store afloat," Eve said. "This stuff isn't that great anyway. My customers expect quality."

Joanna locked eyes with Eve. "I don't know what you're talking about. I just got in a Lanvin coat from the 1930s."

Eve's eyes lit up.

Uh oh. She should have kept her mouth shut. Eve probably had some rich customer in New York who'd shell out whatever it took for the Lanvin. Marnie's Lanvin. No way Eve was getting that coat.

"Really." Eve's voice was studied nonchalance. "It's at Tallulah's Closet now? I might need something like that for my new store."

"I didn't know you were opening a space." Portland could only support so many vintage clothing stores. At least Eve's would probably be in a ritzier part of town and wouldn't compete with Tallulah's Closet. She hoped.

Eve gave Joanna a mysterious smile. "Look, I'd love to talk, but I'd better get to the rest of the sale before the best things are gone." She hoisted her Birkin bag to her shoulder. "Ta."

Joanna shifted the coats over her arm and staggered toward the check-out table. Eve opening a brick and mortar store? Please, no.

While an acned teen wearing a "Chick Remmick for Senate" button tallied her purchases, Joanna sifted through a box of keys and loose jewelry near the checkout. She picked one of them up and thought of the safe deposit box key that fell from the Lanvin coat, then replaced it gently.

There had to be some way she could help Marnie. How, though? It didn't seem right that she should die so alone. At her store. Something was very wrong about the whole situation.

Chapter 6

Hours later, Joanna's ancient Corolla hatchback, nicknamed Old Blue, groaned under its load. Besides the morning's estate sales, at the opera warehouse sale she had scored two large boxes of costumes, including a complete Brünnhilde outfit from *Siegfried* and some of the chorus's costumes from a mid-century take on *Carmen*. The day's haul had been so successful that superstition compelled her to try her luck at the thrift stores along 82nd Avenue, too.

It was just after seven, she was starving, and the closest parking she could find to Tallulah's Closet was three blocks away. She unloaded one box from the hatchback, then impulsively stacked another on top. By looking to the side she could just about make out where she was headed.

As Joanna turned the corner at the end of the block, her heel caught on a crack in the sidewalk. She gasped as she dropped the boxes and fell backward. Ready to hit the pavement, she closed her eyes, but instead fell into flesh. Someone else's arms righted her.

"Whoa! Are you all right?" It was Paul, the workman from the store.

She stepped back quickly. One of the boxes had toppled open, and costumes lay splayed on the sidewalk. "I'm fine." She pulled up her shoulder bag. "Lucky you were here."

"I just finished the front door locks. Thought I'd get some dinner."

"Oh." She stooped to pick up a poodle skirt and stuff it back into a box. "How's it going?"

"Pretty well. Just a little sanding and painting left. It looked like a busy day at the store, too."

She cringed. By now Apple had probably extracted Paul's complete relationship history and named his and Joanna's children. "Apple was, uh, all right?"

"Sure. She was helpful. She even told me I had a shiny aura." They were right outside the Reel M'Inn tavern. Paul helped her put the clothes back into the boxes. With one hand he gestured at the tavern. "Why don't you join me? It's not fancy, but the chicken and jojos are pretty good."

"I really need to get these clothes back to the store. There's even more in my car. I should check in with Apple, too." She glanced at the tavern's battered door. She'd never been inside and suspected there weren't enough antacids in town to stand up to a plate of the Reel M'Inn's jojos. Besides, the rest of last night's steak and a bundle of watercress waited at home to be made into a salad.

"At least come in and have a drink. By the time you're through, traffic for the dinner crowd on Clinton will have let up and you'll be able to park in front of the store." Paul picked up a box of costumes as if the matter were settled and stepped into the Reel M'Inn.

She paused, then followed him. After all, a girl had to eat sometime.

Inside, the small tavern was dark, and smoky. Heads turned as Paul and Joanna entered. Along the bar sat grizzled biker types, and a table of tattooed hipsters played Boggle in the corner.

A large woman with long, black hair polished pint glasses behind the bar. "Well, hello Paul. The usual?" He nodded. "And you?" she asked Joanna.

Joanna didn't like beer much, and the wine looked to be a row of small, screw-top bottles. Not promising. She was debating ordering a plain seltzer when the bartender, who had been watching her deliberations, said, "We have liquor, too."

"Great, could you make me a Martini?"

"This is a bar, honey, and, yes, we make Martinis here. That is, unless you'd prefer a vintage champagne? I can send the butler to the wine cellar." The bartender put down the pint glass and reached below the counter for gin.

Paul laughed. "Five kids at home. She's a little short sometimes. Hey, how did Matt do on his science project?"

"An A-plus — his first ever. He's so proud of that volcano. We had to put it on top of the TV, even though it's half blown up now. Thanks for helping him build it."

Paul glanced at Joanna then back at the bartender. He seemed genuinely pleased.

"Volcano?"

"I'm a man of many talents. Lock installation, volcanos, you name it." He nodded toward a bar-height table with stools on the other side of the room. "Let's sit over there." Fishing hooks and lures were shellacked into the table's surface. Paul set the boxes of costumes behind his chair, against the wall. Creedence Clearwater Revival played in the background.

"Is there a pay phone in here?"

"No cell phone?" He pointed toward the rear of the bar. "Back there, by the bathrooms."

Apple answered on the first ring. "Just checking in," Joanna said. "I cleaned up today. I'll drop off a couple boxes at the store tonight, and we can sort through it all tomorrow." A slender brunette in formfitting jeans smiled broadly when she saw Paul. She crossed the room toward him.

"Sounds good. Not much going on today. The lock guy was there. I'm telling you, that man is hotter than the sun."

"Uh huh." Joanna opened her mouth to tell Apple she had Paul in plain view right then, when the brunette put her hand on Paul's arm. Joanna closed her mouth again.

"Oh — and the Lanvin coat sold."

The coat. Joanna felt a moment of relief, bittersweet as it was. Part of her wanted to keep the coat since it had belonged to Marnie, but it seemed tainted now, too. Besides, Tallulah's Closet needed the money from the sale.

"Where are you?" Apple asked. "Sounds like a bar."

"It is. I'm getting some dinner." The brunette traded a few words with the bartender as she slid her empty glass across the bar, then cast a glance Paul's way as she left. He was studying the shellacked table top. "That's great about the coat. Anything else?"

"Well, I'm not sure it's anything to worry about, but twice today I've seen a stocky guy checking out the store. He was lurking around the front window, and when he saw me looking at him, he pretended to go into Dot's. I saw him again a few minutes later. Something felt really off about him."

"Did he look like, you know — " Vintage clothing stores attracted some unusual types, including a few lingerie fondlers. These were mostly middle-aged men who wanted to caress nylon slips and lace-trimmed camisoles and talk about them. They never bought, and they chewed up time she could be mending or helping customers.

"No, not one of the regular fondlers. And he didn't come in. I just got a desperate vibe."

"I suppose it's nothing to worry about." Apple's "vibes" flowed freely. But then Marnie… "I don't like the sound of it, though. If you see him again, can you let me know? I wrote the detective's number next to the phone."

Joanna replaced the heavy handset and returned to the table, where the bartender was setting down an O'Doul's, a glass, and a surprisingly good looking Martini. "I don't need the glass," Paul said.

"I thought you might want to class it up a bit with your friend here," the bartender said without looking at Joanna.

"I think two orders of chicken and jojos will be class enough, thanks — is that okay?" Paul said to Joanna. The bartender left. "I hope you don't mind that I ordered for you. You look hungry, and I know I am. And you're going to need something in your stomach if you plan on drinking that," he said, pointing to the Martini. "I have a feeling the gin here doubles as paint remover."

She took a sip. "Paint remover or not, it tastes pretty good right now."

Paul leaned back. "Sorry it's taken so long to get the locks done. I've had a couple of other projects going on. I can't believe you went so long with only a lock in the door handle."

"I've been making do for three years now. I guess an extra day doesn't matter."

"Three years — that's a while. How did you come to own a vintage clothing store?"

"It wasn't my first plan. I thought I'd be practical, so I went to law school right out of college. But it didn't feel right."

"What do you mean?"

She considered her answer. "It's hard to explain, but it was like I was living in a strange country, and all my people were on some other island. You know what I mean?"

He leaned forward. "I'm not sure."

"I was doing okay at law school, but I kept thinking, 'Is this all?' After I interned at a law firm that first summer, I knew I couldn't be an attorney." She took another sip of her Martini. "One Friday I went to a party at one of the partner's houses up on Alameda. The living room had a mammoth leather sectional and a postmodern painting that they probably never looked at. The partner kept trotting out cult Cabernets and talking about his latest trip to Italy, but I felt like he didn't really care about either, he just liked having them." She winced remembering what the women in the firm wore: expensive but ill-fitting suits, generic David Yurman necklaces, and loads of chunky highlights in their blown-out hair. The host made a production out of cooking his "special" paella on the grill.

"So, in desperation I took a career test. It was a test where you look at a list of qualities and then rank the ones most important to you. You know, 'organization,' 'idealism' — things like that. One of the qualities was 'beauty.' I'd never thought about it before, but I realized that beauty was really important to me. Not that things have to be beautiful in a traditional way — "

"But that they're beautiful in how they are what they are," Paul said. "I get it."

"Yes." The gin absorbed seamlessly into her bloodstream. It must have been weeks since she'd talked this much, except to Apple. She looked at Paul more closely. "For instance, think about a model home or a hotel lobby. No matter how perfectly everything in them was chosen, often they're not beautiful, because they're not honest. They're dead." Reminded of Marnie, she paused at the last word. "Anyway, I'd always loved old clothing, and one day it occurred to me that it was what I should be doing — finding and selling vintage clothes." Gosh, she couldn't shut up. She raised her glass to her lips again. "Am I boring you?"

"Not at all. Do you want another drink?" Surprisingly, her glass was nearly empty. Paul signaled to the bartender. After a minute she brought a second Martini and another O'Douls along with their food.

"For you," the bartender said as she set a plate of fried chicken in front of Paul, "And for the princess. Bon appetit, as they say in France." Joanna was a little lightheaded and glad to see food to soak up some of the gin, but noticed that the bartender could benefit from a few sessions at Berlitz. And maybe charm school.

Paul looked up, ready to continue the conversation. It was unfair that a man would have such long, thick eyelashes. And her skin felt awfully warm. Must be the alcohol. "So, how did you end up working for my landlord?"

"During summers in high school I used to help out my uncle. He was a woodworker, among other things. Finish work. We replaced pieces of the altar in the old chapel at St. Phillip Neri, for instance. It turned out that I had a knack for it." He fastened his gaze on Joanna. "I know what you mean about beauty. Anyway, he went — away — and my aunt agreed to sell me his shop. So I'm still doing woodwork, but I'm moonlighting to make a little extra money to pay off the shop and some of the tools."

"Woodworking. That must be really satisfying." She leaned back. The Reel M'Inn wasn't such a bad place after all. "The past few days have been hellish," she said, then paused, surprised she had actually spoken.

"And now you need new locks," he prompted.

"Yes, I, it's just…" She didn't know if she wanted to get into it, but the combination of exhaustion, gin, and a sympathetic stranger was hard to resist. "Yesterday I found a body in the store. I guess I'm still a little bit in shock. It was a woman who'd sold me clothes. I can't stop thinking about it and wondering what happened to her."

Paul put down his O'Doul's. "Apple told me a little about this. She was supposed to come back for some money but never did, and you were worried. Then she turned up at the store."

"She was getting up there in years and didn't look very healthy. I don't even know if she has family around here. She lived alone. Plus —"

"Plus what?"

"She wanted me to give her back a coat I sold her, and I told her to wait." She looked up. "I found her under that same coat two days later."

He pulled a handful of napkins from the dispenser and passed some across the table. "That doesn't mean she died because of you."

"The police seem to suspect me. They said they'd be following up." She wiped grease from her fingers.

"Of course. They suspect everyone. You saw her alive a few days ago, so they'll want to ask you questions. Only natural."

She shook her head. "I think I still can't believe it. The last time I saw Marnie she was smoking, looking for cash, complaining about my store's decor — all the usual things." A quick laugh escaped. Her tone grew solemn again. "Then I see her and it's, well…" She took a breath. "I'm really going to miss her." Her voice broke and she looked away. She focused on one of the hipsters who had taken a break from Boggle and was playing a video game involving a rifle and a digital safari. She slowly let out her breath. "I wish I could do something for her."

Paul watched her. "Would it make you feel better to talk to her family, or maybe some friends? It shouldn't be too hard. Portland's such a small town."

She tore a piece of skin from her chicken breast, and steam escaped. Standing outside the store that last day, Marnie had been so tiny and frail. And stubborn. Maybe talking with some of Marnie's friends would be a way to dispel the burning knot in her stomach — not helped, incidentally, by the fried chicken and Martinis. "She used to dance at Mary's Club."

"Mary's Club? No kidding. I bet she had a few stories."

"Oh yeah, every once in a while she'd talk about them. From the sound of it, she was pretty busy in her day. But she never said much about her life now."

"She was older, right? My uncle used to know the manager. They used to work together."

Her focus sharpened. "Really? Maybe he could introduce me. Maybe he knew Marnie."

"It's not really a good time now. He's not really available for visitors." He toyed with his fork, then backed up his chair. It hit one of Joanna's boxes. "Hey, what do you have in these, anyway?"

She pulled open the box next to her and lifted out a pink poodle skirt with a full crinoline. "Costumes from the opera. This one's from a 1950s *Carmen*." She laid it across her lap and unfolded a leather vest and blue pantaloons and held them up. "*Don Giovanni*."

A tall, bearded man undoubtedly with a few pints under his belt came up to their table. "What's this?" He lifted the pantaloons. "May I?"

Joanna looked at the pantaloons and shrugged. They had already survived a month of performances, surely a biker monkeying around in them for a minute couldn't hurt. The pantaloons were made for a man of Pavarotti's dimensions, but the skinny beer drinker pulled them over his jeans and tucked the extra fabric into his waistband. "Hey, look, Ruthie," he yelled to a woman smoking at the bar. "Wait a minute." He hustled to the juke box. A few seconds later the throbbing bass of Michael Jackson's "Billie Jean" flooded the tavern. He began to moonwalk in front of the bar.

Ruthie stubbed out her cigarette and came over to Joanna and Paul's table. "What else have you got? What's in this one?" She reached into the box next to Paul. She tried to pull up one of the poodle skirts, but it was too small, so she buttoned on a nightshirt and stuck a silk rose between her teeth. Then she went to join Don Giovanni by the juke box.

Paul put on Brünnhilde's horned hat. "Hello, dance party."

Before long, Joanna's boxes were empty, and the tavern's patrons were dancing to the BeeGee's "Staying Alive." Only the Boggle players declined to dance. They did, however, push their table closer to the corner to open up the floor.

"Shall we?" Paul asked.

"I don't know — we don't have any more costumes." She'd drunk the second Martini faster than she'd intended.

He leaned forward. "Come on," he whispered.

She laughed. "Oh, all right." She slipped off her 1970s Céline sandals. Too tall for dancing. Paul took her hand and they squeezed into the melee just as the juke box flipped to "Magic Carpet Ride."

The last time she'd danced was years ago, at a wedding with Andrew. He was a competent dancer and proud of it, but he kept checking over her shoulder to make sure someone influential wasn't at the punch bowl. Paul, on the other hand, was relaxed and easy. He touched her briefly on the upper arm to direct her away from the video poker machine behind her. The spot he touched stayed warm.

Before "Magic Carpet Ride" ended, a skinny man with prominent sideburns and arms tattooed from wrists to shoulders cut in front of Paul and grabbed her hands. As he flung her around the room, she wondered if anyone had ever danced swing to Steppenwolf before, especially to such a strong lead. Joanna's head whipped back from the force of his twirl. "Smile, darlin'," he said. "It's not that bad."

The bartender had emerged from behind the bar, hands clapping above her head, and edged up to Paul. After a turn through the highlights of *Saturday Night Fever*, some Led Zeppelin, and a few Marvin Gaye tunes, Joanna returned smiling but exhausted to the table. She was in sore need of something to settle her stomach. The tavern's customers had already stuffed some of the costumes back into the boxes, and the few remaining dancers, seeing Joanna was getting ready to leave, took off their costumes and piled them on a chair. She glanced across the bar to see that the brunette who had greeted Paul earlier had returned and cornered him by the video poker machine.

"Could I get the check?" Joanna asked the bartender, who was pulling a draft beer and still wearing a mantilla from *Carmen*. The bartender reached up to unpin the mantilla. "Please, keep it."

The bartender smiled. "Tonight's dinner is on the house, darling. Now, I'm expecting you back soon. And you, too," she said to Paul, who had left the brunette and joined Joanna.

Joanna reached into her purse to get money for a tip just as Paul was pulling out his wallet. She laughed and put a hand to her warm face. "What do they put in those Martinis, anyway?"

Paul shook his head and smiled, showing the gap between his front teeth. "Let me get the tip. It's the least I can do. It's not every night the Reel M'Inn turns into a disco," he said. "And I'll help you get these clothes to the store."

Paul easily picked up both boxes. Night had fallen, and outside the temperature had dropped just enough that she hugged her bare arms. The rain from the day before had cleared the sky and the moon cast a faint shadow over the bar.

"This is your car?" he asked.

"Uh huh. You sound surprised."

"Your store is so — meticulous. I expected something different. A vintage Bel Air, say, or a Volvo Ghia."

Joanna unlocked the Carolla's hatchback. "I get that a lot."

He stacked the boxes in the car, shoving aside a few bags of estate sale clothes, and sat in the passenger seat. If she lifted her elbow, it would touch his. Sober all at once, she picked through her purse for her keys, avoiding looking at him.

The starter whined, then quit. She turned the key again after giving the engine more gas. This time it started.

As Paul had predicted, parking had freed up on the block in front of Tallulah's Closet. She unlocked the store's front door, and he began to unload the car. A few minutes later, Joanna set the last box in the store. Paul was on the curb, closing the hatchback.

"Thanks for your help," she said. "I can't believe I'm saying this, but thanks for the intro to the glories of broasted chicken, too."

He laughed, then hesitated. Should she say something more? They stood a moment, looking at each other.

"I guess I'd better be going," he said at last. "Wait." He stooped to the sidewalk and picked something up. "We must have dropped this."

It was a frayed silk rose from the *Carmen* wardrobe. As she reached for its green wire stem, her fingers brushed his. Electricity shivered through her body. Crazy. Just like the movies.

He set the rose on the car and gently moved his other hand to her back. His lips slowly and softly met hers. His lower lip slid to her cheek as it lifted.

"Joanna," he said. "I'd like to see you again."

"I..." Adrenalin rattled her bloodstream. For such a chaste kiss, she could hardly breathe. Say yes, say yes, she told herself. Her lips froze.

The streetlight cut across his face, highlighting the curve of his lower lip. "You're probably already seeing someone."

No. No, she wasn't. *Tell him, idiot.* She still couldn't speak. Between fight and flight, flight always won.

"I see. Well, thanks for the evening," he said. "I should be able to finish up the painting tomorrow or the next day, at the latest."

She wanted to say something to keep him there, to try to explain, but she wasn't sure she could.

"Do you need a ride?" she finally managed to get out.

"No. I don't live far." He met her eyes. "Bye." He walked to the end of the block and turned the corner.

Chapter 1

The next morning Joanna rose with a sense of purpose. Paul had been right: finding Marnie's friends and family and telling them about her death was something concrete she could do. What she'd tell them, she didn't know. That Marnie had somehow materialized at Tallulah's Closet dressed for an evening in front of the television and died? That she had no idea why Marnie was there or even what had killed her?

As Joanna put the kettle on to boil, the shock of finding Marnie returned, this time mingled with unease. She still hadn't heard from the police about the autopsy. Detective Crisp's business card lay on the dining room table. Should she call? No. The police could do their job, and she'd do hers. But she'd slip the card in her purse just in case. In the bottom of her purse her fingers touched the silk rose.

"What is this, Auntie V? I mean, honestly. A silk rose. Could it get any cornier?" Joanna asked the portrait. "Besides, it's not like it was some steamy kiss." Joanna swallowed as she remembered the tremor that had passed through her when they touched. "He probably kisses everyone goodbye like that." Like that brunette at the Reel M'Inn. She tossed the rose on the table. Well, no chance of anything happening anyway. She'd scared him off for good.

As for Marnie, the first step was to find her friends. She knew Marnie had danced at Mary's Club and that she'd even had a bit of celebrity in her time. Another potential lead was that an old lover had given Marnie her house. She'd heard the story from Marnie more than once. It was a long shot, but maybe the ex had still been in touch with Marnie or would at least know how to contact her family. Joanna could put her legal research skills to use. Public records should show who owned the house before it was transferred to Marnie, if it actually had been. She could go to the courthouse and try to figure it out, but it was Saturday. She'd have to wait two full days. Or, the computer. Surely that sort of information was online now.

She wrapped her silk kimono closer and brought a cup of coffee to the second bedroom she used as an office. She pushed aside the stack of dry cleaning receipts covering her computer and narrowed her eyes at the closed laptop. Apple had insisted she get one to keep track of expenses, but after one frustrating session with a spreadsheet program she gave it up and returned to her ledger book. To the shock of her professors, she'd made it through college with a typewriter and sheaves of erasable paper she found at Goodwill. The words, struck unevenly on onion skin paper, were so much more beautiful than anything a laser printer could produce.

Joanna took a fortifying sip of coffee and pushed the laptop's power button. It sounded a "ta-da" opening chord and the image of a 1940s rainbow suede Ferragamo platform sandal — a photo Apple installed to lure her to the laptop — filled the screen. The computer's whirr demanded action. What should she do? She dragged a finger on the touchpad, and an arrow circled the screen. One of these programs hooked up to the internet, but which one?

Forget this. She picked up the phone. Letter writing and rotary phones may have largely disappeared, but reference librarians were still on the job.

"Joanna. Long time, no hear. What has it been — a week?" Peter, one of the weekend reference librarians on duty teased her.

"I need to find out who used to own a certain house in town. I have the name here," Joanna said.

"This is a new line of inquiry for you. I was ready for something obscure about stains and rayon crepe." Clicks from a keyboard traveled the telephone line. "All right, give me the name."

Marnie's house had been owned by someone named Donald Cayle and transferred to Marnie in 1962. After a few more prods, Peter came up with more data. Donald Cayle had been the manager at Mary's Club in the 1950s. By the early 1960s his name showed up in business journal articles citing Cayle Investments. Most of his investments were industrial property — warehouses and strips of land along the river where old factories and docks had been torn down. He'd also been a defendant in a few property-related lawsuits and had given the maximum contributions allowed to a number of Republican political campaigns. Joanna wrote his name on an index card and slipped it into her purse.

"Thank, Peter. I owe you," Joanna said.

"No problem, and you don't owe me a thing. I'm wearing the tie tack right now that you brought me last month."

Her first stop would be Mary's Club. After a moment's reflection by the closet — after all, she didn't dress to visit a strip club every day — she chose a crisp cotton blouse with a sweetheart neckline and a late-1950s Mexican cotton skirt with a hand-painted spray of flowers across its hem. She pulled her hair into a loose chignon and grabbed the keys to the Corolla.

*
**

The sign for Mary's Club flashed the outline of a busty woman in pink and blue neon. Surrounding the door was a faded mural of a brunette dressed in a cheongsam who waited for a boat full of sailors disembarking in the background.

She pushed open the naugahyde-padded door and stood for a moment adjusting her vision to the club's interior, dim after the midday's brilliant sunlight. The room was long and narrow and much smaller than the club's front led her to believe. Stale cigarette smoke hung in the air. To her right was a small bar, and just beyond that a stage no bigger than the bed of a pickup truck with a pole on one side where a blonde gyrated absently. A juke box hung on the stage's wall. To the left of the stage opened a hallway Joanna assumed led to the office and dressing rooms for the dancers.

A mural glowed under black light across the back wall. It showed a handful of buff men in tight shirts loading bananas onto a ship. Two women uncannily resembling drag queens adorned the painting's front, one on each side. Joanna raised her eyebrows. No straight man painted that mural.

Lunch was over, and Mary's was nearly empty. A few customers drank beer at the bar, and another, his back to the stage, played video poker.

"What'll you have, honey?" asked the bartender, a matronly woman in a polo shirt with Mary's Club embroidered over the pocket. Both men at the bar turned to stare at Joanna while the dancer punched another song into the juke box.

"I'm here to see the manager, please."

"What for?"

Just as she opened her mouth to reply, a young woman with bright pink hair, wearing a ripped tee shirt and denim miniskirt pushed her way through the front door.

"Hi, Stella," a man at the bar said.

"Leave it." The bartender cast him a warning look.

Stella stopped short at seeing Joanna. "Hey," she said, "What are you doing here?" Stella was a semi-regular at Tallulah's Closet. Joanna knew she was a dancer, but had pegged her for one of the bigger clubs at the edge of town known for cheap steak dinners and a deep stable of girls. Stella sometimes stopped by the store after having a beer or two at Dot's. Usually she was with a man who happily bought her whatever cocktail dress or fake fur coat she fancied.

"So this is where you dance. It's nice to see you. I'm trying to track down an old manager of this place, Donald Cayle."

"Don? Why do you want to see him?"

"You know him? He might know a woman who used to dance here. She died, and I'm trying to find her family, or maybe some friends."

"Really? Don still comes to our summer picnic. Who was the dancer?" Stella leaned against a bar stool.

"This was a while ago. Have you heard of Marnie Evans? I think she danced here mostly in the '50s and maybe the early '60s." Joanna raised her voice as the jukebox switched to a song with a heavier bass.

"No, never heard of her. Talk to Mike, the manager. He might be able to give you Don's phone number. Hey — do you still have that lemon quartz cocktail ring? The one with the big stone?"

"No, it sold. We have a blue one, though, you might like."

Stella shrugged and turned toward the main room of the club. "Follow me." She led Joanna to a small, warm office adorned with a movie-house sized poster of Liza Minelli in *Cabaret*. A thin man sat on a kneeling chair and tapped at his computer. One hand reached for a mug of herbal tea, its tag still dangling over the cup's edge.

"Stella, you're late. Monica has had to run over her shift again, and you know the afternoon crowd is cheap." Then he noticed Joanna. He looked her up and down. "You have a kind of glamour, that's for sure, but you're not our type. Don't get me wrong, but I'm sensing a little stand-offishness. You have experience?"

"No," she said, smoothing her skirt. Did she really look like an aspiring stripper? "That is, I'm not here for a job. I'm trying to get in touch with Don Cayle. One of your old dancers died, and I want to find her friends and family, let them know."

The manager considered Joanna's request as he fiddled with a bracelet of Hindu prayer beads. "We don't give out employees' or formers employees' numbers."

"I get that. But it's about someone who danced here ages ago. Marnie Evans."

"Marnie Evans, huh? No kidding." The manager leaned back and smiled. "She was big in the late 1950s, you know. A headliner. They called her Goldilocks."

"Goldilocks?" Marnie's wig had been ash blonde. She must have been a natural blonde at one time.

"Yeah. Let me show you a picture."

"Mike's kind of the Mary's historian," Stella said.

The manager clicked a few keys on his computer, and a photo of Marnie filled the screen. She wore a silver bikini and high silver heels, and her hair was teased into a large tuft on her head. A ringlet of a ponytail hung down her bare back. One leg perched on a stool, a hand rested on one hip, and her head turned toward the camera. Joanna's throat tightened as she remembered Marnie's face as she lay on the floor at Tallulah's Closet.

"After her show, she'd work the front room. She brought in a lot of money. The mayor used to come to see her. They snuck him in and out through the side door, the door that goes to El Grillo now. She had some other high-toned—" here the manager made quote signs with his fingers "—customers, too." He picked up his mug. "She died, huh? Too bad."

"Just a few days ago. I'd really like some of her old friends to know."

"Tell you what. Why don't I give Don your phone number and have him call you?"

Joanna wrote her home number on a Tallulah's Closet business card and handed it to him. She started for the door, then turned again to the manager. "One more question. I noticed the mural out there. It's—striking." Especially for a club catering to straight men.

"Oh, you like it? It was painted a long time ago by a guy named Monty LaMontayne."

Questioned answered.

"Peace." The manager returned to his computer.

Chapter ⊖

Apple was at the front of the store, settling the Lanvin coat on a mannequin over a psychedelic-patterned Leonard of Paris dress. She had set a pair of fringed boots at the mannequin's feet for a Janis Joplin effect.

"What? I thought the Lanvin sold yesterday," Joanna said with a mixture of relief and disappointment. "Didn't you say Gisele bought it?"

Apple stepped down from the platform that held the window display. "She brought the coat back. Said it just wasn't right. She hadn't even taken it out of the trunk of her car. I think it needs to be smudged. She said her house was broken into last night, too."

"Was she okay?" Gisele was a fashion writer for the local weekly. Joanna had been to her house once for a cocktail party after an event showcasing local designers. Gisele had done up the place in glam-rock luxe with a white fake fur couch and a large, arching silver lamp. She had hugged the designers, praised their work, and pressed them to drink up the marionberry Martinis, but she viciously panned the show in the newspaper the next week.

"I guess she was fine. Nothing was even stolen. I bet you fifty bucks it was Tanya at Steam Fittings. She's still fuming over that 'Soviet vacation wear' comment from Gisele's review last winter."

"Another thing, I saw Eve at the estate sale yesterday, and I mentioned the Lanvin," Joanna said.

Apple's hands dropped to her side. "Why'd you do that? Now she'll try to buy it off you so she can resell it. You know how stubborn she is, too."

"I know. She made a mean remark about Tallulah's Closet, and I couldn't help bragging. Whatever you do, don't sell it to her." Joanna tipped a veiled pillbox hat to a more flattering angle on its stand.

"Good Goddess. She must be the only vintage clothing dealer in town who doesn't even wear vintage."

Joanna remembered the anguished look of the student Eve had paid to wait in line for her. "The guys sure love her, though."

Apple snorted. "Sure. She has all the beauty money can buy."

"She said she's opening a store. She was kind of mysterious about it, too."

"I haven't heard anything about that." Apple walked back to the counter. "Who knows if it will actually happen, though. Remember Eve's party planning business? Then her interior design consulting idea?" She picked up a pink phone message slip. Joanna had bought a case of them when a tire store went out of business. "Message for you. Andrew came by with a stack of flyers for the Remmick rally, too. And Paul was here to paint the door where he chiseled out the lock."

Joanna looked at the phone message. Don Cayle hadn't wasted any time getting back to her. This was turning out to be easier than she'd anticipated.

"Did you hear me?" Apple said. "I said Paul had been by. He asked about you."

"Yeah, I heard you."

"What's going on between you two, anyway?"

"Nothing," she said in a voice that warned not to press the subject. The memory of dancing at the Reel M'Inn and the parting kiss flushed her face. If only Apple knew. "Anything else?"

"Just that guy I told you about. The one lurking around yesterday. I'm telling you, bad energy."

The bell at the door clanged as a customer came in, and Apple turned to greet her. Joanna returned Don Cayle's call.

An old Coasters song droned from speakers hung in the awnings outside the downtown address Don Cayle gave Joanna. She'd have to break her rule about never patronizing restaurants that piped music to the sidewalk. Television sets dotted throughout the restaurant silently showed sports. Toward the back, a waitress rolled silverware into napkins. Other than shoppers, the restaurant was empty but for an elderly man sitting at a booth near the bar.

"Mr. Cayle?" Joanna approached the booth.

Don Cayle stood up and took her hand in both of his. His hands were large and soft, and his nails freshly manicured. A thick gold ring studded with rubies gleamed on his pinkie. He was handsome in a rough sort of way, despite the expensive suit. In his youth a lot of handkerchiefs must have been dropped at his feet.

"You must be Joanna. Please, call me Don. What'll you have?" His voice was gruff but friendly.

She slid into the booth across from him. "Coffee would be great."

"Cream?" He asked and Joanna nodded. "Glenda, some coffee for the lady, with cream." His hands clutched a tumbler of brown liquid and ice. Johnny Walker on the rocks was Joanna's guess.

"You must come here often." The restaurant didn't look like the sort of place where a person would get to know the servers on a first-name basis.

"I own it. Folks seem to like it. The burgers are good, anyway." The waitress poured coffee and set a few plastic containers of half and half on the table. "The club manager called this morning and said that you wanted to talk to me about Marnie. Is that right?" He looked intently at Joanna.

"Yes, she, well — I'm afraid Marnie isn't with us anymore. I wanted to tell some of her friends in person." She realized how stupid that sounded. There just wasn't any gentle euphemism for death.

Don's hand trembled as he lifted his glass and drained it. He raised a finger and nodded at the waitress across the room. "Was it her lungs?"

"No. Or at least I don't know for sure." She wasn't sure how to say what she needed to say. "I found her." She looked up at Don. "I'm sorry."

"There's nothing to be sorry about, honey. That must have been tough on you. Tell me about it."

Joanna winced at the memory of lifting the Lanvin coat. "She was in my store. I have a vintage clothing store on the east side. She'd somehow got in overnight, and I found her there the next morning. I can't figure it out."

The waitress put a fresh drink in front of Don. He removed the tiny red straw and set it on the paper cocktail napkin before lifting the glass. His hands were steady now. "Marnie. What a shame."

"I don't — didn't — know her very well, and I don't know if she has friends or family around here. But I'd like her friends to know. I think she should have some sort of goodbye. I hoped you might know some of the people close to her."

"That's real nice of you." He leaned back in the booth. "I don't know who she was spending time with lately, but when she was at the club and I was the manager, she was good friends with the cook, Ray. And she used to room with another one of the dancers, Nina. I'm not sure what Ray's doing these days, but Nina comes to the club's picnics every summer. You can find her at the Wet Spot tropical fish shop. She and her husband own it."

"You were a friend of Marnie's, right?" She didn't want to stop talking about Marnie just yet.

"Sure. At one time we were close. A long time ago." Don looked into the distance. From the side he resembled Kirk Douglas, including the cleft chin. "She was something else, that Marnie. A real pistol on stage. Off stage, though, a different person. Private. She and I went together a few years, but half the time I never really knew what she was thinking. One day she called me and told me it was over. That's it. No explanation. I haven't seen her in probably twenty years." He pulled his gaze back to Joanna.

She responded to the regret in his voice. "I don't know what she was like when she was younger, but Marnie could be difficult to talk to."

"I suppose it's my own fault more than anything. I was a young man trying to build my business, and I didn't give her the attention she deserved. I left her alone too much."

"I'm sure she enjoyed going out on the town with you, though." Don and Marnie would have turned heads back in the day.

"Marnie didn't like going out as much as other girls. She was real self-conscious, embarrassed about being a dancer. I told her that I didn't care — hell, I used to manage the place she danced, and it's

not like we were dining with the queen when we went out, anyway."
He paused and then laughed. "Sometimes we went to the Desert
Inn over on Stark. I don't suppose you've heard of that place? No?
You're too young. This was back in, oh, '57 or '58. They had some
gambling in the back room, and the entertainment might have, well,
crossed the line from time to time.

"Anyway, they were raided one night when Marnie and I stopped
by. While the uniforms were at the front door, Marnie took a little
piece of paper from her purse and asked the bartender for the phone.
She called the head of the vice squad. Got him out of bed. He was
known for enjoying the sights at Mary's Club, see. I guess he didn't
waste any time calling police headquarters and telling them to lay
off the Desert Inn. A few minutes after the call, another police car
pulled up, and the officer came running in like his pants were on
fire. He rounded up the other policemen and shoveled them out the
door before Mick even had time to freshen up my drink."

Don's smile faded. "I don't know where she got the idea that
anyone was looking down on her." The waitress swapped Don's
empty glass for another drink, his third by Joanna's count. Hopefully
he wasn't driving.

"I wish I could have known her then." She imagined Marnie young,
with soft curves instead of the thin, bony frame she knew.

"Are the police following up on her death?" Don asked as pulled
out the cocktail straw and laid it next to the others on the napkin.
His voice quavered slightly at the word "death." Whiskey or emotion?

"I suppose so. The detective said the medical examiner decides if
the death was suspicious, and if there should be an investigation." She
recalled the detective's questioning. The police hadn't called her. Yet.

"You don't happen to remember the officer's name, do you?"

Joanna pulled his card from a pocket on the side of her purse. Her fingers touched Marnie's cash and the safe deposit box key that had fallen from the coat. "Detective Foster Crisp."

Don nodded. "Yep, she was quite a gal. They don't make them like that anymore."

Chapter 9

The Wet Spot was just off a busy stretch of Sandy Boulevard in a squat 1960s storefront. A bell jingled when Joanna pushed open its door. The humid room glowed eerily from row upon row of lit fish tanks. Scores of filtration systems hummed and burbled, muffling the noise of the traffic outside.

"May I help you?" An Asian man stood behind the counter polishing the walls of an empty tank.

"Yes, I'm looking for Nina."

"Nina? May I tell her who wants her?"

"My name is Joanna Hayworth. I understand she knows — or knew, at least — Marnie Evans."

"Marnie? Old Goldilocks?" He cocked his head slightly and yelled toward the back. "Hey Nina. There's a friend of Goldilocks out here."

A woman built along the lines of Jane Russell emerged from the back. She towered over the Asian man. She wore a wrap dress tied high on the waist that emphasized her bust, and her hair was dyed the color of charcoal briquettes. Only as the woman walked nearer did Joanna notice the crepey skin on her chest and lined face that told her age. "I'm Nina. How can I help you?" she asked in a low, silky voice. The scent of gardenias rose above the chlorine.

Joanna told her about Marnie's death. It hadn't got any easier since she told Don that morning.

Nina tucked her hand under Joanna's elbow and turned her toward the door. "Gary," she said to the man, who was now sprinkling flakes into a large tank full of long-finned fish, "We're going down the street for a little while. If the lady comes by for the Ink Fin Kapampa, it's in tank thirty-nine."

Nina led her out onto the sidewalk and a few blocks to Poor Richard's, a restaurant and bar known more for its stiff drinks than fine cuisine.

Happy hour had just started at Poor Richard's, and a few seniors were enjoying the early bird special of roast beef in the dining room. Nina and Joanna sat at a booth in the Almanack Room, a dim bar with faux beams straddling the ceiling, stamped-brass platters displayed on a plate rail, and a large TV tuned to a baseball game.

Nina extracted a pack of cigarettes from her purse and tapped one out. She lit it, her fingers tipped with long, frosted pink nails. A charm bracelet dangled from her wrist. She pointed the cigarette at Joanna. "Is that blouse an Alex Coleman?"

Joanna was surprised. "Yes, it is. You know your labels."

"I used to have quite the wardrobe. Marnie and I both did. I may have had a blouse exactly like yours."

A waitress came over from the bar. "The usual?" she said to Nina, who nodded. "And you?"

She could order another coffee, but it was getting late in the day and her nerves were on edge.

Nina said, "You need a drink, honey."

Joanna glanced toward the bar where a young guy pulled a beer. He wore a stringy beard but had a face straight from a Botticelli. Could he possibly know how to make more than a rum and coke?

"She'll have what I'm having. Bring us some garlic bread, too, and some fried clams. Sound good?" Nina directed the last part to Joanna.

She realized she was hungry and nodded. She hadn't eaten since breakfast. As for "what I'm having," she feared it would be a glass of white Zinfandel, but too late now.

"So, Marnie was murdered," Nina said.

"They don't know that it was murder." Joanna stifled a shocked laugh.

"Found dead in your store, and you didn't let her in. Doesn't sound like the Marnie I know to do something like that."

"I admit I've wondered myself. She wasn't dressed to leave the house—didn't even have on her wig. But who would kill her? And why?" Her thoughts flashed to the story Don had told her about the head of the Vice Squad. So much of Marnie's life was a mystery to her.

"Lots of people. Some folks might even say I'd do it."

"You?"

"Sure. At one time Marnie knew a lot of secrets and pissed off a lot of wives." Nina sighed. "I just wonder what she got herself into. When I married Gary—that was him at the store—she made fun of me. I always thought it would've done her some good to settle down. A lot of girls got screwed up by dancing."

"What do you mean?" She noticed Nina hadn't said why she might have killed Marnie.

"When you're up on stage with all these men looking at you, you start to see that you have some power. Well, a certain kind of power, anyway. At the same time, you can't trust it, you know what I mean? These men have some crazy idea in their minds about who you are, but they don't know you from Joan of Arc. Naturally, when a man truly was interested in you, you didn't trust it."

"Have you been with your husband a long time?"

"Sure. He used to stick around after my shift and walk me to the car to make sure I was all right. He did it every night for a year and a half before I'd go out with him. He's never let me down." She took a long drag off her cigarette. "Although I admit that I get tired of fish. Maybe that's why I like this place. I can eat the suckers."

"Two Pink Squirrels." The waitress placed drinks on the table. "Food will be up in a minute."

"Been drinking them for years," Nina said as she touched her glass to Joanna's. She flipped ash off the tip of her cigarette. "So, how'd you get my name?"

The drink was sweet and thick with cream. "I stopped by Mary's Club this morning, and the manager gave me Don Cayle's phone number. I had coffee with him this afternoon." Or at least one of us had coffee, she thought, remembering his grip on the tumbler of whiskey. "He's the one who told me where I could find you."

"Don, huh? What did you think of him?" Nina's green eyes focused on her. Expertly applied kohl swept up from their outer edges.

Was this some sort of test? "He seemed very nice, helpful."

"He had a thing for Marnie. He bought her a house, you know, but that was a long time ago." Nina blew a stream of blue smoke to the side. "What'd he say?"

"Not much, really. He wanted to know what happened, talked a little about the old days."

"Did he hit on you?"

"No, no. Not at all." Joanna didn't expect this question. Don had been fatherly more than anything. She had seen her share of Lotharios and wouldn't have pegged Don as one.

"He's a passionate man, Don. I don't know why he never married."

Nina stubbed out her cigarette.

"Maybe he's still hung up on Marnie." She remembered the regret in Don's voice when he had talked about not paying Marnie enough attention.

"No." Nina was firm. "No, that's not it. It doesn't sound like you know Marnie at all. Why are you going to all this trouble? Finding her friends and all?"

"I don't know. I feel responsible for her, I guess. I hate to think of her dying alone. I know she could be difficult, but—shouldn't she have some sort of goodbye?" A memorial service. She hadn't thought of it until now. Even just a handful of people would be something.

"Are you married?"

"No."

Nina nodded, as if this was the answer she'd expected, but asked, "Why not?"

If Nina hadn't been old enough to be her grandmother, Joanna would have laughed off the question. She wasn't sure if Nina broke the conventions of her generation—former stripper, afternoon cleavage, pink cocktails—or if she was a prime example of her generation—all the above plus a firm emphasis on marriage. "I guess I don't feel a rush to get married. And I know I'd rather be alone than stuck with someone I'd be unhappy with anyway."

"So you think you might end up like Marnie, and you feel sorry for her, so you want to throw her a little goodbye party. It sounds to me like it doesn't have much to do with Marnie at all."

Joanna's face burned. "No. No, that's not it. I mean, I do feel bad for her. She was obviously struggling for money, and she didn't seem to have many friends." Maybe she made a mistake assuming Nina was one of them. What did she say to set her off like that?

"But for all her crankiness, I did like her. She deserves more than an anonymous burial."

Nina's demeanor softened almost as fast as it had prickled. She patted Joanna's hand. A small rhinestone decal of a shark fin adorned the tip of her thumbnail. "I'm sorry. Don't feel bad about Marnie. She had plenty of opportunity not to be alone, if that was what she wanted, and don't believe for a minute that she was hurting for cash. If Marnie was anything, she was a survivor. She just didn't show her hand is all."

Joanna nodded, although she remembered Marnie's frequent complaints that she needed cash.

"And don't write off marriage, either. No one tells you how long you spend being old. Got to follow your heart, you know? Got to take a few risks." Nina's gaze lost focus, as if she were remembering something, or someone. She slowly drew a finger down the condensation on the side of her cocktail glass then looked up at Joanna. "So, what next?"

"About what?"

"A memorial service. You want to hold one, right?"

"Well, so far I've just talked to you and Don." She drained the end of her cocktail. What had she got herself into? "To tell the truth, the memorial service idea only just occurred to me," she said tentatively, "And I'm not sure who to invite. Who else do you think would want to come?"

"There's more than a few men around town who might want to pay their respects but wouldn't necessarily want to show their faces."

"How about family?"

Nina shook her head. "I recall Marnie's mother dying some years ago. I don't think she has any family. Living, that is. When she moved to Portland, started dancing, most of her family cut her off. Tell you what. Why don't you let me plan the get-together? I can call Mike. I bet he'd let us hold it at the club some morning before they open."

"Are you sure you want to do this? A few minutes ago —"

"You can help. I'll give you Ray's phone number, and you can call him. He used to cook at the club and was like a younger brother to Marnie."

Joanna nodded. "Don mentioned him."

"I'll call some of the other girls. I have some photos, and I can put together some sort of tribute. Monday morning, before the club opens, would be good. Most people my age have time weekdays. I'll call Don, make sure he can come. Is that all right with you?"

"Nina, thank you so much."

"Oh, don't thank me. After all, I'm sure we'd all want the same, wouldn't we?"

Chapter 10

The Sunday paper lay spread over the bed's cotton matelassé cover. Joanna sorted its sections, separating the ads from articles as she performed what she called the paper's "filet." The National section featured an article about the election. A photo of Congressman Remmick showed Andrew's tiny image in the background. Polls were still close.

The Metro section opened to a grainy black and white photo of Marnie circa 1960. "Margaret Eleanor Evans, aka 'Goldilocks' dies at 71" the headline read. Joanna pulled the newspaper closer.

> Margaret Evans, known as "Marnie" to friends and "Goldi-locks" to her many admirers, died on Wednesday of cardiac arrest. She was 71 years old. Evans had advanced ovarian cancer at the time of her death.
>
> Nicknamed "Goldilocks" for her long, blonde hair, Evans made her reputation as the star attraction at Mary's Club in the late 1950s and early 1960s. At the time, Portland was home to a handful of burlesque clubs, many reputed to have ties to organized crime. Mary's Club was one of the few clubs to escape investigation by Robert Kennedy's 1957 vice probe.

After stepping down as a dancer, Evans lived quietly in northeast Portland. She leaves no known survivors.

So, Marnie had died of a heart attack. Joanna stared at the paper. She had always figured Marnie looked so frail from too many cigarettes and a lot of hard living. "Not the years, but the miles," as Apple would say. Cancer explained the skeletal build, and maybe even her wig. She'd never said a word about it to Joanna, not once. Since Marnie had died of natural causes, the police probably weren't investigating her death, which must be why they hadn't returned to question Joanna. They must have decided Marnie had broken in for the coat then died. Interesting. Mob activity, too. She thought of Don.

The death notice should have eased her mind. After all, it left out that Marnie's body was found at Tallulah's Closet. She wouldn't have to worry about people too freaked out about the death to come in — or worse, too curious to stay away. But it still left a lot of questions. Why was Marnie at the store to begin with? Did she really pull the coat over herself and die behind the counter? Or, as Nina had suggested, did someone "help" her?

Joanna took her empty coffee cup to the kitchen. She smoothed the Poor Richard's napkin with Ray's number written on it in Nina's girlish scrawl. Hopefully ten in the morning wasn't too early to call.

Unlike Nina and Don, Ray didn't seem to need much explanation for why she was calling. He invited Joanna to come over right away. She slipped out of her dressing gown — this one from the pre-code film era with a print of broad blue stripes and brightly colored anemones — and into a blue 1950s sundress fitted through the bodice and hanging in pleats mid-hip. She pulled her hair back and secured it with an elastic hair band, quickly spritzed vintage Je Reviens down her cleavage, then headed into the already warm morning.

⁂

"Damn it." Joanna pulled the car to the curb. Every street in this neighborhood of southwest Portland seemed to end in a hilly cul de sac. And they were all named after flowers — Daffodil, Marigold, Primrose. Who laid out this neighborhood, anyway? Martha Stewart on acid?

She looked at the map again and shoved it back on the passenger seat. She shouldn't be far now, at least as the bird flies.

Ten minutes later, she parked in the driveway of a small, yellow house that backed into a ravine. Pots of miniature roses crowded the steps to the porch. The Corolla shuddered as she shut off the ignition, and a man opened the house's front door.

"Joanna?" he said, holding out a hand. "Ray. Come in." Ray looked to be in his sixties with gray-streaked hair and skin craggy from sun. He wore a silver ring with a Chinook-style salmon engraved on it. The ring combined with his strong, solid build pointed to Native American. "You said you wanted to talk about Marnie."

She hadn't told him about Marnie's death. It didn't seem right for a perfect stranger to deliver that kind of news on the phone. She took the obituary from her purse. "I'm afraid Marnie died last week. I wanted you, and her friends, to know."

Ray's expression remained calm, his voice soft. "I saw the obit in the paper this morning. A pity." He sounded sincere. "Would you like a cup of coffee? I was just going to pour myself some."

She followed him into the kitchen where a coffee pot filled the air with its aroma. Through the adjoining hall she could see the living room filled with morning light. Twittering finches jumped perch to perch in two large cages set back from the windows. Ray walked ahead of her with a slight limp, as if one leg were slightly shorter than the other.

"Let's go to the back. We can talk there."

They took their coffee through the dining room to a glassed-in porch overlooking a grassy yard with a vegetable garden on the edge of the ravine. Tomato cages strained to hold up fruit-heavy vines, and green beans grew up and over bamboo tripods. Ray opened the back door slightly to let in the morning air.

Joanna settled into a wicker chair with wide arms and a soft cotton blanket draped over it. The tension over finding the house melted away. She set her coffee cup on a low table in front of her. Next to a stack of typewritten papers stood a framed photo of a middle-aged woman in Native American ceremonial dress. She picked it up. "That's a gorgeous cape she's wearing."

"My aunt. She was on the tribal council."

Ray didn't seem prepared to say anything more. The mug's comfortable heft, the house's light and calm—Joanna recognized a kindred spirit. Even the coffee met her high standards. Maybe he wasn't overly talkative, but Ray's relative sanity was a nice change after her encounters with Don and Nina.

A large crow alit on a bird feeder, scattering the wrens who had been feeding. Its black beak pecked at seeds. Sun flashed blue on its feathers. Ray's eyes narrowed for a moment.

She replaced the photo. "You like birds."

"That's a raven. He comes to visit from time to time."

Joanna waited. She was beginning to see that Ray liked a stretch of quiet between observations.

"In my culture, the raven is a trickster." Ray's eyes stayed on the bird.

"He plays tricks on people?"

"Sometimes. But not like Coyote, another Indian symbol. The raven brings truth."

The crow — raven — crouched and launched into the air, its feathers ruffling at the wing. Ray watched it fly off.

Joanna lifted her mug. "I talked to Nina yesterday. She gave me your phone number."

"She still at the fish store? How's she doing?"

"She seems to be well. We're planning a memorial service for Marnie and she asked me to get in touch with you. She said you and Marnie were close."

Ray looked thoughtful. "No kidding? Nina wanted to do something for Marnie, huh?"

Joanna remembered Nina's erratic behavior. "Yes. At first — well, she said she'd take care of the rest if I talked to you. I talked to Don, too." There was no point in getting into Nina's conversation at the restaurant.

At the mention of Don, the corners of Ray's mouth turned down, but he nodded as if something had become clear. He didn't speak.

"I'm surprised that *The Oregonian* picked up on Marnie's death."

"Oh, not me. Forty, fifty years ago Marnie was pretty big news." He sank back into his chair. "I know Nina and Marnie from when I cooked at the club. Now the club uses the kitchen mostly to reheat frozen pizzas. They used to put out quite a spread."

"Really?" She figured a strip club would rely on something like beer nuts.

"Oh yes. When the ships came in at Rose Festival, the club was full of sailors eating pancakes and eggs. I cooked there for ten years.

Started when I was sixteen."

"Do you still cook?"

"Nah. The gig at Mary's was good because my shift was short. I hurt my leg in an accident when I was a kid, and I don't like to stand too long. My brother died a little while ago. I've been helping out at his business."

"What was Marnie like, back then? The manager showed me a picture from her Goldilocks days."

Ray looked out the window, and for a moment she wondered if he had heard her, if he would lapse into monosyllables again. Then he spoke. "Oh, Marnie, I never could figure her out. When she hostessed after her show, she hopped from lap to lap, laughing, talking, the life of the party, you know? When the next girl would go on, instead of going back to the dressing room, Marnie'd come to the kitchen and sit in a little wooden chair I kept for her. She didn't talk much, she'd just watch me cook and watch the waitresses come in and out with orders. Sometimes she'd soak her feet in an old dishpan. She was always dieting, but she did love my cinnamon rolls."

"Mike, the manager, said she was really popular."

"Biggest thing since Tempest Storm left town. She used to do a 'three bears' routine. She'd start out pretending to sit on a bed and say, 'This bed is too big,' and take off—well, you know—all the way to 'This bed is just right.' Sounds pretty corny now, but the crowd loved it." Ray shifted in his chair. "How about you? How do you know Marnie? It surprises me that she'd have a new friend these days."

"I have a vintage clothing store on Clinton called Tallulah's Closet. She used to sell me clothes."

"You have the store?" He leaned forward.

"Yes, for almost three years now." He shouldn't sound so surprised.

She smoothed her vintage dress. Maybe she didn't exactly look like an executive, but she was perfectly capable of running a small business.

Perhaps realizing the effect of his reaction, he changed topics. "Clothes, huh? She loved her clothes. Hard to imagine her getting rid of them."

"She sold me a few hostess dresses from the club. I had to scrub the glue from her pasties out of one of them." She and Apple had spent a morning the spring before trying first soapy water, then dry cleaning fluid, to dissolve the dried glue from one particularly cantankerous silver cocktail dress. "But for the most part she sold me a lot of day wear. Just a few evening pieces. And a gorgeous old coat, a Lanvin." Maybe she'd keep that coat after all. "You've known Marnie a long time."

Ray shifted in his seat again and moved his left leg with both hands. "She grew up in Oysterville, too, you know. I'm a little younger, but we went to the same schools."

"Oysterville. Beautiful country." Joanna's grandma grew up near there, on the ocean. They'd visited once or twice.

"Indeed. I don't know if Marnie ever went back after she moved to Portland."

"Had you seen her lately?"

"First time in years at my brother's funeral. She didn't look so good, to tell the truth. At the time I chalked it up to the funeral." The raven had returned and cawed from the edge of the garden shed.

"I didn't know about her cancer, either. I wonder if she told anyone at all." Joanna took another sip. "I'm sorry about your brother."

"He was in construction. Died in an accident." They both sat for a few minutes in silence. Clouds moved over the sun, momentarily dimming the light through the sun porch's windows. Ray put his hand on the loosely bound sheaf of papers on the table. "My brother left me the tribal history he'd been working on for years. I was just looking through it again."

"That must be fascinating." She craned her head to see it more closely. Penciled figures — Native American symbols, maybe — inscribed the front. Apple might know what to make of them. Ray pushed the papers further back on the table, out of her view. An opened envelope slid from the sheaf, and Ray quickly tucked it aside.

She stood and placed her empty mug on the table. "Thank you for the coffee. The store's due to open soon. I just wanted to tell you about Marnie and the memorial service. Tomorrow at Mary's Club, before opening. I'll see you then?"

Ray frowned. He opened his mouth as if to say something, then shut it again and shook his head. "No, I can't make it." He stood up.

"Is the time not good? I could call Nina — "

"No." The steely edge to his voice jolted Joanna. "Don't bother. I won't be there. I'll see you to the door."

Chapter 11

As soon as Joanna unlocked the door to Tallulah's Closet the next morning, she knew something was wrong. She held her breath a moment and listened. Nothing but the rumble of the bus on Clinton taking morning commuters downtown to start the work week. Inside, headless mannequins stood like actors on a darkened stage. She flicked on the light closest to the door, hesitated, then walked toward the back to click the switches that illuminated the rest of the store. Her unease persisted. What was it?

Breath quickening, she glanced behind the tiki bar. No, no body this time. She checked the cash drawer and saw the usual assortment of small bills, although the Bakelite box holding loose change was askew. The stereo and stack of LPs were in their places, too. She laughed nervously. Must be shock from finding Marnie's body last week and the memorial service in just a few hours, she decided. Besides, she'd just had a new lock put in, a better one. Her perceptions were out of whack, that's all.

She passed through the working area formed by a glass-fronted display case holding jewelry on one side and the store's wall opposite, and opened the bathroom door to wash her hands. Shards of glass lay on the floor, and a footprint dirtied the toilet lid. *Damn it.* So there had been someone in the store. The alley's muggy air filtered through the broken bathroom window. But nothing seemed to have been stolen. Or so it seemed.

Joanna's gaze wandered the store. Her eyes widened. Those blouses clumped together, that red satin Susie Wong dress dangling by a shoulder on its hanger. There's no way she or Apple would leave the store like this. At the end of each day, she always made sure all the clothing faced the same direction on the rack, so their pink tags dangled out and the hangers were spaced evenly along the bar.

She scanned the store again. No one could possibly still be in the shop, unless...She cleared the counter in a few, fast steps and yanked back the dressing room curtain. Empty.

She let out her breath and turned to face the store. Who would have broken in but not stolen anything? Maybe someone thought they were getting into the bar next door, found out they were in a vintage clothing store, and left. But if that were true, why would they rifle through the racks?

Joanna had come to the store to find something appropriately somber to wear to Marnie's memorial service — nothing in her closet seemed quite right — but now she wondered if she'd better forget the whole thing. The store wasn't secure. Then again, Nina went to so much trouble to set things up at Mary's Club. That is, if Nina showed up at all. She hadn't returned Joanna's call about Ray refusing to come to the service, and she'd been so squirrelly when they met. No, Joanna had to go. She had to say one last goodbye to Marnie.

Frustrated, she flattened a cardboard box and leaned it against the shattered window. She found a roll of duct tape and sealed its edges. It should keep out intruders — and flies — for the few hours she'd be gone. When she returned from the memorial service, she'd call the police.

From the row of black dresses, she pulled a demure 1940s black crepe dress with short, gathered sleeves and gold buttons running up its center, and clipped off its price tag. It was when she emerged from the dressing room that she noticed the empty hanger where the Lanvin coat had hung.

"No," she moaned. Could Apple have sold it again and not told her? Joanna rushed to the receipt book and flipped through it. No receipt for the coat. It was definitely missing. She slammed the receipt book on the counter.

Why would someone steal the coat? Her thoughts flashed to Eve, but she had to admit even Eve wouldn't stoop that low. The coat was beautiful, sure, but hardly museum worthy. Tallulah's Closet had a Schiaparelli parure and a beaded flapper dress worth more than the coat.

She glanced at the clock. She had to hurry to get to the memorial service, but first she'd call the landlord. Maybe while she was away he could repair the window. She rummaged through her purse searching for the landlord's business card. Her hand stopped at Marnie's safe deposit box key. She placed it on the tiki bar and examined its small brass shape.

Then it hit her. The store. The apartment of the fashion writer who first bought the coat then returned it. The coat's slashed lining.

Somebody wanted that key.

As she sped across town, Old Blue protesting with occasional pings, Joanna thought back to who knew she had Marnie's coat. She had told Don, Nina, and Ray that Marnie had sold clothes to the store. Eve knew, too. They all knew she had, or at least could have, the coat. In fact, she'd specifically mentioned the coat to Ray. Then, of course, there was whoever Marnie had told about selling her coat. And everyone who walked by the store and saw the coat in the window. She sighed. That was a lot of people.

Until now, in all the break-ins nothing had been stolen, and except for a shattered window, nothing had been destroyed, either. But Marnie had ended up dead. At the store. Sure, the medical examiner had ruled it was natural causes, but Joanna wasn't so sure. Despite the August heat blowing in the Corolla's sun roof, she felt a chill. Now she had the key. Was she at risk?

At Mary's Club, Nina was setting up an easel near the stage. A sheet of foam core and a box of photos rested on the table next to her. Good, Joanna thought, Nina showed. At least that's one less thing to worry about.

"I'm sorry I'm a little late. I stopped by the store, and someone had broken in."

"Oh no, that's too bad, honey. Did they get the money? From the cash register?" Nina continued to pin photos to the sheet of foam core.

"Just—a coat. Someone stole a coat."

She nodded. "Lucky you. Maybe it was some kids and they were scared off before they could take more. You should get a security system. Mary's used to get broke into all the time before they put one in. Hey, Mike's here, too, in his office printing out a few Goldilocks photos."

A bank of floral bouquets lined the front of the stage, and the fragrance of lilies competed with stale beer, cigarette smoke, and pine-scented cleanser. A few of the bouquets were still wrapped in plastic, and many were shot through with yellow and gold flowers.

Joanna laid her bouquet—flesh-pink dahlias and spikes of fragrant stock—next to a vase of gladiolas.

"Impressive, huh?" Nina said. "Mike says they've been coming in since Marnie's obit in yesterday's paper. Most are addressed to Goldilocks. The paper did a nice little article on her. Did you see it?"

"I did. They said she died of a heart attack."

"So I read."

Joanna touched the green and scarlet cymbidium orchids in one particularly lush bouquet. Nina watched her bend down to read the card. "It doesn't say who it's from, but it's from Don," she said. "I'm sure of it." Was that bitterness she heard in Nina's voice? "Would you like coffee, honey? There's a pot on now behind the bar."

"Thank you." She brought the cup of coffee laced with powdered creamer back to the table where Nina was sorting through photographs. She sipped the coffee, grimaced, and abandoned it at the edge of the stage. Mary's Club dancers had better be good, because their coffee wasn't going to earn them repeat customers. She picked up a black and white photo of Marnie and Nina posing in their hostess dresses. Nina wore a tight Chinese silk dress with a high collar and a slit up the thigh. "Nice dress."

"That one was gold silk. Absolutely gorgeous. I wore stilettos with it, and let me tell you, the dogs were barking at the end of the night. I did my routine barefoot, though. It was a sort of tropical dance, and Don said barefoot was all right. Marnie did all her routines in feathered mules. I don't know how she did it. Look, here's a picture of Don."

Joanna held up the photo. Don leaned over Marnie with one hand on the wall behind her and the other holding a cigarette as if he were gesticulating to make a point. Don had dark, wavy hair, and his sleeves were rolled up to reveal strong forearms and part of a tattoo.

"He's a handsome man. It's so hard to imagine Marnie that young. When was that—late '50s?" Joanna asked.

"About then. Not long after I met her, actually. She'd just moved here from the coast. She must have been eighteen or nineteen then. She auditioned for a spot at the club, and Don gave her my name. I was looking for a roommate."

"I wonder why she decided to be a dancer?"

"I wondered, too. I was surprised she didn't look for some other job, you know, as a secretary or working at one of the department stores. She was good looking enough. I'm sure they would have hired her. I guess she thought the money would be better at Mary's. Anyway, she came to Portland because she was wild about Franklin, a boy she'd gone to school with, and he'd moved here. She must have spent half her nights at his place. He was living on a little boat at Sauvie Island then." As she talked, she pinned photos to the display.

"A boat?"

"Mm-hmm. His family were fishermen. When he first moved to town he didn't have enough money to rent a place, so he just stayed on the boat. I saw it once. It looked real cozy."

Nina pulled another photo from the box, this one a faded Polaroid of a bedroom with twin beds. Marnie sat on one bed painting her toenails. Her hair was in curlers. One hand was held up in front of the camera.

"She was mad at me for taking this one. Marnie never went out without eye makeup. She'd go without lipstick, but never without eyeliner."

"What happened between Marnie and Franklin?"

"Not sure. One day Marnie came home. Gary and I were watching TV—I still remember what was on, it was *Gunsmoke*—and Marnie went straight to the bedroom, sobbing. I think she'd been drinking, she was having a hard time standing up without holding the door frame. She and Franklin had broken up. I thought they'd get back together. You know how it is, ups and downs. But they didn't. I'm pretty sure they still saw each other from time to time, but that was that. Not long after, Marnie started seeing Don. They were together for years."

"But they never married."

"Oh, some people think Don would have, but Marnie wouldn't do it. Me, I don't know. I don't think Don ever wanted to settle down."

Nina had filled the board with old photos of Marnie. She moved the easel closer to the stage and posed the board on it. "What do you think?"

"Looks good." The mostly black and white collage was full of emotion — people laughing, waving cigarettes, kicking a leg in the air. "People should be here before too long. Should I see if we can get some music?"

"Mike is still in the back. He might have some CDs. They're probably mostly Liza Minelli, though. If we're lucky he'll have Judy Garland. Or we can see what's on the jukebox." Nina nodded toward the stage.

When Joanna returned, two women had arrived and were oohing and ahhing at the flowers. One wore a diaphanous flowered caftan, and other woman wore shorts and practical shoes and had a book of large-type crossword puzzles under her arm.

"Wendy and Liz, I'd like you to meet Joanna. She's the one who first told me about Marnie."

"Wendy," the caftan-wearing woman said, extending a meaty hand. "They called me 'Veronica' when I danced."

"Liz," the other woman said. "Used to wait tables. I like your dress. My mother had one just like it."

"Louise would be here, but she's on a cruise in Mexico," Wendy said.

It crossed Joanna's mind that her grandmother would have liked being part of this gathering. Maybe not the strip club part, but she could imagine her settling down with a cup of coffee for a good, long gossip about the old days.

The front door opened, and Ray entered carrying a platter of cinnamon buns. Joanna did a double take. "I always forget what a dump this place is until I see it with the house lights up," he said. He avoided Joanna's eyes.

Nina took the platter and hugged him. "It's so nice to see you. I was sorry to hear about your brother. Did you make these?"

"Yes, fresh from the oven. How's Gary?"

"He's all right. Oh, here he is now." Nina's husband came in carrying a pink bakery box. "Let me take those."

Joanna went to the bar to make another pot of coffee. It looked like they'd need it. "Somewhere over the Rainbow" began to play over the loudspeakers, its melody languorous and oddly beautiful in the dingy club. When Joanna returned, Don had arrived. He stood next to Gary, with his back to Ray. Ray moved away from him.

How strange it must be for them all to be back here, Joanna thought. When the club was part of their daily lives fifty years ago, they were young, and if they thought of their futures at all, it's hardly likely this is what they had imagined. Nina seemed such a frustrated romantic. Joanna watched her arrange the flowers next to the stage. Don looked pensive. She couldn't read Ray. Wendy was showing Liz some photographs she had taken out of her mammoth bag, probably of her grandchildren. None of them appeared particularly sad, but

Joanna didn't see them as a very emotive group, except perhaps for Nina. Not that she should be surprised, she reminded herself. None of them had seen Marnie in years.

She thought of the shattered window at the store. None of Marnie's friends looked like burglars, either, let alone capable of killing someone for a safe deposit box key. Nina was strong enough to do it. Ray might be able to break in. Of course, Don could hire someone easily. She had a hard time picturing any of them climbing through the store's bathroom window. Had the landlord fixed the window yet? She saw a pay phone on the wall by the door and was fishing in her purse for quarters when Nina called for attention.

"All right, I think just about everyone is here." Nina smiled at the small gathering. Don sat next to Gary, and Ray was at a table by himself. The club's manager, Mike, brought the coffee pot from behind the bar and poured himself a cup. Joanna sat down with Ray.

"Joanna was good enough to get in touch with us to tell us about Marnie's death. I thought it would be nice if we could go around the room and everyone could say something about her. We'll start with Joanna."

She hadn't been warned about this part of the program. She stood up. "Thank you for coming on such short notice. I didn't know Marnie nearly as well as any of you, only for about a year. The first time I met Marnie, she came by my vintage clothing store with a box of dresses. She had a way about her that made you feel she had an interesting past. Now, whether or not she'd tell it to you, that's another story."

A knot of emotion gathered in her throat. No more Marnie bringing in tattered pedal pushers but surprising her with the occasional knock-out gown. No more Marnie reminding her to wear sunscreen or giving her tips on how to put on false eyelashes or suggesting she line the back wall with mirrored tiles. No more Marnie at all.

"She wasn't always easy to talk to, but I knew she was a kind person. I'll never forget her." Self conscious, she sat down and felt that she hadn't really done Marnie justice. "I was so sorry to hear about her heart attack."

"Heart attack, right," Nina said under her breath.

"The paper said they did an autopsy, and she died of a heart attack. Leave it be," Ray said.

Joanna was surprised he had even heard her, and was startled by the sharp edge to his voice. He hadn't even wanted to come, and now he was defending Marnie.

"I bet someone encouraged that heart attack," Nina said, this time more loudly. "Some people might say she had it coming."

"Nina, Ray's right. Maybe Marnie wasn't perfect, but who is?" Don said.

Nina glanced at him, then looked down at her coffee. "I'm sorry. Ray, would you like to talk next?"

Ray stood up. "Yes, thank you." He cleared his throat. "I grew up in the same town as Marnie, though I didn't really get to know her until we were adults. But since she was close with my brother I thought of her as an older sister. I feel like I always knew her, really. She even helped me get my job cooking here. Marnie wasn't meant to be a country girl, and when she followed Franklin to Portland, I came, too, a few years later."

Don's chair creaked.

Oh, Joanna thought, so Marnie's boyfriend, Franklin, was Ray's brother. And it was most likely Franklin, then, who died recently.

"What most people don't know," Ray continued, "Is that Marnie could be very tenderhearted. When I had the operation on my leg, she came to see me every day and read from *The Jungle Book* to me. She was hard to get to know, but once she accepted you, you became family, and she was as loyal and generous as a person could be."

Marnie's words came back to Joanna. "You're family," she'd said.

"I admit I hadn't seen her in years," Ray said. "But it's hard for me to think she's not here anymore. I'm sorry, too, that she never did have her own family. And that she died alone. I guess it's a reminder for all of us to appreciate each other while we can." Ray sat down. "And please help yourself to cinnamon rolls."

Just as Nina's gaze turned to Don, the front door of the club opened and a man entered. His pale skin contrasted with his long dark hair, which he'd pulled back into a ponytail. He couldn't have been much older than thirty. The summer morning's warm air and brash light surged in with him.

"May I help you?" Nina said.

"Is this the memorial service for Marnie Evans?" The man looked at the few people gathered. "I'm her son."

Chapter 12

"Is it all right if I come in?" the man asked.

A few seconds elapsed as the people at the memorial service stared at him. "Yes, yes, come in and sit down," Nina said. "Here, let me take those." She lifted a cellophane-wrapped bundle of birds of paradise from his hands.

"I'll be damned," Liz said.

"My name is Troy." He hovered near Don. "I hope I'm not interrupting."

"You'll have to excuse our silence, son," Don said. "It's just that some of us didn't know that Marnie had a child. Have a seat."

All eyes were on Troy. He set his backpack next to his chair. He wore what was probably concession to dressing for a memorial service: black jeans and a muted grey dress shirt Joanna recognized as a DaVinci from the early 1960s. He could have been any one of a thousand men who moved to Portland to join a band, build bicycles, or simply acquire a few tattoos.

He waved toward the flowers Nina still held. "Something about them reminded me of her." Nina laid the birds of paradise on the stage. Impressive choice. The flowers did feel more like Marnie — at least the Marnie in the photos — than did the bouquets of lilies, gold mums, and gladiolas the others had sent.

Troy surveyed the quiet room, questions lingering in the air. A wide, warm smile broke over his face. "I hope you don't mind my coming. I saw Marnie's obit in *The Oregonian*, so I called the club about sending some flowers. The person who answered told me about this morning's gathering."

He certainly was charming. Nina's expression softened. "We're happy to have you, of course. Would you like some coffee? Maybe a cinnamon roll?"

Joanna sat back. So, Marnie had a son. She had never said anything about children or a husband. From the looks on the faces around the room, she wasn't the only person caught off guard. She remembered an article she'd read somewhere about a man who trolled obituaries, then went to funerals to steal from the families of the deceased. Could Troy be one of those?

Troy helped himself to a cup of coffee and two donuts. He wrapped a cinnamon roll in a napkin and set it aside. He held his coffee cup with both hands, elbows out, like a child.

Ray cleared his throat. "Uh, Troy, it sounds like you've been out of touch with your mother for a while. How did she keep you hidden away so well?"

For a second, Troy looked confused. Then he relaxed and again flashed a melting smile. "Oh, I see. You're probably wondering if I'm for real. Marnie was my birth mother. She gave me up for adoption right after I was born, and I only met her about a year ago. I always wondered who my birth parents were, so I registered with the adoption agency. I guess Marnie was curious, too." He reached into his backpack handed a folded letter to Don. "Here."

"It's from Marnie. Says she's his mother and wants to meet him." As Don returned the letter, he studied Troy's face.

"I keep the letter with me all the time," Troy said. "I remember exactly what I was doing when it came in the mail. And now…" He pushed his donut away.

Joanna was still skeptical. Sure, he had a letter, but there was something a little flim-flam about him. The men, especially, seemed to be calculating Troy's age. Marnie must have been near forty, or even slightly older, when Troy was born. He was fine-boned, like Marnie, but dark haired. Any of these men, or who knows how many others, could have been his father.

"Your father never got in touch with you?" Mike, the manager, asked.

"No. Never. As far as I know, he's not even aware I exist. Marnie knew how to keep secrets, that's for sure." The tension in the room dropped a notch. "Although she never did talk much about herself, she told me she'd been a performer here. Are these her?"

Troy went to the easel to look at the photos Nina had pinned up. Nina pointed out a few of Marnie as Goldilocks and then another of Marnie smiling, leaning against the hood of a Peugeot, with her hair blown against her face and a hand lifted to brush it from her eyes. In the distance was the ocean.

"Where was this one taken?" Troy asked.

"Why don't you keep it?" Nina said, obviously smitten. "It was taken at the tip of the Long Beach peninsula, near Oysterville. Where Marnie grew up. Ray, too." She nodded at Ray.

"That's where the guy running for the Senate grew up, isn't it? He came to speak at the law school last winter. He's doing some great work on roadless issues. I'm focusing on environmental law."

Remmick. Andrew's congressman.

Nina glanced at her husband. "Yes, I believe they knew each other."

The service took on a new energy. Everyone stood, talking to each other and trying to chat up Troy, the women especially, giving him maternal pats on the shoulder to which he'd respond with shy smiles. Nina took Don aside for a moment. Don shook his head and pulled away, and Nina, head down, walked toward the restroom. Troy and Joanna chatted a little about law school, and Troy gave her a card for his art installation business. "It doesn't pay much, but it's helping me get through school."

Mary's was scheduled to open for the day soon, and Tallulah's Closet would, too. She rose to leave. She should feel happier and more settled about Marnie. After all, she'd had her chance to talk with Marnie's friends — and her son, if he was her son — and to say goodbye to her. She'd even found a potential source of stock for Tallulah's Closet with Wendy, who said she still had some of her show clothes, now several sizes too small for her.

But the thought that someone wanted Marnie's key, and the uncertainty, at least in Joanna's mind, about Marnie's death kept her uneasy. Maybe once she talked to the police she would relax again. Since Marnie had died, her world seemed to have turned upside down. She looked forward to the day she could kick back on her chaise longue with nothing more taxing to think about than mapping out the next Friday's run of estate sales.

She hugged Nina and inhaled her aura of cigarette smoke and gardenias. "Thank you for arranging all this. I'd better get back to the shop, it's almost time to open it." On impulse, she gave her a little squeeze at the end of the hug before letting go. "Let's not lose touch."

"Maybe we can have lunch. Soon. I'll tell you some stories about Marnie back in the day." She glanced back at Troy. "Crazy about the son, isn't it?"

"That would be nice." Nina might have been moody to begin with, but she was a good friend to Marnie, even after all these years.

"Will you take one of these photos? How about this one?" Nina handed her a photo of Marnie standing outside the club in a silver lamé cocktail dress.

"Isn't that one of her hostess dresses? She sold me that dress."

"Yes, it is. Perfect, then," Nina said.

On the street, Joanna tucked the photo into her purse. She slid it in an inside pocket next to the key that had fallen from the Lanvin coat.

Chapter 13

Joanna hoped to find someone fixing the bathroom window, but Tallulah's Closet was dark. She flipped on a few lights and picked up the phone to leave another message for the landlord. She'd call the police, too. As she began to dial, the door behind her chimed.

"Finally," she said under her breath and turned, expecting to see the landlord. But standing at the door was Laura Remmick, the congressman's wife. Although they'd never been introduced, Joanna recognized her from events she'd attended with Andrew. Laura stood out even among Joanna's carefully tended racks of vintage clothing like a Manolo pump in a box of Hush Puppies. Joanna's expression morphed from surprise to a welcoming smile. Outfitting a congressman's wife would be a real coup. The broken bathroom window could wait a little longer.

"Hello. Are you looking for anything special today?"

Laura Remmick ran a hand through her caramel highlights. "Oh, I'm just looking. But I wonder if you have any cocktail dresses, maybe from the early- or mid-1960s? My husband drags me to all sorts of events, and I'm so tired of what's in my closet."

"You're Laura Remmick, aren't you? I admire your husband." Silently, Joanna thanked the vintage clothing gods. No matter how boring the congressman's wife might find boutique cocktail dresses and designer suits, few women of her sort ended up on the working class side of the river at a vintage clothing boutique. Laura was spot-on about choosing 1960s dresses, made for women with her slender hips and a modest bust, rather than 1950s dresses which tend to suit curvier figures better.

"Why don't you check the rack behind you?" Joanna said. "Most of our best black cocktail dresses are hanging there. I'm just opening the store. I'll put out the sidewalk sign and be back in a second to see what I can find for you."

When she returned, Laura was still standing where Joanna had left her.

"Where do you get most of your clothes?" the congressman's wife asked.

"Oh, all over. I get some from thrift stores and estate sales. People come in and sell me clothes, too. Of course, I dry clean and steam everything before I put it out for sale." She pulled from the rack a black lace cocktail dress threaded with a thick, sky blue ribbon around its empire waist. "You look like you're about a four. What do you think of this one? The vee in the back is really nice. And see how the ribbon makes a sash to the hem? It looks Audrey Hepburn in front, then you turn around and it's Sophia Loren."

"How cute," she said without conviction. "I bet a lot of interesting people come in to sell clothes. Real characters, I mean."

"Definitely. Definitely characters." Joanna pulled another black cocktail dress for Laura to try, this one a form-fitting sheath with a trapeze of silk chiffon over it, weighed down and given motion by a quadruple row of tight ruffles along its hem. She took a pole made from a broom handle from behind the counter and lifted a Pucci dress, the pride of store, from a hook on the wall. Finding a mint condition Pucci these days was akin to stumbling on a Picasso at a garage sale. It was more expensive than most of her customers could afford. Laura could definitely afford it, and its high-waisted cut and swirling pattern of pink, mauve, and celery green would accentuate her blue eyes.

"Sweet dress," a trim black man said as he came in the store.

"Hi, Kevin," Joanna said. "I put aside a few pieces for you."

"Thanks, doll." Kevin was better known in some circles as the drag queen Poison Waters. In street clothes he looked like a junior architect. Only his carefully plucked eyebrows gave away his profession.

Laura ignored Kevin and plowed ahead with her questioning. "Who brought in those dresses, for example?" She pointed at the cocktail dresses Joanna had put in the dressing room for her to try.

"One came from an estate sale in Sellwood, and the other I found at a thrift store. I bought the Pucci at a church rummage sale, believe it or not." Why was the congressman's wife so stuck on where Joanna got her clothes? Most women cruised the racks eagerly and methodically, intent on snagging the best of the one-of-a-kind gowns. This one seemed to want to stand around and talk. Finally Laura went in the dressing room and drew the leopard print curtains.

"Laura Remmick?" Kevin mouthed and raised his eyebrows.

"Can you believe it?" she mouthed back, then said to him in a normal voice, "I thought you might like these Vendôme pearls. Look, gumball-sized baroque, perfect for the big girl. I had to wrassle them off Barbara Bush."

"I bet that was easy," Kevin said in Poison's voice.

"And I found some size twelve lucite mules for you, too, although they might be a little narrow."

Laura emerged from the dressing room wearing the Pucci dress.

Her shoulders and arms were perfectly sculpted, and she had the smooth, evenly brown legs of a woman with regular appointments at the tanning booth and the waxer. The dress's wild pattern might make it a risky choice for a Washington cocktail party, but it fit like it was made for her.

"You look fabulous," Kevin said.

"Thank you," she said, although she barely glanced at herself in the mirror. "Do you ever get clothes from, oh, I don't know, entertainers around town?"

"No one particularly famous, if that's what you mean." She was definitely fishing for information. But why?

"What about Marnie?" Kevin said. "Wasn't she a dancer in the fifties-sixties?"

"That's interesting." Laura seemed to perk up. "She just died, didn't she? I read about it in yesterday's paper."

Well, well. Joanna rested a hand on the back of Kevin's chair. So, all this questioning was about Marnie. Didn't someone at the memorial service say Remmick knew Marnie? "Yes, not quite a week ago."

"What was she like? She must have been attractive to be a showgirl and all."

"She used to be a real bombshell. Wait, I have a photo right here." Joanna retrieved her purse from under the tiki bar and pulled out the photo Nina gave her. "I have the feeling she did what she wanted without caring what the rest of the world thought."

Laura studied the photograph, the thumbnail from her French manicure resting over the black and white image. She paused a moment, as if uncertain where she wanted to take the conversation. Finally she said, "What kind of clothes did she bring in?"

"A lot of dresses with Polynesian prints, strangely enough. A few items from her working days, too. She did bring in a gorgeous coat, a Lanvin."

"I'll try it on, please."

Her stomach clenched. "I'm afraid you can't. It was stolen last night."

"Oh. Pity." The word 'stolen' had no effect on her. "The showgirl, Marnie—did she tell you much about her life?" Laura asked as she closed the dressing room's curtains behind her.

"Not much." Joanna cast a glance at Kevin, who was sliding a pedicured foot into a pearly beige pump. If it had been she and Kevin alone, she would have spent half an hour filling him in on finding Marnie's body, the broken window, the memorial service, and Marnie's surprise son while he sat in the big, zebra-striped chair by the shoe display and ate take-out from Dot's. "I heard she used to live in Oysterville, where I understand your husband grew up."

"Yes, I asked my husband if he knew her, and he said they went to high school together." When Laura pushed aside the curtains of the dressing room, she had changed back to her street clothes. Joanna noticed something new, a little vulnerability.

Laura brought the Pucci and the black cocktail dress with the chiffon overlay to the counter. "I'll take these."

"I can't imagine what it would be like to have to dress for constituents." Joanna thought of her own wardrobe. She wouldn't be marrying a senator any time soon.

"Once I wore red nail polish when Chick and I were interviewed for a morning show. By the time we got back to the office, they'd already had five calls saying that it wasn't proper for a congressman's wife to have red nails." She examined her tasteful manicure. "That was early on. I know better now."

"You can't please everyone."

"No. That's true. But when Chick and I got married—well, people said things."

Joanna remembered the brouhaha in the papers and the sniping Laura took for being the "trophy wife." "Oh, people always say things. Likely, they're jealous." Laura's hopeful face made Joanna realize she was looking for comforting words, even after all these years of parrying public opinion. "As long as you and your husband are happy together, they should be happy, too."

"Oh, we are. Happy, that is." Laura looked earnest. "It's just that, well, Chick is a little older than I am—"

Joanna nodded. A "little" older being close to thirty years. The congressman had to be near seventy. A well-preserved seventy, but not exactly in the first blush of youth.

"And, naturally, he had a past. He was a bachelor for a long time, you know. He has to spend a lot of time away from home. So people talk."

"He was a bachelor for a long time, but he married you. That should tell people something." The intimacy of trying on clothes had sparked discussion of everything from stretch marks to fears of eternal spinsterhood, but Joanna never thought she'd be talking to the wife of a congressman about her insecurities.

Laura picked up her purse. "Sorry for going on and on. I'd better be leaving."

"I'll wrap these up for you. I'm so glad you found a few things you like." Selling the Pucci would pay the store's rent for a few weeks. Laura hadn't even glanced at its price tag.

Joanna pulled a sheet of hot pink tissue and laid it on the counter. "How did you hear about the store?"

"From my husband's chief of staff in town. I understand you know him."

"Yes, Andrew."

"With the polls so close, we've stepped up the functions, and I really needed to boost my wardrobe."

She wrapped the Pucci then slid the second dress off its hanger. "Did you get the chance to try this on?" She held up the black cocktail dress. "Sometimes they fit differently."

"I'm sure it will fit fine." Her voice had reverted to the confident, indifferent tone of someone who is always pleasant without really being engaged. She smiled, showing perfectly aligned, china white teeth. She tapped her credit card on the counter.

Chapter 14

After Laura Remmick and Kevin left, Joanna returned to the broken bathroom window. She moved the cardboard to the side, and, using a hand towel, carefully pushed the window the rest of the way open. She brushed shards of glass to the floor and lifted her skirt to step up on the toilet and look outside. There was just enough clearance for her shoulders. If a bigger person had tried to come in, he wouldn't have had much room to maneuver.

She leaned out further and looked down the narrow alley. Tallulah's Closet didn't have a back door. To the right, dumpsters hulked. To the left, light shone between the buildings.

Joanna's imagination replayed the scene. The intruder would have parked a few blocks away, then, without drawing attention to himself, slipped into the alley behind the video rental store. Keeping close to the buildings, he'd be less conspicuous. Dot's closed at two in the morning. Maybe he waited until then. She swallowed hard.

"Hello?" said a man's voice close behind her. She pulled back into the store so quickly that she bumped her head against the window frame. A piece of glass knocked loose and clinked to the floor.

Paul stood outside the bathroom. "Are you all right?"

She rubbed her skull where it throbbed from hitting the sash. "I'm fine. Don't you ever knock?"

"You didn't hear the doorbell? The landlord called and said you'd left him a message that someone broke in, this time through a window. He wanted me to come over and replace the glass. He didn't tell me to bring a first aid kit."

Joanna felt her face redden. "Sorry. I guess I was distracted."

Paul took a paper towel from behind the counter and wet it in the sink. "Here, let me get this."

He put a hand under Joanna's chin to steady her, then with his other hand lifted the hair from the side of her head. "It's bleeding a little. Looks like you scraped it." A freckle flecked the iris of one eye. He smelled of soap and wood.

He started to dab the paper towel to her head, but Joanna snatched it from his hand, controlling her breath. "Thank you, but I'm fine."

He stepped back and looked at her for a few seconds while she held the paper towel to her head.

"Aren't you here for something?" she asked.

"Yes, I am. Unless you'd rather I call the landlord back and tell him to send someone else."

"No. I'm sorry. It's just—I went to Marnie's memorial service this morning." She looked up. "I took your suggestion and tracked down some of her friends."

He smiled. "And they wanted to have a memorial service?"

"Yes, and before I left for the service, I stopped by the shop and found the window broken. Plus, someone stole one of my coats. Marnie's coat, actually."

"Did you lose much money?"

"That's the funny thing—other than the coat, nothing seems to have been taken."

"You've had a rough morning." His voice was sympathetic, but he kept his distance. "I can take care of the window, at least." She moved to let him in the bathroom. "Anyone could have pushed the window open once it was broken. There's not even a latch."

"Yeah, I can see that now. I'm guessing he came in through here but left through the front door. There's no way he could have shoved the coat out the window."

"You can push a button on the edge of the door and it will lock after you. It's not impossible to pick, either." Paul's body was hidden by the bathroom door. She heard the tinkle of glass as shards hit the trash can.

She gingerly touched the side of her head where it had hit the window frame. Could this day get any worse?

The bell at the door jingled. Joanna put on her customer face and turned. Her smile froze as she saw Eve.

"Hey Joanna." Eve flipped her hair. "Thought I'd come down and see this Lanvin coat I've heard so much about."

"You can't. It was stolen last night."

"You're funny," Eve said, but she wasn't laughing. "Get serious. I have a customer who totally goes for 1930s clothes. I could give you a good price for the coat."

Eve could give her a gold brick and Cary Grant's hand in marriage, and Joanna still wouldn't sell her Marnie's coat. Not that it mattered now. "It's the truth. Someone broke in last night and stole the coat."

Eve put a hand on her hip. "Someone broke in and took some old coat and didn't steal the flapper dress?" She pointed to a pale yellow beaded chemise so delicate that Joanna hung it high on the wall and only took it down for serious customers.

"Uh huh. They—"

Paul's voice interrupted. "I'm going to need to get a few tools and then go to the hardware store."

Eve looked over Joanna's shoulder. Her face lit up, her expression sweetening to pure honey. She brushed past Joanna, leaving a trail of jasmine, and held out her hand. "Eve Lancer. I don't believe we've met."

Joanna turned to see Paul smile in return. Was that simply a polite smile or something more? Eve held his hand a second longer than necessary. Joanna cleared her throat. "I'm sorry, but there's no coat to sell." She forced a smile. "But thank you for your interest."

Eve's eyes narrowed. "Well I don't really care about the coat anyway. I just wanted to tell you we'll be neighbors soon."

"Neighbors?" No, it couldn't be.

"My new store. I'm moving into the theater on the corner."

"But—but that's a theater." Joanna's mind raced. Profits were slender as it was.

"It's going to be a sort of combo vintage clothing store-movie house. High end."

"But—" Having another store so near would devastate Tallulah's Closet. "Don't you need a special permit or something? It's been a theater so long."

"Approval from the neighborhood association and a lease. That's it. I'm sure it won't be a problem. I'm seeing the landlord in a couple days and—" Eve examined a manicured finger "—the neighborhood association meeting isn't for another month or so."

"I see." A month. At least that was some time to prepare, although she had no idea how. Thanks to family money, Eve had limitless resources. She could buy up the best stock, offer it at rock bottom prices, and lure in every customer who might have wandered into Joanna's store instead. Then, when Tallulah's Closet was shuttered—which wouldn't take long, unfortunately—she'd jack up her prices again. And she'd do it laughing the whole time.

Eve smiled at Paul, who was pulling out his keys. "Leaving? I'll walk with you."

After they left, Joanna stood still a moment. Maybe Eve's store wouldn't be anything all that great, and customers would still prefer Tallulah's Closet. Maybe people selling clothes wouldn't stop by Eve's first before selling the leftovers to Joanna. She looked around the store—the softly lit jewelry case, the red bench where so many people tried on shoes, the racks of cocktail dresses that had danced at parties across town, across the decades.

Joanna had spent three years building Tallulah's Closet, but Eve could take it all down in a matter of months.

Chapter 15

While Joanna was showing a customer sundresses for a vacation to Mexico, Detective Crisp and a uniformed police officer arrived at last. Her heart quickened. Why was Crisp here? He investigated homicides, not break-ins. She calmed herself. Maybe it was for the best. She could tell him about the key.

Crisp, thumbs tucked into his belt, surveyed the store. The younger man, probably his first year on the job, cast an eye at the customer, who was holding up a filmy peignoir and trying to decide if she needed it for vacation, too.

"Nice store," the uniformed man said. "You call these clothes, what? Retro?"

"I usually call them 'vintage'," Joanna said.

"My grandma had a purse like that." He pointed to a black Koret handbag with peach silk lining.

"I hear that a lot." "My grandma had one of those" was probably the comment she heard most at the store, followed closely by "Everyone sure was small back then."

Crisp held out his hand. "You remember me? Foster Crisp. This is Officer Bryce."

"Yes, of course I remember you." She hesitated a moment. "They sent a homicide detective for a robbery?"

"I needed to talk to you anyway." Crisp wore a neatly ironed Western shirt, its yoke trimmed in blue piping. Today's bolo tie featured a polished agate. The fan ruffled the hair around his ears.

"I need to talk to you, too. Remember the—"

Impatient, Bryce cut in. "So, what was stolen? A ballgown? I guess it would be easy to get a bead on a fellow wearing an old ballgown around town." He laughed and slapped his thigh.

What a joker. "A coat from the 1930s. A Lanvin."

Officer Bryce said, "That's it? A coat?"

"Nothing else, at least not that I can tell. The stereo is still here, and the credit card receipts are locked in a cupboard under the jewelry case. I put the cash drawer in there every night, too."

"Is it a valuable coat, then?"

"Yes and no. It isn't in mint condition. It has a new lining, for one thing, so collectors wouldn't be interested. The leather's dry and won't stand up to much wear. But it's a beautiful coat. From a famous designer. The thing is, I think the burglars wanted the—"

"Where'd they break in?" the uniformed officer asked.

She led them to the bathroom. "In here. But I've been trying to tell you—"

This time it was Crisp who stopped her. "The stolen coat. Is it the one that covered Marnie Evans when you found the body?"

Joanna nodded. "I'd just stopped in to get something to wear to her memorial service this morning, actually. I found the bathroom window broken and a footprint on the toilet lid."

Officer Bryce opened his notebook. "When was the last time you were in the store, before today, that is?"

"I locked up just after six last night, then came in again at about nine-thirty this morning."

The men squeezed into the bathroom. Bryce rested his hand on the back of the toilet, and the tissue holder, a pink metal box decorated with poodles, clattered to the floor.

He snapped his notebook shut and tucked it into his back pocket. They moved back into the main part of the store. "I'm going to be honest with you. We get a lot of criminal mischief in this neighborhood. Graffiti, things like that. Some petty theft, too. None of your neighbors reported break-ins, and this kind of incident is common enough that I don't even think it's worth sending someone in to take prints."

Joanna drew a deep breath to quell her rising frustration. "There's one more thing."

Officer Bryce opened his mouth, but Joanna put up a hand to signal him to stop. She went to her purse on the shelf below the tiki bar, drew out Marnie's safe deposit box key, and handed it to Crisp.

"Remember how the Lanvin coat's lining was slit? I think whoever did it was looking for this. It fell out of the coat just after I bought it."

The detective turned the key in his hand. "What makes you think someone wanted the key?"

She sat down. "A lot of strange things have been happening since the coat came to the store. First, Marnie died. I found her there." She pointed at the tiki bar for Bryce's benefit.

The younger man leaned back, his leather belt creaking. "How'd she die?"

"The medical examiner said it was a heart attack—or at least that's what I read in the paper. But I'm telling you, her death couldn't have been natural," Joanna said. "It's too odd. She broke into the store and lay down and died? I don't think so. Then Apple—she works here, too—saw someone lurking outside. Plus, one of our customers bought the coat, and while she had it her apartment was broken into. The coat was in the trunk of her car the whole time. Nothing in her apartment was stolen. She ended up returning it. And now it's gone."

Joanna glanced toward the back of the store, where a customer was trying on cocktail rings and pretending not to listen.

The officer folded his arms. "In this neighborhood, it was probably kids on a dare, or someone who had had a few drinks next door and decided it would be fun to see if they could get into your store. To tell the truth, you're pretty lucky."

"So you're not going to follow up." Joanna wouldn't meet the officer's eyes. She knew he heard the frustration in her voice.

"I'm sorry ma'am. We'll take a report and put it on file. But it sounds like a whole lot of coincidence, and breaking and entering and stealing something of relatively low value isn't high on the list of priorities. If anything else happens, give me a call." The officer jotted a number on the back of a business card and put it on the counter. "Here's a report number if you need it for insurance."

Detective Crisp stepped forward. "Slow down, Bryce. Homicide is interested. I don't know why the murderer didn't take the coat the first time."

"Murderer?" She'd been half expecting something like this, but the word still shocked. The customer at the back of the store had given up all pretense of shopping and listened, slack-jawed.

"That's what I came to tell you. The autopsy report showed that when you found Ms. Evans, she'd already been dead for a day and a half."

This new information took a moment to sink in. "But I…"

"She didn't die here, Ms. Hayworth. She was brought here, already dead."

"What?" Joanna reached behind her for the bench and sat down. "Already dead?" A day and a half earlier. That would have been not long after Marnie had called her to demand the coat back.

Removing a pair of red mules jumbled on the bench, Detective Crisp joined her. "That's what I'm here to tell you. We've been to Ms. Evans' house. Someone broke in through the back door. Evans died, and the assailant drove her in her minivan to your store and left her here."

"But I thought she died of natural causes, a heart attack. You said 'murder.'"

The doorbell rang, and two women, one pushing a stroller, came in. Officer Bryce ushered them outside.

"She did die naturally. Her body was weakened by ovarian cancer. But the stress of someone breaking into her house may have brought on cardiac arrest. That's manslaughter."

Joanna shook her head. "I don't get it. Why would someone haul Marnie's body to my store? They had to have a reason for coming here, so they would have had to talk to Marnie first, hear about the store in the first place. She couldn't have died right away."

Bryce came back inside and flipped the sign to "closed."

Joanna raised a finger. "Couldn't the broken window have come later? Maybe someone — someone totally different — realized Marnie wasn't home and broke in to steal something."

"I see what you're getting at," Crisp said. "But nothing was stolen as far as we could tell. The last time we talked, you said you'd called her, correct?"

"Sure. She never picked up."

Crisp looked thoughtful. "I wondered."

"What?"

"The messages were erased on her answering machine. But that's the only thing out of place we noticed. No fingerprints, nothing stolen." He toyed with a pillbox hat near the bench. "It's the one piece I haven't figured out — why he didn't just leave the body at home."

The air in the store stifled. Joanna rose and turned up the fan another notch. Still standing, she faced Crisp. "Marnie sold me the Lanvin coat and some other clothing Tuesday morning. She called that afternoon and insisted on getting the coat back right away. Thursday morning I found her. So she must have died Tuesday afternoon or evening. Does that sound right?"

"Yes. That's correct."

"This is how I see it. Someone went to Marnie's house and demanded the safe deposit box key." She lifted the key to chin level. "Marnie called me to get the coat back because the key was in it, but I couldn't bring it. Maybe she was intending to come get the coat herself, but she didn't. She died. The — the person who was with her decided to break into the store himself to search for the coat and dump off Marnie's body." Yes, it was all coming together. "It's the safe deposit box key. I'm telling you, someone wants it."

"I think you're making too much of the coat. Why not steal it right away when he brought Marnie to the store? Why wait to come after the key?" Crisp asked.

"Well." She bit the corner of her lip. "Could there be two people after the key?"

Crisp shook his head. "So now you suspect two people."

"Think about it. The second person — the one who broke in — he might have called Marnie, but she was already dead. He erased the answering machine's messages so no one could track them back to him."

Crisp rose. "Look, I'm going to put all this speculation to rest right now. I see where you're going, but it's a dead end. Yes, someone stole the coat, undoubtedly to hide something—maybe hair or skin—that gave away his identity. We should have taken it as evidence right away."

"But the key. What about the key?"

"I told you, we've been doing some investigating, and we have a few promising leads. I can't tell you more than that."

"No. I'm not convinced." She folded her arms. Didn't he get it?

"Listen to me, Joanna." For the first time, Crisp let irritation cross his placid face. "We've been doing a lot of investigating, including Marnie's financial records. Marnie Evans didn't have a safe deposit box."

The customer shopping for her trip to Mexico emerged from the dressing room and handed two sundresses to Joanna. Officer Bryce and Detective Crisp parted to make way for her.

"No peignoir?" Joanna tried to sound upbeat, but the thought of Marnie dead in her minivan, then driven to the store and dumped, rattled her.

"Not this time."

She packaged up the customer's purchases while the policemen started for the door.

Just then, Paul walked in, carrying a bag from the hardware store. As Paul and the detective passed, each stopped in his tracks.

"Hello, Crisp."

"Hello, Paul."

Curious at the strained greeting, Joanna glanced up from the tiki bar.

The detective spoke first. "How's your uncle?"

"You probably know better than I do."

Crisp turned back to Joanna. "Does he have a key to the store?"

"I don't know. Maybe. I suppose so." Confused, she looked from man to man.

"Do you know him very well?"

Now alarmed, Joanna focused on Crisp. "What do you mean?"

He fixed his eyes on Paul. "No, I suppose you've always kept your hands clean." He turned to Joanna. "As for you, I'm just saying you need to be careful who you give access to the store. If you have any more problems, you have our number."

Officer Bryce backed up a step and knocked two pairs of pumps off their display rack.

"Uh, sorry," he said.

"Come on, Chet."

Joanna watched them get in the patrol car. Once the customer had left with her purchases, Joanna turned to Paul. "What was that all about?"

Paul set the paper bag on the counter. "Detective Crisp arrested my uncle. A couple of times, actually. They go back a long way, when Crisp was investigating robberies." He drew a small bottle from the bag and looked at her. "I brought you something for your scrape."

"He seemed concerned about the store." Joanna took the antiseptic from Paul's hands and sprayed some on a tissue, but her gaze remained on Paul.

"My uncle's a burglar. High-end stuff—jewelry and art, mostly. He had quite a reputation. Crisp chased him down for years before he finally caught up with him. He knows my uncle and I were close, and I suppose he wondered—" Paul picked up his toolbox. "Anyway, no need to worry about him. Uncle Gene's at Deer Creek state pen."

No need to worry about me, either, his tone implied. Aware of Paul watching her, she wandered to the stereo and pulled a record from the stack. Detective Crisp's cowboy boots had put her in the mood for this one in particular. She dropped the needle, and "Take Me Back to Tulsa" twanged from the speakers.

"Bob Wills and the Texas Playboys," Paul said. "You're kidding."

"I love it," she said stubbornly.

"I do, too. It's just not a popular choice these days."

"Story of my life."

They looked at each other. Joanna felt her skin flush. The phone rang, but she didn't move to pick it up. After a few rings it stopped. Bob Wills sang about Little Bee getting honey while Big Bee got the blossom.

Paul broke the silence. "I'd better take care of the window."

She surprised herself by touching his arm. "Have you had lunch yet? I was just going to order something from next door. They do a Middle Eastern plate that's pretty good if you eat your way around the hummus."

"No, but thanks." He picked up his tools and started toward the bathroom. "This shouldn't take long, and I'll be out of here."

Chapter 16

Later in the afternoon, Joanna took the safe deposit box key from her purse and pressed it on the counter. It was small and made of brass, with a five digit number and "U.S. Bank" inscribed on it. If Crisp wasn't going to follow up, she was. Marnie might have had an alias. Who knows? She picked up the phone.

After a few seconds of a jazzy version of "The Long and Winding Road," a woman answered. "U.S. Bank Personal Services. May I help you?"

"Yes, I wonder if you have a safe deposit box registered to Marnie — or Margaret — Evans?"

"I'm sorry. We can't give out that information."

Joanna had expected as much. "It's like this. Marnie Evans died, and I found the key in her things. What happens to the contents of her safe deposit box, assuming that she does have one?"

The woman on the phone explained that the executor of Marnie's will would have to prove Marnie died before getting access to the box, unless Marnie had authorized someone else to have access to it, too. That is, if she did have a safe deposit box.

"I see. Thank you." She clunked the phone back in the cradle. So she wouldn't be able to walk into the bank herself and see what was in the box. She picked up the phone again to order a bowl of soup from next door. After Paul left, a flurry of customers had kept her busy until now, and she was starved. As she waited for the food to arrive, she tapped a pen absently on the counter.

The police thought she was overreacting about the key, but she wasn't buying it. Someone broke into Tallulah's Closet and slashed the coat's lining first before stealing it. Gisele's apartment was broken into. The coat and Marnie were the only things common to both situations. And Marnie had ended up dead. Whoever wanted that key must be the same person who moved Marnie to the store and slashed the coat's lining.

She stared at the key on the counter. Her first instinct was to get rid of it. She could toss it off the Hawthorne Bridge. If the key was gone, the threat was gone. On second thought, whoever wanted the key wouldn't know it was gone. He — or she — would think Joanna still had it.

But who would even know Joanna had the key in the first place? It would have to be someone who suspected that the key was in the coat and also knew that the coat was at Tallulah's Closet. Laura Remmick had seemed unnaturally interested in Marnie, and she had wanted to try the coat on. She was slender and fit enough to have come in the bathroom window. But she wouldn't break into a store and steal the coat, then come back the next day.

The oscillating fan whooshed in the background. Marnie, oh, Marnie. How could Marnie have knowingly put her in this kind of risk? Joanna fidgeted with a pen, then threw it down. Blossom Dearie's baby-talk crooning on the stereo began to irritate her, and she replaced the LP with the *Barbarella* soundtrack. She shouldn't be mad at Marnie. She probably hid the key so long ago that she'd forgotten it was even in the coat until after she sold it. Whoever wanted the key hadn't forgotten, though.

Her thoughts were interrupted by the waitress from Dot's carrying a bowl of soup on a tray. "Here it is. Tomato today. I tossed in an extra roll."

"Thanks," Joanna said and handed her cash. The ringing phone pierced the store's calm. Joanna's hand hit the edge of the soup bowl, and it crashed to the linoleum floor. A large, red stain spread slowly at her feet. She grabbed a handful of paper towels from the bathroom to soak up the soup as she answered the phone. It was an automated call encouraging her to refinance her mortgage. Cursing, she slammed the soaked paper towels into the garbage and went to the bathroom for the mop. At least it was almost time to close. She could make something comforting to eat at home — maybe tagliatelle with truffle oil, Pecorino Romano, and a little parsley from the garden. Or a tomato pasta.

The bell at the door rang as a pregnant woman with bleached platinum hair, roots showing, and a raft of bluebirds tattooed over her shoulders entered the store. "Still open?"

"For another five minutes." Joanna leaned the mop against the wall. Damn it. Hopefully the customer would be quick about it. "Looking for anything in particular?"

"Maternity wear." The customer picked up a pair of shoes. "Look, it says 'Henry Waters Shoes of Consequence.' That's hilarious."

"We have a few pieces over here. Two 1950s smock tops by Lady in Waiting."

"Lady in Waiting. Where do they get those names?"

Joanna forced a smile.

"I don't know if I'll get this big." The pregnant lady examined one of the tops and patted her belly. "I'm vegan. My doctor says I should be eating more protein. Dairy, even. My doula says vegan is fine if I do supplements."

She could eat a whole canned ham for all Joanna cared. "We have some house dresses, too. A couple of wrap dresses in cotton. They'd see you up to the last trimester."

"Look at that." The pregnant lady ignored Joanna and picked up a navy patent slingback with suede trim. She read from the inside of the shoe. "'Fiancés, Go Steady With,' it says."

"Yeah, those names are really something." Would she ever leave? It didn't look like she wanted to buy anything.

She put down the shoe. "Bug's father—I'm calling him 'Bug' for now," she said as she rested a hand on her belly "—thinks dairy is a good idea. Sometimes I get a little lightheaded. My blood pressure is low, you know. But I'm like, hey, you're just the father. We're not even married. You don't have a real say at this point."

An unmarried mother, like Marnie. And the father had no say. Could that be it? Could that be what's in Marnie's safe deposit box—the identity of Troy's father? Joanna directed her focus to the pregnant lady. She didn't want to rush her—after all, she needed the sale, especially with Eve's store opening—but she had to think. What else could it be that someone would be so desperate to hide?

"I'm sorry there's nothing here for you today. We get new stock all the time, so make sure to check back. If you leave your phone number, I can give you a call if anything comes in."

When at last the customer left, Joanna flipped the sign at the front door to "closed."

It's not stocks or jewels in the safe deposit box. It must be proof of the father of Marnie's child. A secret someone is desperate to hide.

*
**

Joanna shut off the lights and closed the shop for the night, making sure that the bathroom window was also locked, and left for home on foot. Neighbors were walking their dogs after work, and the jasmine-like scent of blooming Glorybower trees wafted through the late summer evening. She unlocked her front door and stood just inside the house for a moment, listening. The house was quiet. Normal. The portraits stared in the dim light. This is ridiculous, Joanna thought. I'm getting paranoid.

In the garden she plucked a large, ripe Caspian Pink tomato still warm from the sun. She pinched the tips of a basil plant and put the leaves in her skirt, which she'd gathered up and held in one hand as a basket. She picked a handful of green beans and added them to the pile of vegetables. She'd peel and cook the tomato with the green beans, add a few tablespoons of cream, and toss them with pasta. After a day like today, a starchy dinner was just the ticket.

She double-checked doors and windows before bed to make sure they were locked, but that night she slept uneasily. The neighbor, home from swing shift at the sewage treatment plant, woke her as his car pulled in the driveway outside her bedroom window. A blast of Crosby, Stills, and Nash quit suddenly when he cut the engine. The predawn train whistles at the Brooklyn yards a few miles away woke her, too, even though she normally slept through them and even liked their faraway eeriness when she did hear them. She thought about the key resting in her purse's inside pocket. Someone broke into the store to find it. Would he come here, too?

Worry held her in the strange world between consciousness and sleep. Images of Marnie on the beach with Ray and his brother,

Troy holding a bouquet of birds of paradise, and Eve smiling at Paul floated in and out until Joanna finally woke. The sun was still soft on the horizon.

Chapter 17

Pioneer Courthouse Square overflowed with people. Some clutched to-go cups of iced lattes. Others balanced children on their hips or in front-packs against their chests. Still others out on the sidewalk waved signs reading "Environmentalists for Remmick" or simply "Remmick for Senate." Loudspeakers played music fuzzy with static.

Joanna and Apple wedged themselves between a man with a patient Labrador retriever and a group of junior high school girls with pink and blue hair.

"So you really think Marnie was hiding a birth certificate or something like that in her safe deposit box?" Apple asked.

"What else could it be?"

"Maybe she was blackmailing him. The father, I mean."

"If she was, she wasn't very good at it. She always seemed to be broke. What I wonder is, why now? Troy must be thirty-ish. Why wait so long?" Joanna frowned at a teenager holding a skateboard who pushed his way past her.

"Maybe because Marnie knew she was dying. Maybe she needed money to pay the doctor. I guess we'll never know." Apple peeled up the edge of her broad-brimmed hat to look at the stage. "Do you see Andrew?"

"No, but I'm sure he's here. He'd better be. I had to close the store this morning to be here." She surveyed the crowd. "How is it that Portlanders manage to look like they're camping even when they're downtown?"

Some of the crowd were street-cool with tattoos and clothes likely scavenged from the Goodwill bins. But much of the rest of the crowd, the people who wrote the larger checks to Remmick, Joanna guessed, wore tee shirts with hiking shorts and flip flops or rubber clogs. Some even sported the horror of sandals with socks. In the 1950s — the years of vintage clothing she loved best — downtown on a Sunday afternoon, men would have worn straw fedoras and ladies would have worn cotton dresses with pumps that matched their handbags. The women would have put on lipstick and set their hair. These days, everyone from a janitor to the mayor wore fleece vests.

A handful of women in cotton tees and leggings edged near Joanna and Apple. They looked to have just come from yoga class, leaving a flotilla of Subaru wagons in the parking lot.

"I bet they're all on the board of the same Montessori school," Joanna whispered. "I wonder where the kids are?"

"At Suzuki camp, probably. Or terrorizing the labradoodle."

Heat rose from the square's brick pavement. A woman jostled Joanna as she made her way closer to the stage. The light rail train's bell sounded twice as its doors opened and more people disgorged onto the sidewalk bordering the square.

At last the music shut off, and the crowd's noise began to rise. Congressman Charles Remmick took the stage. Remmick wore khakis and a button-down shirt open at the neck and looked entirely at ease in front of the crowd that now roared with applause and whistles. His arms and face were tan, maybe from his much-publicized river rafting trips or from training for the Portland marathon he ran each year, even at his age.

"Thank you," Remmick said, his voice reverberating through the square. The crowd quieted. "Thank you all for coming out. I always know I can count on Portlanders to want to talk about the issues.

"As you know, I wasn't born with a silver spoon in my mouth. I grew up watching my father come home from the cannery every night, tired, worried about the broken arm that might plunge my family into debt we couldn't shake, or thinking about the college that he couldn't afford for me.

"But I'm not here to give you a sob story about growing up poor. I just want you to know I understand where so many Oregonians are coming from. And living on the coast also gave me a keen appreciation of our wilderness. I played in the woods with my friends, pretending we were Lewis and Clark. I got to know our Native American friends and see, firsthand, their daily struggles."

The crowd cheered again. Joanna remembered Andrew telling her one night that Remmick's big break as a young lawyer had come when he had defended a tribe that sought federal recognition. Ultimately, the bid failed, but Remmick made headlines that boosted his first run for Congress.

"All my life I've loved Oregon and known I wanted to do what's right for its people. I want to make sure that we all have healthcare and that we have the best colleges and universities. I want to know our pristine wilderness stays that way — " this brought a whoop from the audience " — that salmon runs are strong, and that our air and water are pure."

Joanna began to tune out Remmick's words. She supported him one hundred percent, but over the next half hour he would lay out why he was the best candidate for the Senate, mostly for the benefit of the television cameras that would broadcast snippets to Pendleton, Baker City, and points east. She'd heard it before. The crowd pressed against her.

"Look, there's his wife," Joanna whispered to Apple and nodded toward the stage. "Doesn't she look like she could have walked straight out of central casting for 'politician's wife of uncertain age'? I still can't believe she bought the Pucci." Laura Remmick tossed her artfully dyed hair and laughed with the crowd at something her husband said.

Apple looked intently at the stage. "He has a waxy aura."

"Andrew?" Joanna asked.

"No, Remmick. He has a huge blue reach, but a waxy residue on the edges. And pointed on top." She shot a glance at Joanna. "You know what I think of Andrew's aura."

"What does a pointed aura mean?"

"Dishonesty, usually."

One of the Montessori moms glared at Apple and made a "hush" noise. Apple flashed her a "peace" sign.

Dishonesty. As far as most people were concerned, Remmick's reputation was unimpeachable. He'd done so much good for his district. From the stage, Laura Remmick smiled at her husband. No children joined them — too bad, the papers would have loved that. No children. Unless…Marnie? Could Remmick be the father? The crowd cheered to something he'd said, and Remmick beamed, a light wind ruffling his hair. No. Impossible.

They stood for a moment, listening to more platitudes about jobs, the environment, and the need to turn out for the election. Antsy, Joanna looked at Apple, and Apple nodded. They wove their way out of the crowd and across the street surrounding the square.

"Air, at last," Joanna said.

"You seem distracted."

"I can't help but think about Marnie and wonder why she hid that safe deposit box key. The store just doesn't feel the same anymore." Their footsteps hit the sidewalk in unison. "Hell, my life doesn't feel the same. Ever since she brought in that coat, everything has turned upside down. Marnie died, the store's been broken into, and now Eve plans to run me out of business."

"I never felt good about that coat from the get-go," Apple said.

"It's not the coat's fault. It's that key. I'm sure of it."

"The store's closed until lunch, right? I have some mugwort in my bag. Why don't we do an energy clearing? The coat's gone, Marnie's—gone. Maybe if we clear the energy things will get back to normal."

"I don't know. Last time you smudged, you set off the smoke detectors. I thought we'd never get them turned off again."

"You have to admit that things went much more smoothly around there after I cleared that load of Jantzen bathing suits. The toilet started working again, remember?" Apple's bracelets jangled as she lifted a hand to push up her sunglasses. "It can't hurt."

"Oh, all right. I'm meeting up with Nina, Marnie's old roommate, this afternoon, but I guess we have a couple of hours."

"That's plenty of time. The car's just around the corner." Apple picked up her pace.

Joanna was skeptical. Turning around her life now was way too much work for a little bit of herbs.

"First, let's move these mannequins. We need privacy." Apple lugged two mannequins—one adorned with a sky-blue lace dress with a full skirt and three rhinestone brooches pinned in a cluster, the other in a dusty brown 1950s suit with a thick mink band encircling the wrist of each sleeve — to build a screen between the tiki bar and the wall the store shared with Dot's. With a rack of hats between them, they shut out the view of the back of the store from the front window.

"Where should we sit?" Joanna asked.

"There." She pointed to the leopard rug near the dressing rooms.

Joanna arranged the folds of her broad-skirted sundress around her on the floor. She reached over to straighten the lace hem on the mannequin. "Okay. What's the plan?"

Apple moved a 1960s *Vogue* from the end table and replaced it with a lunch plate from Dot's. She pinched some herbs from a tin container in her purse and made a pile on the saucer. "Can't say. It depends. I'll clear my mind and see if I get any messages." She struck a match from an old Brown Derby matchbook — amazing they still worked — and lit the herbs. She sat back and closed her eyes.

Joanna sighed. When Apple was communing with the spirits, it could take anywhere from a few minutes to half an hour. To pass the time, she looked around the store. She didn't often see it from this angle. The hems of the black cocktail dresses against one wall hung in flounces, lettuce edges, and stiff shantung silk. The feathers on one cocktail hat shivered as if they adorned a head in conversation at a mid-century party. Funny. There must be a draft somewhere.

If Eve had her way, Joanna would be posting a "store closing" sale sign at Tallulah's Closet soon. Eve didn't care who paid the price as long as she got what she wanted. Joanna's chest ached. She didn't have the money to set up shop somewhere else. And the neighborhood was getting so much better. If she could hang on for another year or two, she might start to see enough profit to build some savings.

She leaned against the zebra chair behind her. The sweet, weedy smell of the mugwort reminded her of the woods where she grew up. Once, when she was ten or so, she lost her way in the forest. At first she didn't care. She sang and threw rocks in the creek. No one bothered her there. Then the woods darkened. She found an old logging road and ran down it, crying, until she heard her grandfather yelling her name in the distance. His flashlight barely pierced the thick night. That's how she felt now, but no one was in the wings to save her.

She wanted to look at the time so not to be late for Nina, but Apple appeared to be deep in spirit communication mode.

"Apple —"

"Hush." Apple held up her hand. "Marnie. She hasn't yet moved on."

"Moved on?"

"Passed over. She's still here, and she's — well, it feels like she's disappointed."

"Angry or confused, I understand. But disappointed?"

Apple seemed troubled. "I don't know. I can't say I've ever felt this from a spirit. There was something else, too, but I can't put my finger on it." She closed her eyes again. "Wait."

A bus rumbled by. Someone, her voice undoubtedly amplified by too many vodka tonics, came out of the bar next store saying, "— Takes me for granted. Like he thinks I'm just going to sit home while — " The voice faded.

Apple opened her eyes. "Oh Joanna."

"What?"

She hesitated. "It'll get worse. Maybe much worse."

The back of Joanna's neck prickled.

"Something about a baby, too. Something about a baby, and she's sorry." Despite the store's stuffiness, Apple rubbed her arms. "I don't think we should be messing around in this."

"I thought you said you were clearing energy so that everything could get back to normal."

"You don't believe in any of this, uh, hocus pocus anyway, right?" Apple quickly replied. She took a deep breath and exhaled. "We need to leave all of this alone and let the police do their jobs. Give the safe deposit box key to the police. And I'm glad we're rid of that coat."

Joanna stood to return the mannequins back to their original places. "Well, I'm not glad about losing the coat. It was special to Marnie, and it's special to me. Plus, I tried to give the key to the police, but they didn't want anything to do with it." She fluffed the skirt of the blue-dress clad mannequin.

Apple turned a glass over the mugwort to extinguish its smoke. "Then don't say I didn't warn you."

Chapter 18

Driving across town, Joanna pondered Apple's warning. The "baby." Surely that meant Troy. She wanted her old life back: calm evenings with a novel, a good dinner, a hot bath. Marnie's safe deposit box had to be at the crux of her troubles. If she could figure out what was in it, who wanted it, all this trouble would go away.

She pulled into a parking spot on the street around the corner from Pal's Shanty, a seafood bar not far from the Wet Spot. The emergency brake squawked as she yanked it. Nina was so nice to suggest they meet again. Maybe she'd even know something about Troy's father.

Nina was already seated at a bar-high table when Joanna arrived. A beer and a tin bucket of clams sat in front of her. The murmur of friendly conversation drifted from the bar running across the other side of the room. Nina raised a hand in greeting, the charms on her bracelet glinting.

"Have some clams. Garlic bread is on the way. It's just a beer bar, but they have a decent house white wine." Nina waved at a waitress. She'd twisted her coal black hair into a side bun and planted a silk orchid in it.

"Glass of house white for me, thanks." Joanna perched on a bar stool. "More fish eating?"

"You got it. Every time I see a fish stick hit the pie hole, I smile."

She seemed relaxed. "I thought the memorial service went pretty well, don't you?"

"I do. Thank you for everything you did to make it happen."

"I was glad to do it. It was nice to see everyone together again. Been a long time." She focused on Joanna. "What's with you? You seemed kind of worked up. I thought the service would calm you down. Isn't it what you wanted?"

"Yes. Sure." White wine in a thick glass alit in front of her. She took a sip. From a box—the bubbles, if not the taste, were a dead giveaway—but passable. "Yesterday I found out Marnie had already been dead at least a day when I found her. That means—"

"Somebody brought her, dead, to your store and dumped her. Honey, I'm sorry." She reached out and patted Joanna's arm. "It just gets stranger, doesn't it?"

"It was strange enough when I thought she broke in, then died. But now…." She took another sip of wine.

"Now you're wondering why you were chosen?"

"That's it."

Nina shook her head. "Marnie's life has been a cipher. Always. She couldn't even die in a normal way, poor thing."

"It's funny, but I—" She paused, feeling embarrassed. "I feel like she chose me somehow. Like I was special to her. The last time I saw her she called me 'family'."

Nina leaned back and examined Joanna. "I don't want you to take this the wrong way, but you come off as a little reserved. Maybe even stand-offish. So was Marnie. She might have connected with that."

"Maybe." Nina's remark, though true, stung.

"She made a lot of choices that alienated her from people, but those choices never seemed to get her anywhere." Nina signaled to the waitress for another beer. "Not that you'd do that, honey."

"Like what?"

"Her choices? Well, moving to Portland to dance at Mary's Club for one thing. Her father disowned her, and her mother had to sneak away to write letters to her. She lost family, friends, to do what she did."

"Marnie reminded me a little of my grandmother. I always kind of wished they could have met. Grandma even grew up somewhere near Marnie, I think."

Nina touched her hand. "What was her name?"

"Helen. Helen Miller." Saying her grandmother's name warmed her. "Pretty common name, I know."

"Funny. I heard Marnie talk about a Helen. Who knows?"

Nina was humoring her, but Joanna appreciated the gesture. "She moved to Portland for Franklin, her boyfriend, right?"

"Sure. But look how far that got her. You'd think if he really cared for her he wouldn't have let her dance. Or he would have married her. Instead, he went and married someone else and left her —"

"To hook up with Don."

"Among others." Nina played with her beer bottle. "Don wasn't the only one, you know."

The regulars along the bar, mostly retirees, chatted. Talk about the Trail Blazers basketball team drifted over. "And then there was Troy. I wonder who his father is?"

Nina pressed garlic bread into the juice left behind by the clams. "I've been wondering about that, too. You know, I even wondered if it might be Chick Remmick."

"The congressman? You're joking."

"They knew each other. Had an affair, even, when he was

district attorney."

"Wow. I'm surprised — and yet, not really surprised after all." Chick Remmick and Marnie. That would explain Laura Remmick's interest in Marnie. "I went to Remmick's rally this morning. I admit, the same thought crossed my mind when I saw him on stage, but I couldn't believe it."

"Their affair was no secret. Didn't last long, but still."

Coming to see Nina had been a good idea. Nina was the first square lead she'd had about the key. Joanna lowered her voice. "Marnie sold me a coat, and a safe deposit box key fell out of it after she left. I keep thinking she must have put a birth certificate in the safe deposit box. Something proving who Troy's father is. And now — "

"Now with the election — "

"Exactly." Joanna tapped the table. "The election is tight. If it got out that he fathered a child by a stripper, he'd be toast."

Nina pushed her now-empty plate away and leaned forward. "This key. Do you still have it?"

Joanna hesitated a moment before responding. No. It couldn't be Nina who broke in. What would be her motive? "It's in my purse right now." At some point, though, whoever wanted the key was going to figure out she had it. She dropped the clam shell she held on a napkin and pushed it away. "Detective Crisp, the one investigating Marnie's death, says she didn't have a safe deposit box."

Nina shrugged. "Marnie was no dummy. If she had something to hide, she would have figured out a way to have a safe deposit box that didn't tie straight back to her name." Nina leaned back and nodded. "A shame, really."

"What do you mean?"

"He's a good congressman, and he'll be a good senator. Why should something that happened years ago get in the way? I mean, Remmick was a bachelor then. It's not like he was cheating on his wife."

"But what about Marnie? Someone killed her and moved her to my store then stole the coat."

"Killed her? The papers said she died of natural causes. A heart attack."

Joanna remembered Nina's outburst at the memorial service. She hadn't been so sanguine about Marnie's death then. She'd insisted Marnie was murdered. "But moving her to my store?"

Nina took a long draw of her beer. "Maybe he wanted her to be somewhere someone could find her. Not leave her alone at home for God knows how long." She tucked the silk flower firmly behind her ear. "Honey, I've seen a lot in my years here on planet Earth. I wish we could say that good and bad are as clear as black and white, but they aren't. Take marriage for instance. Gary wasn't my first choice, but you know what?"

"What?" Joanna answered as expected.

"He's done right by me every step of the way." She waved a hand in front of her. "Oh, I'm not easy. No sir. I've put him to the test, but Gary has been there for me. Sure, maybe he's no Alan Ladd, but I can count on him. You know what I mean? In the end, that's what matters. After all, passion dies." Nina's beer was empty. Maybe that accounted for her lost look. "Right?" Nina prompted.

"Right."

"If Chick Remmick had a kid by Marnie, well, good by him. I wouldn't hold it against him. It was a long time ago." She sighed. "And look at the alternative. That bigot, Mayer. Now that one. I could tell you stories about that one."

Nina went on to regale her with a story about Mayer's indiscretions at the clubs in the 1960s, but Joanna's thoughts were on Remmick. Nina might be right. Perhaps Marnie had a child by him, put the baby up for adoption, and locked up the birth certificate. With the election, Remmick wanted to make sure no one found out about Troy. Sure, in this day and age it wouldn't matter to most people, but a surprise love child could definitely be a distraction. Remmick may have visited Marnie, and in her weakened condition she died. Maybe Marnie had told him about her, and he brought her to Tallulah's Closet so she'd be found. It could have happened that way.

If Remmick were Troy's father, what was the harm in giving him the safe deposit box key? Then her troubles would be over. Then everything could go back to normal.

Back home, Joanna reached for the phone and wandered to the front window, the phone's cord dragging behind her. She dialed Andrew's number.

"Hey there," Andrew answered. "Calling to pledge receipts from every disco dress you sell to the Remmick campaign?"

"Funny." She didn't laugh.

"Did you make it to the rally?"

"Sure did. It was inspirational." Or would have been had she stayed for the whole thing. "I didn't know if you'd answer the phone, you're so busy these days."

"I'm in my car now on the way to a prep meeting with City Club, but I'm glad you called. Why don't we meet up for a drink later this week?"

She ignored his question. "Do you have any fundraisers coming up for Remmick? Soon? Maybe something not too large? But not too small, either." She rushed the last part as she thought about the gossip that might arise if Andrew showed up with her and not his wife at an intimate function.

"Sure, practically every night. Tonight there's a dinner hosted by one of the execs at Bowman lumber."

"Will you take me?" No point in beating around the bush.

"Oh, Jo, I don't know. I'll be working all night. Besides, why do you even want to go? You never were interested in going to these things when we dated."

"Remember how you always told me I should market the shop to women on the west side? I thought this would be a great chance to meet more people. You know how these events are. All the men will be chatting in one room, and the women will gather on the patio and talk about each other." Joanna was appalled at how well she lied, but it wasn't too far off. With Eve trying to move into the neighborhood she'd need all the business she could get. "I could give them someone new to talk about."

"I told Laura Remmick about Tallulah's Closet, you know. I saw her reading the obit for that old showgirl who used to sell you clothes, and I told her about you."

"Yes, thanks. I really appreciate it. She came in and bought a few things yesterday." Andrew paused. Joanna could hear traffic in the background. She knew she almost had him. "I have just the perfect dress for a nice dinner party. I'll do you credit."

"All right," he said. "I suppose it wouldn't hurt to add a new face and shake things up a little. I'll pick you up at six-thirty."

"Thanks, Andrew. Say hi to Heather for me." Joanna thought it wouldn't be a bad idea to remind him of his wife.

Chapter 19

Joanna turned off the taps and leaned back in the warm water. A bath always calmed her down.

She wasn't looking forward to the evening ahead. Her excuse to Andrew about trolling for new business felt weaker by the hour. Portland's society women clung to a social order more rigid than Louis XIV's court. Conservative women joined the Portland Garden Club and crafted elaborate centerpieces for fundraising dinners at the art museum, while more liberal women joined the Hardy Plants Society and arranged garden tours to support farmers' markets. Conservative women shopped at boutiques, and it wouldn't cross their minds to wear "used" vintage clothing. Meanwhile liberal society women stuck to practical shoes and pant suits. They might, however, wear a vintage velvet evening coat or a splashy 1950s crystal brooch pinned over a scarf hand-woven by African villagers.

Laura Remmick fit the liberal society woman mold, but chances were high the rest of the wives would be more conservative. In fact, Joanna was surprised Remmick would even bother trying to raise money from timber executives.

Tonight she'd wear a mid-century lavender cocktail dress by Ceil Chapman, one of Marilyn Monroe's favorite designers. Chapman made dresses the media had dubbed "tabletop" gowns for the display they made above the waist. This dress had Ceil Chapman's signature wrapping across the bodice over a straight skirt that ended at the knees. The sleeves dipped just off the shoulder, but not scandalously so.

She rummaged through her jewelry box until she found the bracelet her grandmother had left her, gold chain links dangling a large faux pearl charm. The last time she'd seen her grandmother wear it, it had been just a few months before the accident. Her grandparents were driving into town for an anniversary dinner, and her grandmother had even troubled to paint her fingernails, leaving the moons exposed as she'd been taught in beauty school during the Depression. The bracelet wouldn't fetch more than a few dollars at Tallulah's Closet, but she wouldn't trade it for diamonds. As she fingered its links, she felt a familiar pang of guilt mixed with sadness. She tucked the safe deposit box key into her evening clutch.

Andrew pulled up to her house on time and honked the horn. He was talking on his cell phone. He honked again, then waved when he saw her. She remembered clearly why she had broken up with him.

"Hey Jo. Do you mind if I keep the top down?" he said when he finally slid the phone into his suit jacket.

"That's fine." She settled into the leather seat, pulling the skirt of her dress up slightly so that she could sit. "A little air would be nice."

"It was Heather on the phone." He sighed and started the car.

"You told her that you're taking me to tonight's dinner, right?" It dawned on her that Andrew might have "forgotten" to mention it to his wife.

"Yes, of course. I was just telling her that I was here to pick you up. I might have hinted that it was a boring event at the historical society. I figured there wasn't any reason in getting her too upset."

She looked away. He hadn't changed at all.

"You know, you always understood me." He cast a quick glance at her cleavage.

Same old tune. It was easier to take Andrew's calls and meet for the occasional coffee than not see him. At least, it used to be. She remembered the night they stayed up late years ago playing cards with friends in a cabin on Mount Hood. He was relaxed, happy to be winning a pun-fest inspired by the word "egg." He had locked eyes with Joanna across the worn card table and lifted his lips in a conspiratorial smile. She touched the charm on her bracelet. The sooner they arrived at the dinner party and were surrounded by other people the better.

"I need to stop for gas. Shouldn't be a minute." He pulled the BMW up to a pump across from an old pickup truck. Andrew honked the horn. "Where's the attendant?" Andrew's impatience could flash so quickly into anger. The same weekend on Mount Hood he was so loving, they blew a tire on the way home. The flat wasn't anyone's fault, but he tore a branch from a tree along the road and thrashed it against the tree until its bark shredded. Joanna had moved to the other side of the car and watched intently, measuring her breathing, until his anger was spent.

He honked again. "Why does everything take so long? I don't know why this state has such a stupid law about not letting you pump your own gas."

"I'm in no hurry." Despite her irritation, she fell into her old habit of calming him. "It's a nice evening."

"Yes, I guess it is." His voice relaxed. "Where did you find this dress? I like it." He leaned forward to stroke the fabric at her shoulder.

He had crossed the line. Just as she raised her hand to push him away, Andrew leaned back and waved his hand. "Over here. We don't have all day, you know. Fill it up."

"Then I guess you'll have to tell that to the guy who actually works here. Hi Joanna."

She turned in her seat to see Paul standing next to the truck. He held a squeegee and must have been washing the windows on the other side when they had pulled up. "Oh, hi Paul." Damn Andrew.

Paul dropped the squeegee into a bucket. Andrew might be wearing Gucci, but Joanna knew plenty of people who would pay good money to look like Paul in his faded jeans and tee shirt. "I think the attendant is checking the oil on the Honda over there." Paul nodded at the far end of the lot. He opened the truck's door and slid in. As he started the engine, he rolled down the driver's side window and said, "You look great. Have fun tonight."

When the truck pulled out of the lot, Joanna turned to Andrew. "Why are you so rude? Just because a man is washing his windows you think he works here?"

"I don't see why you're so worked up. I mean, he could have been the attendant. He looked like it."

"And even if he was, that's still no excuse for yelling at him." When they were dating, she never would have risked Andrew's anger by talking to him like this. It felt good to let loose.

"What's got into you? Who is that guy, anyway?"

The attendant strolled over to the BMW. "Fill 'er up?" Andrew nodded and handed him a credit card.

"What's it to you who he is?"

"You're just so defensive. You're not interested in him, are you? I mean, he doesn't look like your type."

"That's none of your business. Besides, what makes you think you know my type?" The genie had officially left the bottle.

"I mean, he hardly looks like an Ivy League graduate. What does he do for a living? Deliver beer?" Andrew drew back. "Wait a minute. That was the guy changing the locks at the store, wasn't it? Do you have a thing for him?"

"Maybe he didn't go to Harvard, but that doesn't mean that he's not worth knowing. At least he's not the kind of guy who makes passes at an ex-girlfriend while his wife is home with the baby." The gas station attendant lifted his eyebrows. Joanna knew she was making a scene, but for once she didn't care.

"Listen, just because you're sorry we broke up, you don't have to take it out on me. You have no idea what's going on for me at home. It isn't as easy as you think. I'm under a lot of stress."

It figured that the discussion would roll back around to Andrew. It always did. "I'm not sorry I broke up with you. In fact, I'm happier about it every day that goes by."

"Why? I treated you well."

"No. You didn't." She had wanted to say those words for a long time. "I treat you well" had been one of Andrew's stock phrases. To avoid a fight, she had always let it slide. Apparently she was looking for a fight today. "You didn't treat me well at all. You put me down in a thousand little ways. You didn't listen to me. I didn't dress well enough for you. I never finished my law degree. I never was good enough, and I almost believed it. No, the best thing I ever did was to leave you."

Joanna braced herself for his anger. Would she be able to make it home walking in her evening pumps? Instead, he was quiet. Maybe her words had been a little harsh. Regret replaced the thrill of letting loose. "Look, I'm sorry. Let's forget this ever happened."

The attendant handed back Andrew's credit card and receipt and replaced the cap to the gas tank. He glanced at Joanna, fascinated.

Andrew started the car. He sounded subdued. "Heather says we need to see a counselor. She says if we don't, she'll leave me. I know things between her and me haven't been perfect, but I'm so busy these days with the campaign."

Oh lord. She pushed back in her seat and looked straight ahead. "I'm sure you'll work it out." It was shaping up to be quite an evening.

Chapter 20

The sun sat low on the horizon, casting the lilac light through the sky the French called "the blue hour." They drove in silence for a few minutes before Joanna spoke. "Who will be at the dinner?"

"The host is a senior vice president at Bowman, and he's invited some people from the Forestry Institute. And Chick and Laura, of course." His confident tone had returned. He shifted down as they approached a curve. "There's one other person you'll know, too." He kept his eyes on the road.

"Who?"

"Eve Lancer."

Great. Just great. "Andrew. Why didn't you—"

"I know you don't like her, but she's dating Marlene's brother. Marlene and Denny are the hosts." When Joanna didn't respond, Andrew continued. "What's the big deal with Eve, anyway? I know you've got something against her, I just don't know what."

"She's just not—it's that—well, she doesn't really love vintage clothes." She knew that sounded lame. Andrew would never get it.

"That's no crime. I'm not totally wild about vintage clothing, either—except on you, of course."

She shot him a warning glance. "And now she's opening a shop just down the block from me. It'll devastate Tallulah's Closet, and she knows it."

"Maybe it will help the store by drawing more vintage clothing buyers to the neighborhood. It sounds like she's a good business-woman. What's wrong with that? You could probably pick up a few tips from her."

Joanna folded her arms. "That's not how she plays. But never mind. Don't worry, I promise I won't make a scene." Now not only did she have to figure out if and how to hand over Marnie's key, she'd have to weather Eve's veiled barbs.

They pulled up next to a mid-1960s house perched on the edge of a hill overlooking downtown Portland. The newly rich bought faux Tuscan villas on lots carved out of the rapidly disappearing blueberry fields on the other side of the hills, but more established families had houses here, in the West Hills. The house was a hexagon partially circled by a deck. On one side, a patio and lawn ran between the house and the edge of the steep hill. The patio stepped up to the deck, which in turn led into a large open dining and living room.

Andrew handed keys to a uniformed valet. Parking was notori-ously difficult in the West Hills, especially along the crest where the houses — many supported by stilts — hovered at the edge of cliffs to better take advantage of the views of downtown with Mount Hood, Mount Adams, and Mount St Helens in the distance.

They stepped from the stone-paved side entrance into the house and were met by a server in black with a white apron and a silver tray of champagne glasses. Andrew ignored the server and hurried deeper into the house, probably to find the host and get the full guest list. Joanna took a glass, then did a double take.

"Colette. I didn't expect to see you here."

"Hi, Joanna. I can't live off my paintings, but at least with catering

I get a free meal. Hey, is that the dress you had in the window a few weeks ago? It looks great on you."

"Thanks. In the end I couldn't bear to sell it." Colette was called away, and Joanna glanced after her, certain she'd know more people working in the kitchen then she would at the party. The Remmicks hadn't arrived yet. Eve neither.

Andrew returned and led her toward the living room. Its glass doors opened to a small group of people, champagne flutes in hand, talking on the patio. "Mrs. Porter," Andrew said, "I'd like you to meet my friend, Joanna. Joanna, this is Mrs. Porter."

"Call me Marlene." Someone caught Andrew's attention, and he strode across the patio, leaving her alone with Marlene. She wore a crisp beige dress, probably Narciso Rodriguez, and demure gold hoops. She was preternaturally tanned.

"It's nice to meet you," Joanna said.

"Yes." Marlene's eyes wandered towards the guests behind Joanna.

"You have a lovely house. Such a wonderful view," she tried again.

"It's a Pietro Belluschi. We love it." She looked at Joanna with an eyebrow raised. "My, what a fun dress."

Joanna tipped the last of her champagne down her mouth. Maybe coming to the dinner was a mistake. She could have just mailed the key to Remmick with a note. "It's crazy isn't it? The dress came from the Honey Black estate."

The mention of Honey Black got Marlene's attention. Honey Black had inherited a fortune in timber money, and the millions she gave away through her foundation barely made a dent in it. Joanna had found a folded blank check in the pocket of one of her coats. The rumor was Black always kept a blank check with her in case she met someone without much money but whose roof needed replacing or daughter a tonsillectomy. "Really? I guess you are about her size."

"She had wonderful taste. I feel lucky to wear her dress."

"Marlene." Eve swept up behind Marlene and looped an arm around her waist.

Marlene's expression warmed immediately, and she returned the hug. "Eve, darling. You look spectacular."

She did, Joanna noted sourly. Her honeyed hair was thick and shiny, pulled back behind her ears to reveal shoulder-dusting earrings. She seemed perfectly at ease.

When she saw Joanna, Eve looked momentarily surprised, then her lips widened into a smile. "Why, I didn't know you'd be here." She pointed at the seam of Joanna's dress, just below her bust. "The seam's loosening a little there. You might want to get that fixed before it gets worse." Eve looked over Joanna's shoulder at an arriving guest. "Got to go say hi."

Joanna turned to see the red soles of Eve's Louboutins crossing the patio as Eve left to pour her charm on a suited executive. She chided herself for not taking the time to get a manicure. Kevin knew a good place on Broadway. And maybe a touch of concealer around her eyes wouldn't have hurt. Women like Eve seemed to have a gift for perfectly smooth legs and magazine-worthy eye shadow.

When Joanna turned again to face Marlene, she was gone. Colette took Joanna's empty glass and handed her another full one. She held out a tray of hors d'oeuvres.

"Try the sliders. They're pretty good."

Joanna took one and a small linen napkin.

"Don't let Marlene get you down. For all her airs, remember she's just a real estate agent. In the platinum club, sure, but still a real estate agent. And that other one—" They both watched Eve mesmerize the executive and a woman who had joined them. The man's hand dropped suspiciously low on Eve's back. Thankfully his wife didn't seem to notice. "Well, I'm not sure what to say," Colette finished. "Good luck."

The patio's flagstones radiated heat. Besides Eve, Marlene, and a man who must be Marlene's husband — he looked like he'd rather be in his office reading timber sales estimates — Joanna saw six other couples. Some of the women smiled and nodded at her, but after looking her over decided that she wasn't worth the trouble of crossing the patio. Snippets of conversation floated toward Joanna, mostly about a new golf resort under construction near the coast. Remmick and his wife still hadn't arrived. Not that she knew how she would get the congressman alone once he did show up.

At last a black towncar pulled up to the house. This one wouldn't require the valet and would remain in the place of honor at the head of the driveway. Marlene trotted to the living room while the rest of the guests watched expectantly.

Remmick and his wife appeared on the patio, each holding a champagne flute. Laura wore the black cocktail dress with the chiffon overlay she'd bought at Tallulah's Closet the day before.

"Hello, Joe. Hello, Diane. Marty, how are you?" Remmick shook hands with the people assembled on the patio.

Andrew drew Joanna forward. "Chick, I'd like you to meet Joanna Hayworth."

The congressman took her hand in both of his and looked straight in her eyes. His hands were strong and warm. "Joanna, I'm pleased to meet you."

Despite herself, she felt drawn by the politician's charisma, felt everyone watching them. A vague trail of expensive cologne rose from him. "Congressman Remmick, it's nice to meet you. Your speech downtown today was so moving."

"Please, call me Chick." He moved on to greet the woman next to her.

"Hello, Joanna, what a nice surprise to see you again," Laura said and touched her bodice. "What do you think of the dress?"

"I can't imagine it looking better on anyone else." How strange to be in the public eye, Joanna thought. Wherever the Remmicks go, people watch them, and they know it. What happens to a man who is surrounded by people always ready to tell him that he's right? His popularity is their popularity, and his influence is theirs, too. It would be hard to stay down to earth. You'd start to believe being right and powerful was your destiny. Maybe even enough so to think that you're above the law. That breaking into a store or threatening an old lover was fine. Just as long as certain information never reached the public.

"Laura, so nice to see you." Eve hugged Laura, each shooting air kisses past the other. "I didn't know you wore vintage or I would have sent you some truly special dresses." She smiled. "Not that this dress isn't wonderfully flattering on you, of course."

Marlene called the guests in to the dining room for dinner. Darkness was just starting to settle. The taper candles running down the middle of the polished wood table cast warm pools of light that reflected in the tall windows.

"Please, everyone, take a seat. Congressman, Laura, I've put you here," Marlene said, her hands on the backs of two chairs at the head of the table. Joanna pulled out the teak chair nearest her. Andrew sat closer to the head of the table, near Remmick. The table ran parallel to the windows, and Joanna's seat faced the inside of the house. A frisée salad was already set at her place.

"The salad greens are from Sauvie Island and the lardons are from a farmer in the Hood River valley," Marlene said. "Laura and Eve, your salads are vegetarian, as you like them."

Servers began pouring a Willamette Valley Pinot Gris, and a discussion of the merits of various single vineyard Pinot Noirs started up at one end of the table. Joanna nervously sipped her wine then pushed the glass away. She needed to keep her wits about her if she was going to talk to Remmick about the key.

The woman to Joanna's right looked up the table to Laura. "I just have to tell you how marvelous you look tonight, Mrs. Remmick." Laura's hair was pulled into a sleek chignon. A glittering diamond bracelet punctuated one bare arm.

"You like my dress? I bought it yesterday at a charming vintage clothing boutique on the east side. It's Joanna's store." She nodded at Joanna. Six bejeweled heads swiveled to look at her.

"Thank you. You'd make anything look wonderful," Joanna said. "But that dress truly was made for you."

"Really?" A woman with mathematically-placed highlights in her hair said. "Vintage? How interesting. When I was in high school I used to wear vintage clothes."

Another woman with deep pink lipstick said, "When I think of all the things my mother had, and we just gave them to Goodwill after she died."

Like I haven't heard that before, Joanna thought.

"You look so chic," one of the younger women said to Laura. "You, too." She turned to Joanna, as if seeing her for the first time. "Do you have any suits like Jackie O used to wear? You know, the kind with the jewel neck and jacket that stops here?" She placed a hand high on her waist.

"Lots of them. We have an ivory brocade suit in now that would look terrific on you." She hoped that she'd have enough business cards to pass out after dinner. She made a mental note to vacuum the store in the morning.

Eve's voice rose from a few seats down the table. "Isn't Joanna clever? Such fun dresses she stocks, too. I do love to stop by her store when I need a little something informal."

Playing dirty, Joanna thought. She's going to say something nasty, but not nasty enough that anyone could call her on it. She tensed in anticipation.

Eve continued. "If you like vintage, especially the higher-end dresses, come by my studio for a private showing. I have a few, special things I don't post on my online store, Eve's Temptation. Or you can come by my new boutique. I'm hoping to have it open by the end of the year." Her laugh was truly musical, soft and clear. "That was gauche, wasn't it? I'm sorry. I didn't mean to interrupt your discussion, Joanna."

Joanna stabbed her fork into a lardon. Already getting in her digs.

Laura set down her wine glass and smiled. "Joanna really does have some lovely dresses." Joanna looked at her gratefully. "I bought a Pucci, too."

The clutch of men surrounding the congressman's seat were in deep discussion. Andrew put a few bites in his mouth when he wasn't talking. He didn't seem to taste the food at all. Of course, he was working tonight, but even when they were dating he seemed only vaguely aware of the time and thought she'd put into their dinners.

As the servers cleared salad plates and prepared to bring in the main course, the host stood. "I'd like to thank everyone for coming tonight, especially Chick and Laura. In the timber industry, we've supported the congressman for many years. Some people might be surprised at this, might think, 'How can a bunch of lumber fellers get behind an environmentalist?' But in the end, we all want the same thing—an economically strong region with healthy, productive natural resources. After all, without trees, we wouldn't be in business, would we?"

Shouts of "hear, hear" went around the table.

The host took a sip of his wine. "And yet with stricter environmental laws, we've had to cut back on harvest in some areas. But there are other ways to use the beautiful land Bowman owns. You've probably all read about it in the paper, but tonight I'd like to formally announce our plans for the Willapa Greens Golf Resort. Darling, would you bring those over to me?"

"Joanna." Eve's whisper floated to her. "Did you get the Lanvin coat back yet?"

Joanna kept her gaze fastened on the host but shook her head.

Marlene handed her husband a stack of glossy brochures, and he passed them around the table. Its cover showed a view of the ocean with a golf club and raven drawn in the corner. The brochure opened to a map of the Long Beach peninsula. A black border delineated the resort.

"Congressman Remmick," the host gestured to his right, "Grew up nearby. We'd like to name the course Remmick Greens in his honor."

The guests clapped.

"Marty, I can't tell you how pleased I am," the congressman said. "Is this what the resort will look like?" He pointed toward the architect's drawing of a structure made to look rustic, but undeniably expensive.

"I know you hear me," Eve hissed below the presentation. "Do you have the coat or not?"

Joanna continued to focus on the host. "…Modeling the lodge after a traditional Native American longhouse as a mark of respect for, well, for the same tribe you helped when you were first getting started as a lawyer."

Something small and wet hit her back. A blackberry garnish from dinner. She peeled its pulp off the fabric near her shoulder. Unbelievable. Eve actually threw a blackberry at her. "We can talk later," Joanna said through gritted teeth.

She wiped her hands on the linen napkin and pointedly turned her back to Eve. Damn her. That blackberry would probably stain. It had to be her Ceil Chapman dress, too. The congressman seemed contrite about something, but in the melee with Eve she'd missed it.

A few heads around the table tilted. Marlene said, "Chick, you've been a big supporter of the tribes as long as you've been in office."

"I did my best. But when it came down to it, they just weren't able to meet the burden of proof for continued governance."

"What's continued governance?" a man across the table asked.

"A little jargon, I'm afraid. I keep forgetting I'm not in Washington. The tribe had to prove that they stuck together, with some sort of self-government, continuously."

After a dazzling smile from Eve, the man sitting next to Joanna switched places with her. She leaned her head toward Joanna. "It's just a yes or no. Yes or no."

For God's sake. They were supposed to be paying attention.

"— That means no government money and no reservation," the congressman finished.

"Well?" Eve was relentless.

That was it. Joanna swiped her wine glass with her right hand, sending Pinot Gris across the linen tablecloth and down Eve's lap.

Eve bolted to her feet. "Oh!" Joanna said in mock surprise. "I'm sorry. Your comments were so fascinating, congressman, I must have forgotten my glass was there." One of the servers rushed up with a napkin to mop Eve's lap. Marlene took Eve's shoulder, probably leading her toward the bathroom. Too bad it wasn't the Pinot Noir. Red wine is the devil to get out of silk charmeuse.

"Did you know the contractor who died a few weeks ago? The paper said he was Native American and grew up in Oysterville," the man across from Joanna asked Remmick.

"I did know him, although I hadn't seen him in years. We went to grade school together. His family fished for the cannery that my father worked at. His accident was a real tragedy."

The woman to Joanna's left whispered to her husband, seated on her other side, "He fell off a wall at the new condo complex they're building in northwest. Into a dumpster, impaled by scrap metal. Horrible."

Joanna looked up in surprise. She realized they must be talking about Franklin, Marnie's lover when she first moved to Portland, and Ray's brother. Ray had been so calm about his death. He'd never hinted at anything so grisly.

She flipped the brochure upside down, hiding the raven from view.

After the salmon course, the catering staff began to clear dinner plates. Eve returned but thankfully seemed distracted by the man who had sat between them at dinner. It was completely dark out now, and the lights of the city sparkled like loose rhinestones through the plate glass windows. She still had somehow to pull Remmick aside and feel him out about the key. How would she get him alone? Guests were hanging all over him.

"I thought we'd have dessert in here and then go outside for coffee and pear brandy," Marlene said.

After a dessert of berry crisp, Marlene opened the doors to the patio, where the staff had set up coffee service. The air had cooled a little, but the patio's flagstones were still warm underfoot. Two women, now more friendly than before dinner, asked Joanna for her business card. A few other guests, small crystal snifters in hand, wandered through the paths in the gardens that tiered down from the patio.

Remmick walked toward the edge of the patio and around the corner of the house, just out of view. Joanna might not get another chance to talk to him alone. Nervous, she paused, then followed him. He pulled a pair of glasses from the inside pocket of his jacket and put them on to read an index card he'd taken from the opposite breast pocket. He saw Joanna and smiled.

"Just reviewing my appointments for tomorrow. Did you enjoy dinner?"

"Yes, I did." Joanna extended her hand. "I'm Joanna Hayworth. We met earlier."

"Yes, of course." The congressman shook her hand. "You sold my wife that lovely dress."

"Ms. Remmick could make anything look lovely." Up close, the lines around the congressman's eyes belied his body, lean and strong from years of running. His hair was precisely cut and dyed a gentle brown. She thought he might be examining her, too.

It was time. Joanna drew a deep breath. "I understand that you grew up in Oysterville. I think we may know someone in common. Marnie Evans."

Remmick thought for a moment. "Oh yes, Marnie. Yes, I went to school with her. She was a few years behind me, as I recall. How is she doing?"

No way. Marnie's death couldn't be news to him. After all, his wife had known. It was even in the newspaper. "You know she died, don't you?"

"Did she? That's a shame," he said mildly.

Great, Joanna thought. He wouldn't even own up to knowing about her death. Of course, if he'd fathered a child he didn't want to recognize, he'd want to distance himself as much as he could. "I thought maybe you had known her better than that."

"No. Wasn't she in the entertainment business?"

Was he implying that just because Marnie was a dancer he couldn't possibly know her? Joanna's blood pressure began to rise. Maybe Marnie wasn't a saint or loaded with money, but she was a fine person. Certainly better than some of the guests at tonight's dinner. "I had thought you knew her intimately, even. Or maybe that's something you'd rather not have people know?"

The mood changed abruptly. The congressman put his glasses back in his jacket and looked straight at Joanna. "What are you getting at?" His voice was pure ice.

"You had an affair with her, didn't you?"

"Yes, I did. A long time ago. It's nothing I need to, or care to, hide." He hadn't missed a beat.

Her jaw dropped momentarily. She snapped her mouth closed. "But if you had a child with Marnie, you'd want to hide that, wouldn't you? A baby with an ex-stripper? That wouldn't reflect very well on someone of your stature, now would it? With such a close election?" Her voice hit a high pitch. If she could just give him the key and get it over with.

Laura Remmick came around the corner. "Chick, there you are darling." She squeezed his hand. "And Joanna. How are you? Everyone loves the dress."

Remmick hadn't taken his eyes from Joanna, but he spoke to Laura. "Joanna was just telling me about the baby I had with a childhood friend. Supposedly I want to hide this child so he won't sully my reputation. Did I get that right?"

Laura's eyebrows pulled together. "What are you talking about?"

"You know, darling, that a long time ago, long before I met you, I spent some time with a girl I knew from Oysterville."

"Of course, you told me about that before we married," Laura said calmly. Was it Joanna's imagination, or did she pause just a second before she responded? Remmick broke his gaze with Joanna and smiled at his wife, then returned to Joanna.

"Perhaps you haven't noticed that Laura and I don't have children. It's not because we don't want them or because Laura has any physical problem. The fault, I'm afraid, is all mine. This is more explanation than you deserve. I don't know what you want from me, but I'd appreciate it if you took your accusations and left." Remmick draped his arm around Laura and led her back to the patio.

Joanna froze. Her face stung. She had just accused Remmick of fathering a child he couldn't possibly have had. Maybe he even thought she planned to blackmail him. What an idiot she was. Why couldn't she have kept her mouth shut?

She couldn't go back to the patio and face him. She walked away from the guests and up the side yard to the front of the house. The valet was leaning against the wall of the garage and smoking a cigarette. He stood up expectantly.

"No, that's all right, I'm not looking for a car. Are the caterers still here?"

He gestured with his cigarette toward the kitchen. "Try the side door."

She continued around the house and entered the kitchen. Colette was loading a bus tub with serving platters. The fluorescent light shone bright after the night outside.

"Colette? Are you leaving soon?"

"I just need to load the van. Why?"

"Do you mind if I catch a ride home with you? I'm done with this party, and I don't want to wait around for Andrew."

"Sure, it won't be but a few minutes."

Joanna stood outside the kitchen for a moment. The faraway sounds of conversation pierced by loud laughter mixed with the chirp of crickets. A moth hit the driveway light, struggled, and fell, dead, on the pavement.

She gathered her courage and crept through the dining room to the deck. She stood back until she saw Andrew, fortunately on the opposite side of the patio from the congressman. Eve was with him, her hand resting on his arm. He seemed to have forgotten all about the campaign donors he was supposed to be schmoozing with. Joanna tapped his shoulder. "I have a horrible headache, so I'm going to get a ride home with one of the catering staff. Thanks for bringing me tonight."

"Too bad about the headache," Eve said. Anyone who didn't know better would have thought she was sincere. "I saw you talking to Chick over there behind the house. Anything interesting?"

"Just telling him what a great rally it was this morning." Joanna knew her face flushed. "Andrew, I've got to go."

"I thought maybe we could get a drink on the way home. You know, catch up."

Remmick turned to face her direction. Although he was far enough away to be out of earshot, she backed toward the house. "I know you're busy. I need to leave now. See you later."

Her elbow hit something slick, and a vase of lilies shattered on the stone patio. All eyes were on her. "Clumsy," someone to her right said.

"Sorry. Sorry," she muttered and hurried for the kitchen.

Chapter 21

Although she hadn't had much to drink, Joanna woke the next morning feeling hung over. She groaned remembering the look on Chick Remmick's face when she accused him of fathering Marnie's child. What made her think she could march up to Remmick, say a few words, and hand over the key? He was supposed to be grateful. She was supposed to go home feeling safe and satisfied. Instead she felt like a first class heel.

As long as she had the key, and as long as someone wanted it, she was still at risk. Or was she? Sunlight filtered through the blinds in her bedroom. Maybe she was overreacting. Then her thoughts turned to Marnie's eyes, open in death, and the razor-clean slit in the Lanvin coat's silk lining. She shivered.

She pushed off her sheets and felt next to the bed with her feet for slippers. She'd talk to Troy and see if Marnie had dropped any hints as to who his father was. Troy's father had to be the connection to the key.

Cup of coffee in hand, Joanna called Troy. "Remember me from Marnie's memorial service?" A trace of vintage L'Aimant, a perfume that had always comforted her, rose from her dressing gown. "Could we meet? I'd like to talk to you about Marnie." She wrote "Velveteria, 10 a.m." on the back of an invitation to an art opening and hung up the phone.

She still felt roundly humiliated from talking to Remmick. Aunt Vanderburgh stared disapprovingly from the wall above the couch.

"I know, I know," Joanna said to the portrait. "You don't think I should be giving away the key anyway, especially to someone who would break into the store — and God knows what else — to get it. You're right. That was dumb. I was desperate."

The portrait's lips remained pursed.

"All I want now is to know the enemy. Maybe once I figure out who wants the key, I'll know what to do. Maybe Troy can shed some light on that."

Joanna set down her coffee mug and stretched. The key still sat in her evening clutch, tossed on the dining room table the night before. She slid out the key and looked at it, as if it could tell her something. Apple said the spirits said things had to do with a "baby." If Remmick wasn't Troy's father, who was? She put the key in her hands and closed her eyes as she'd seen Apple do when she wanted to feel an object's energy. Nothing.

She shrugged and went to the bedroom to get dressed.

A few minutes before ten o'clock, Joanna pulled up in front of a storefront on East Burnside. Her destination, a museum of paintings on velvet, was wedged between a store selling raw pet food and another with a window display of western shirts. Through the open door, she glimpsed Troy on a stepladder adjusting track lights. He bit his lip in childlike concentration on his task.

When he saw Joanna, Troy stepped down and smiled. "Thanks for meeting me here. I've been so busy lately that I haven't had much time even to grab a beer with friends."

He was so damned charming. She couldn't resist returning his smile as she set her purse on a 1970s gold velvet side chair with heavy wood trim she thought of as the "Spanish Galleon" style. "I bet it's been hard to keep up with studying, too. Law school is such a time suck."

"Yeah. But it's summer break now."

"That's right. No internship for you this year—you must be starting your second year."

Troy shifted on his feet. "Yeah. Second year."

Something about Troy's response gave her pause. "Who did you have for torts?"

He fidgeted with a pair of pliers. "I can't remember. His name sounded kind of, uh, Scandinavian."

Whoa. There's no way a student would forget a first year professor before the second year even started. "Rasmussen, maybe?"

"Right—that's it. Rasmussen. He was a tough professor."

"I can imagine he would be." If he existed. This was rich. "Does he still wear a toupee?"

"Yeah, a really bad toupee." Troy laughed nervously. He slipped the pliers into his rear pocket and stepped back up on the ladder. "Can we talk while I work? Got to get the show up by noon."

Aside from his dark hair and sharp cheekbones, he resembled Marnie. He was slight and moved gracefully. He squinted as he focused on measuring the placement for the next painting, then looked down and smiled again when he caught Joanna watching him. Troy would have no problem collecting girlfriends with the urge to mother. Although he might be stretching the truth about law school, it didn't mean he wasn't Marnie's son. But it didn't mean he was, either.

"Do you hang all the shows here?" she asked as she looked around. Behind her was a series of Michael Jackson portraits ranging from the Jackson Five days to his last bleached skin and sculpted nose look. Below those were several velvet Elvises.

"No, this is the first I've done here. Mostly I put up shows in cafes and places like that."

"This month it's all about clowns, it looks like." Joanna gestured toward the canvases, stacked two and three deep along the partition, waiting to be hung. In the painting closest to her, a clown in a top hat, its curves slashed with white paint, cocked his head at an unnatural angle.

"Yep, clowns. Creepy, aren't they?"

"And sad."

"So, how did you know Marnie?" He took a pencil from behind his ear and picked up the level resting on the top of the stepladder.

"She used to sell me clothes. I own a vintage clothing store, Tallulah's Closet."

Troy marked a spot on the wall, then picked up a spool of wire. "Oh yeah, the place on Clinton. Next to Dot's. That's yours?"

"Uh huh. It wasn't in the papers, but I was the one who found her. In my store. It was awful."

A curl of wire dangled from the spool. "You what? You found her dead? I guess I thought—" He didn't finish his sentence. A moment passed before he picked up his pencil again.

If Troy really was her son, maybe Joanna hadn't been very sensitive. "You know, Marnie would have appreciated that you hang paintings. She had a thing for watching home decorating shows on television. I'm not altogether sure she wouldn't have liked the clowns, either."

He laughed and snipped a length of wire before attaching it to a cable running along the top of the partition.

"I have to admit that I was surprised when you showed up at her memorial service. She always seemed so—alone." She kept her eyes on him. Lying about law school, indeed.

"I can see that. I was surprised when I met her. I never thought my birth mother would be a stripper."

"Did you see her very often?"

"No, not really." He stepped off the ladder to pick up a painting of a clown with a glistening tear drop on his cheek. "We talked on the phone from time to time, but we only met three times since she first called me about a year ago. She took me out once to Higgins. Lunch was great, but I think it almost killed her to go that long without a cigarette." He paused a moment, the clown dangling mid air. "Bad choice of words, but you know what I mean. Anyway, she was proud that I'm going to law school and used to send me money every month. It was funny—she never sent a check, just cash. Tens and twenties mostly."

So that's why Marnie was so eager to sell her clothes. It would be like her to send Troy envelopes stuffed with cash instead of writing a check. But would she have thought to verify that Troy truly was her son?

"The money really helped out, but I don't have to worry so much about it now, at least not once the house sells."

She raised her eyebrows. No, Marnie couldn't have. "You must have had a terrific job between college and law school to buy a house."

"Oh, no." He turned toward Joanna. "Didn't you know? Marnie wrote me into her will. Her lawyer saw her obit and got in touch with me. She left me everything, including a really sweet Mercedes.

I got myself into a little financial trouble a few years ago, and, well, the money from the house will definitely come in handy."

He finished hanging the clown and straightened it on the wall. "But that's not why you stopped by. Was there something you wanted to talk about?"

She chose her words carefully. He'd already wheedled his way into Marnie's estate. Who's to say he wouldn't try to take advantage of a potential father, too? "Yes, there is, in fact. I wondered if Marnie had ever told you anything about your father? I have something Marnie left behind. It seemed right to give it to him."

"Nope. Don't know who he is. I asked her once, and she ignored me. I sort of figured I was the result of a one-night stand."

"I know she had affairs — or at least judging from the flowers she got at the memorial service, some especially dedicated fans. But she had serious relationships, too."

"I have to admit when I looked around at the crowd at the service I wondered if any of them could be my father."

She thought back to the dim room at Mary's Club, the sound of Judy Garland's voice wafting over the sound system. The black light mural behind them, washed out under the houselights. Ray, Nina, her husband, and Don all looking at each other when Troy walked in. Ray seemed to see Marnie as a big sister, not a lover, although you never knew. Marnie's first love, Franklin, was dead. Besides, they'd been involved too long ago for Franklin to have fathered Troy. Then there was Don.

"She had a long relationship with Don Cayle, the man sitting closest to the stage."

Troy nodded. "I remember him. The guy with the pinkie ring."

"Yes. I think he gave Marnie the Mercedes."

"Hey, pinkie ring or not, the man has good taste. He gave me his card, said he'd be calling about getting together sometime. It seemed a little out of place, but I thought, you know, whatever. You never know when it might come in handy to have someone's number." Troy paused, pliers in hand. "Marnie did mention a guy she used to know. Once or twice she said something about him. Someone she used to work with at Mary's Club. I wonder if it was Don?"

"I wouldn't be surprised." Troy sounded interested. Of course, he would be if he thought if Don were his father. It was no secret that Don had money.

"I had the feeling that she was a little sorry for him. She didn't talk much about her old life, but she did mention she felt she owed someone something. What is it you want to give my dad, anyway?"

"It hardly seems important now," she lied.

Troy waited for more explanation. When Joanna didn't reply, he said, "Well, I'm sorry I can't help you more." He set his pliers on a rung of the stepladder. "It's funny. Marnie seemed to be cleaning things up, as if she knew she was going to die. It's like she sought me out and wanted to make amends by giving me money. She even drew up a will."

"She did have pretty advanced cancer. She must have known she wouldn't live long."

"I don't see why she was so secretive. She could have left a letter with her lawyer telling me who my father was, but she didn't even do that."

Then Joanna had another thought. "Do you know what you're going to do with Marnie's clothes?"

"I guess I thought I'd hire an estate sale company to sell everything."

"I could give you a better price than an estate sale company. I'd love to have first crack at Marnie's wardrobe." It would be another chance to look around Marnie's house. Maybe she'd find something to point her in the direction of Troy's father.

Troy stepped down the ladder and faced her, his hands folded in front of his chest. "That's why you really came today, isn't it?" He nodded as if he'd caught her in something. "You wanted her clothes. You made up some kind of story about my dad, but it was Marnie's clothes you wanted all along."

Yikes. She put her purse down again. "No, no. Really, it was about your father. The clothes are a total afterthought. If you want to wait for the estate sale company, that's fine with me."

He stood silent, arms still folded, watching her.

"I really can give you the best price, though." She guessed when you're looking for the advantage like Troy is, you think everyone else is, too.

He burst into laughter. "It's all right. I get it. I'm no fool. You'll pay faster than an estate sale company anyway, and I can use the cash."

"Really, I — "

Troy waved her away. "I have the keys to the house now to look around a little, but I have to give them back tomorrow. The house isn't really mine until probate is through. I doubt the lawyer is going to come down and count Marnie's dresses. If you want, you could come by later this afternoon."

"Late afternoon would be good." Apple could take over at the store. "Maybe around five?" She glanced at her watch. Almost time to open.

"All right." He moved the ladder away from the wall and stepped back to survey his work. "What do you think?"

The velvet clowns stared back, each creepier than the last.

Chapter 22

Before opening Tallulah's Closet for the day, Joanna stopped by Dot's to order something for lunch. Then she readied the store for business. She turned on the lights, set out the sign, and selected a Judy Collins album for the stereo. Seeing the paintings at the Velveteria had given her an itch for "Send in the Clowns." Apple had left a note by the phone saying she'd put a crystal in the window to ward off bad energy. Its light spangled near the front door.

Even the routine of opening the store brought her pleasure. The lush patterns of fabric on the racks, the faint perfume of a scented candle, the row of leather pumps against the wall confirmed every day that she'd made the right choice in opening a vintage clothing store. Damned Eve. What could she do?

Her sandwich arrived as she was checking the phone messages.

"I'm calling for Joanna Hayworth," a reedy voice played on the answering machine tape. "This is Rick Matthews with Cord Matthew McKeen. I'm calling about the Margaret Evans estate."

Marnie's lawyer. The breath stalled in her throat. She copied down the attorney's phone number, then pushed away her sandwich, where she'd laid out a yellowed linen napkin and a sterling table knife she'd bought at an estate sale. She picked up the phone and was quickly put through to the attorney.

Rick Matthew's voice was businesslike. "I'm handling the probate for Ms. Evans's estate. I called to let you know that Marnie left you something in her will. We've put a certified letter in the mail, but I wanted to tell you firsthand."

"No kidding? I'm surprised she thought of me." So sweet—and unexpected—of her.

"Just a second and I'll read you the passage." The attorney was back on the phone in the time it took Joanna to eat a tater tot. "Here it is: 'To Joanna Hayworth, I bequeath my ivory beaded Helen Rose dress, stored in my cedar chest, and all the clothing in my closet and bureau'."

If the Helen Rose dress was in good condition, it would be a remarkable score. Helen Rose had designed Grace Kelly's wedding dress and Elizabeth Taylor's wardrobe for *Cat on a Hot Tin Roof*. And the dresses. She'd have to make a special "Marnie" section in the store. She could tell customers Marnie's story. A pang went through her as she remembered the stolen Lanvin coat.

"Thank you so much. Marnie meant a lot to me."

"There's more." Matthew cleared his voice. "You were always special to me, Joanna. You're every bit as wonderful as I'd imagined." Paper crinkled. "That's all."

As she'd imagined? As if Marnie knew who Joanna was before they met. Unlike Troy, Joanna was certain of her biological parents. Maybe the police detective was right, and Marnie was starting to lose it just a little. She took a moment to let it all sink in.

"Ms. Hayworth, are you there?"

"Yes, sorry." Joanna stood up straighter. "Thank you for reading that." Her thumb reached across her palm to touch the back of her grandmother's ring. "I saw Marnie's son just this morning. I understand he's pretty much inheriting the whole estate."

"Yes. Troy."

Joanna paused. "So, there's no question that Troy is her son?"

"Why do you ask?"

"Oh, I just—I guess you hear all those stories about impostors."

"All I can tell you is that Troy is in Marnie's will, and she refers to him as her son. If she's sure, then I'm sure."

"I don't know if you can reveal something like this, but did Marnie ever mention Troy's father? Maybe leave something for him in her will?"

"A will is public record, so I'm not betraying any confidences in telling you there's no mention of the father of her child."

Joanna smiled at a customer who entered the store and waved a finger to indicate she'd be with her in a minute. "There's one more thing, since I have you on the phone. Marnie sold me a coat, and I found a safe deposit box key in it. Have you got into her safe deposit box yet?"

"The police asked about that. As far as I know, Marnie doesn't have one. All her papers—the deed to her house, that sort of thing—were in a lockbox in her bedroom. They're in our safe now."

"Why would she have a safe deposit box key?"

"Can't say. Maybe she had a box at one time and never turned the key in."

Deep in thought, she hung up the phone. Marnie knew she was going to die and rushed to prepare for it. The lawyer didn't necessarily know all of her secrets. Maybe bringing the Lanvin coat to Tallulah's Closet was part of a greater plan. She was more interested than ever to get to Marnie's house.

*
**

Older, well-kept homes lined Marnie's neighborhood just below the Alameda ridge. Marnie's house, covered with textured yellow stucco, was up a short flight of concrete steps from the street. In front of her minivan sat a car draped in a gray tarp, perhaps the old Mercedes convertible she'd bragged about. It was Troy's now.

What must have been Troy's bicycle, a well-used fixed-gear, leaned against the garage. The front door was ajar.

"Hello," she yelled into the living room. The low slant of the late afternoon sun filled the room. She shut the door behind her and turned to look at the row of neatly kept lawns undulating down the street. Maybe Troy wouldn't get much for the furnishings, but Marnie's house would earn him some real money. She put her hands on her hips. Troy barely knew her. It didn't seem right.

For an ex-showgirl, Marnie kept a grandmotherly house. Pink swags draped the windows, matching the mauve and rose upholstered furniture. Two Queen Anne-style chairs, probably unused for years, flanked a cherry table holding a silk flower arrangement. Judging from its worn seat, the couch was where Marnie spent most of her time. A pack of cigarettes and a lighter sat on the end table next to it, and a half-eaten sandwich and cup of coffee rested on the table in front. The dirty dishes stood out in the otherwise tidy room.

"Hey." Troy came in from the kitchen wearing cut-offs and an old tee shirt. A bandanna was tied lopsided around his head. "I'm cleaning up. The refrigerator is full of spoiled food, and there's glass all over by the back door."

Where someone had broken in. And shocked Marnie to death? Or was she already dead?

A black cat with a white spot on his chest wandered into the living room and twisted through Joanna's legs. She knelt. "Pepper," his collar read and listed Marnie's address. "I've heard a few stories about this cat."

"I'm allergic. The cat box is disgusting, too. I'm going to call the pound."

Pepper nudged his head on Joanna's calf. Marnie's cat going to the pound? No. "I could take him."

"He's yours." Troy toyed with his sponge. "Rick Matthews, Marnie's lawyer, called me this afternoon and said Marnie left you her clothes. I guess you won't be buying them off me after all."

The Helen Rose. "I'm really curious about one of the dresses in particular. It's supposed to be in a cedar chest."

Troy put down the sponge and moved toward the hall. "I saw a chest in the second bedroom. This way." He led her to the crowded guest bedroom and squeezed between a twin bed and some stacked boxes to open the curtains. "Right here," he said as he moved a stack of romance novels from a wooden chest.

The varnished cedar chest looked almost exactly like one her grandmother had. Her grandmother had called it a "hope chest" and said she'd embroidered pillowcases and tea towels as a girl to save in the chest for her eventual marriage. Joanna opened its lid, releasing a sharp, woody scent. It was nearly empty except for a bundle wrapped in white tissue. When she set it on the bed, a chiffon skirt slid from the paper.

"That's got to be it. If you don't mind, I'm going to get back to the kitchen. I want to get the garbage out before it really stinks up the house. When you're done in here, Marnie's clothes are down the hall in the other bedroom."

As she unwrapped the dress and laid it across the bed, the sounds of the radio and running water made their way from the kitchen.

"My God. Gorgeous," she whispered. The dress was a breathtaking composition of ivory silk chiffon with a buttery silk underskirt and bodice. Mousseline, as delicate as a spider's web, covered the bodice and shoulders, extending beyond the silk lining to form three-quarter length sleeves. The dress's full skirt would have hit at tea length. But what really set it apart was the extravagant beadwork covering the front of its bodice and dipping below the waistline in a vee. The beads, all white, ivory, or glittering pearl, formed a full-blown rose. Some of the beads dangled, designed to move with the woman who wore the dress.

"Oh, Marnie," she murmured. "You were planning to get married, weren't you?" To whom? Don, maybe? She couldn't possibly sell the dress. She stretched its waist between her hands. She couldn't possibly wear it, either. Marnie had been tiny.

She returned to the cedar chest, but all she found was a pair of yellowed gloves. She passed her hands once again over the gown's delicate bodice. She'd have to buy more acid-free tissue to store it. Had Marnie gazed at the dress with sadness over the years or closed it in its chest and never looked back? She gently rewrapped the dress and carried it down the hall to Marnie's bedroom.

Troy had opened the bedroom windows, and warm, fresh air poured in. He must have watered the garden, too. A few sparrows splashed in the birdbath. He was turning out to be quite the homemaker.

On the dresser sat a jewelry box shaped like the Virgin Mary with a tangle of necklaces in its tray. Although most of it looked to be costume, she picked up a baguette-cut emerald ring whose value would put the Mercedes outside to shame. Next to the jewelry box was a framed photo. Judging from the style of the clothes, it had been taken nearly fifty years before. Its color had faded into watery reds and ivories, but she recognized a younger, lively Marnie standing next to a wooden boat on the river. She was laughing and kicking an espadrille-clad foot into the air. A dark-haired man had his arm around her shoulders, and another man smiled next to them. Ray. The second man had to be Franklin.

Joanna pushed open the closet door to a row of tiny but elegant mid-century cocktail dresses from the old Nicholas Ungàr department store. Gorgeous. Two of the dresses shimmered in raw silk with full skirts. One was brilliant coral with a demure neckline in the front but a plunging back with a small bow at the bottom. Next to it hung a green peau de soie strapless dress, slightly lighter green tulle crisscrossing its bodice.

She slid them off their hangers and laid them on the bed. The green peau de soie dress would be perfect for Jennifer, a Tallulah's Closet regular. At the back of the closet were two coats: a smock-style black velvet coat with rhinestone trim that Marnie might have worn with the cocktail dresses, and a leopard print raincoat she guessed was from the late 1960s. The raincoat didn't show much wear. Both coats joined the stack on the bed. At least Eve wouldn't be getting these, she thought.

Only one dress looked as if Marnie might have worn it recently. It was mauve with padded shoulders and a floppy bow that tied at the neckline. It could have been ripped from the set of *Falcon Crest*. That one she put in a pile for Goodwill.

"Are you finding everything?" Troy called from the kitchen.

"Yes, thank you. I'm making a pile on the bed."

"Great. Let me know if you need anything."

She turned to the dresser. Most likely this was where Marnie's more recent wardrobe of jeans and sweatshirts was stored. If she had any personal letters or photos that she hadn't locked up in the safe deposit box, they might be here, too.

The dresser was wide and low-slung with a mirror and two columns of drawers. The first drawer she opened was full of underwear and ratty bras, all carefully folded. She glanced at the door, then slid her hands under the lingerie. Nothing but a lavender sachet.

The dishwasher started up in the kitchen.

The next drawer down held socks and stacks of tee shirts and sweatshirts. In the third drawer was nothing but jeans and cotton pants with elastic waistbands. Other than the jumble in second bedroom, Marnie was awfully neat, but so far the dresser hadn't yielded anything for Tallulah's Closet. Or anything else.

The first drawer on the other side of the dresser was more promising. She lifted a silk, bias-cut nightgown in pale apricot and placed it on the bed. Definitely a keeper. A velvet bed jacket and three boxes of unused stockings, along with a nude silk garter belt, joined the pile. An empty bottle of My Sin perfume lay on its side on the bottom of the drawer. Again she ran her hands around the drawer, and again came up empty.

She was beginning to resign herself to not finding anything to shed light on Marnie's secrets when the next drawer yielded a quilted glove box. She lifted its satin top and saw letters and a few cards. Holding her breath, she stood and crept down the hall to look in the living room. Troy must still be in the kitchen. Despite the Suzie Homemaker business, Joanna didn't trust him. If he wanted to find out who his father was, he could do it himself.

She lifted the box from the drawer and skimmed through its contents. A small plastic bracelet with faded type reading "Baby boy Evans" dropped to the bottom. Although the bracelet was proof that Marnie had a son, it didn't mean the son was Troy. She took a quick look at a packet of letters from Oysterville. Charlotte Evans. Marnie's mother, perhaps.

As the envelopes flipped past her fingers, the familiar handwriting on one jumped out. Joanna pressed a hand to her mouth. She checked the return address, and a gasp escaped her lips. Marnie had a letter from her grandmother? They had known each other. She held the envelope flat between her palms. There was no time to look at it now, but this one was going home with her. She tucked the envelope into her purse and returned to the glove box.

Of the remaining letters, one envelope stood out as newer than the rest. She glanced up at the door again. Other than the dishwasher, the kitchen was quiet. Maybe Troy was in the driveway looking at his new Mercedes.

She slid the letter from its envelope. The stationery bore Don's name and office address, but it was handwritten and clearly not a business letter. It was dated in April, only four months ago. "Dear Marnie," she read, "You know I'm not so good at writing or at telling how I feel. As I said, I will give you whatever you need, but don't threaten me. Don't make this hard on both of us."

"I'm thinking I just might keep the—Joanna?"

Her head snapped up as Troy entered the bedroom. The glove box was on the dresser, its top closed, thank God. She lowered her hand with the letter behind her leg. "Hi. You startled me. Look at everything I found." With her free hand she gestured to the bed.

Troy glanced at the bed, but his gaze quickly returned to the glove box on the dresser. She slipped the letter into the waistband of her skirt in back, hoping the gesture looked like she was casually scratching an itch.

"What's that?" He nodded toward the glove box.

"Oh, I just pulled it out of one of the drawers." Her heart beat quickened.

"Did you look inside?"

"Not yet."

"You know, the will only said clothes. No jewelry or anything like that. I'll take it and look through it later, then." He pulled the box closer, then put his hands on his hips. "What's wrong? Wait. Do you have something behind your back? There wasn't any money in that box, was there?"

She thought fast. Andrew always said that the best defense is a good offense. "Why did you lie about going to law school?"

His hands dropped to his side. "What?"

"There's no Professor Rasmussen at the college, Troy."

"Well, there used to be —"

"No, there's not. You're lying."

He toyed with the corner of the glove box. "Okay, you're right. I'm not in law school." His tone was defiant. "But what did it matter to her? She was old and going to die anyway. If she thought her son was in law school, it didn't hurt anyone."

"But you used that story to get money out of her. If she knew how you really lived, maybe she wouldn't have sent you all that cash. What did you end up spending it all on, anyway? Beer and concerts? Just because Marnie was getting up there in years doesn't mean it's all right to lie to her."

He looked up at Joanna, almost pleading. "But I wanted her to be proud of me. She seemed so frail and had so many questions. I guess the truth just felt like a let down. I didn't want to disappoint her, you know? And then she started giving me money for school, and — well, I needed it."

She could imagine sitting across from Marnie at lunch and feeling like you had to prove yourself. She was his mother, after all. Still, lying about being a law student went too far. "That's no excuse."

"I just took my LSATs. After talking to Marnie, I got kind of excited about law school. Environmental law. Now, thanks to her and all this," he waved his hands at the house, "I can actually go." He unleashed a melting smile.

He seemed to have forgotten she might be hiding something. For the moment, anyway. Her breathing slowed. Keep the conversation going. "Yeah, you're doing all right, now. You should have this jewelry appraised, too. I think there's some valuable stuff in there." She pointed at the jewelry box. Bye bye emerald ring. I bet it goes to buy stereo components.

He didn't move. He looked at her. She grew nervous. As long as she faced him, he shouldn't be able to see the letter. He wasn't a big guy, but he had that strong, wiry look.

Joanna smiled brightly. "Did you see these dresses Marnie had? This one has a built-in underskirt of tulle." She stepped sideways to the bed, keeping her back to the wall, and picked up the peau de soie dress. "The tulle is one way to identify it as a mid-century dress rather than one from the 1940s. Sure, they have similar design, but the 1940s dress wouldn't have a full tulle skirt, just a single, stiff layer to give the skirt some rigidity. A metal side zipper is a giveaway of a 1940s dress, too. It wasn't until later that zippers moved to the back."

Troy's eyes glazed slightly. She continued her lecture. "Now take a look at this evening coat. Silk velvet. Velvet can be made from a number of different fabrics — cotton and rayon were common — but silk is really special. Notice how there aren't any buttons to fasten the coat. Know why? Because it had to be able to accommodate a full skirt. That was the profile of the time. This dress, on the other hand—"

"I'd better get back to the kitchen. The fridge is only half cleaned. Let me know before you leave and I'll find a box for the cat." Troy disappeared into the hall.

She let out a long breath. She put Don's letter in the bottom of her purse with the letter from her grandmother. She wanted to read both right away, but it would be best to wait, continue to look through Marnie's clothes. Act natural. What else was in the glove box? She'd never know now.

She lifted a box of scarves from the closet shelf. She thought about Don's letter. Why did he lie to her? He'd been adamant about not seeing Marnie, telling Joanna so at least twice. But he clearly had seen Marnie, and not long ago, either. Like father, like son?

Chapter 23

At home Joanna took the letters from her purse and smoothed them open on the table. Feeling ridiculous even as she did it, she drew the dining room curtains. No use tempting fate. Pepper had hid under the couch as soon as she opened his box. His eyes glinted citrine.

First she picked up Don's letter.

"Dear Marnie, You know I'm not so good at writing or at telling how I feel. As I said, I will give you whatever you need, but don't threaten me. Don't make this hard on both of us." Don's handwriting was uneven, the "g"s and "y"s dipping into the lines below. She read slowly.

> Yes, it's true that I've been keeping track of you over the years. You aren't always so good at taking care of yourself, and I wanted to be around if something went wrong, so I hired someone to check in on you from time to time. You can imagine my surprise when the man I hired told me you met your son, our son. Why didn't you tell me?
>
> I always wanted a child, and now I find out I have one. I know you want me to leave you alone, and I will. But I won't let you get in the way of my son meeting his father. You can't keep him from me, Marnie. I'll find him. In the

meantime, take care of yourself. You know I'm always here
for you if you need me.

A mark above Don's signature made her think he may have started
to write "love" but abandoned it mid-stroke. He signed the letter
simply, "Don."

Well, well. So, Don really is Troy's father, Joanna thought. Or at
least he sounds sure he is. He isn't trying to hide his paternity at
all — instead, he probably wants to prove it.

As the full implication of the letter settled in, she started to laugh
at the absurdity of her fear. There wasn't some murderer on the loose
ready to do anything to get his hands on Marnie's safe deposit box.
No, it was just Don, and he simply wanted to take responsibility
for his child. Relief flooded over her. Everything was going to be
all right. She set down the letter and pushed herself from the table.
This called for a Martini.

"We're celebrating, Aunt Vanderburgh," she shouted into the living
room as she took an ice tray from the freezer. He must have visited
Marnie after she sold the coat to Tallulah's Closet. He probably insisted
on meeting Troy, and Marnie said no. She might have had a heart
attack from the stress. Her body was already in bad shape thanks to
cancer. But that didn't explain how Marnie ended up at the store. Joanna's hand slowed as it reached for the shaker. If something happened to
Marnie when Don was there, he would have called an ambulance for
sure. Unless he had already left. Or something else entirely different
happened. After all, people kill people they love all the time.

"What do you think, Auntie V?" Gin bottle in hand, she looked
at the portrait. "You're right. The letter is too loving. Breaking into
Marnie's, the store — all that was just to figure out how to find Troy

and maybe get proof that he's Troy's father." She poured the gin and a hint of vermouth into a cocktail shaker. "And to think I was so terrified." And to think of the ugly scene with Remmick. On second thought, she'd make the Martini a double.

After a good shaking—in *The Thin Man*, Nick Charles said to shake Martinis to the waltz, so she hummed a bit from *The Blue Danube*—she poured it into a cocktail glass with bamboo fronds etched on its side. If only she could call Don right then to tell him about the key, just to put his mind at ease, but she didn't have his home phone number. Well, the call could wait until morning when he'd be at his office. In the meantime, she would sleep easily. Don wouldn't hurt her. The safe deposit box held something he wanted public, not something he would kill to hide.

She took a sip of the Martini. Piney and glacier cold. "The pleasures of gin," she said to Pepper, who had emerged from under the couch and sniffed at the fireplace. "Something you'll never know." Now for her grandmother's letter.

This one was brief, just one leaf of writing paper, and not even filled. Her grandmother was setting a time to meet with Marnie at the tea room at the top of Meier & Frank, an old downtown department store. "It won't be for long. We'll have to meet while Bill's at the doctor's. I'm so sorry—I wish it didn't have to be this way. I'll bring pictures of Joanna. She just won the second grade spelling bee." Her heart leapt at the mention of her name. "Love, Nell." Nell. Joanna's grandmother's name was Helen, but she'd been called Nell as a girl.

Grandma, her grandma. This tiny connection to her radiated warmth that the gin couldn't match.

She took her cocktail to the chaise by the window. Pepper was working his way around the room, investigating the baseboards.

Marnie had known her grandmother. Marnie's raspy voice came back to her. "You're family." Maybe not a blood relation, but in a small town close friends were family. Nina said Marnie had been treated like an outcast when she started at Mary's Club. Maybe her grandfather had forbid her grandmother to visit her.

As she lifted her Martini, the tiny ruby in her ring caught the sun. She set down her drink and held up her hand. A smile spread over her face. Her grandmother's ring — Marnie had recognized it. That first day. That's how she knew. That's why she kept coming back, staying longer. If only Marnie had said something. They'd have had so much to talk about.

Joanna took a deep breath and exhaled slowly. For the first time in days, she was beginning to relax.

A raven alit on the roof of the house across the street and tucked in its wings.

Chapter 24

As Joanna lazily finished her second Martini, the doorbell shrilled through the house. Pepper launched off the couch and ran into the bedroom. She put her eye to the peep hole. It was Apple, and even through the fish-eye distortion of the lens Joanna could see she was agitated.

Joanna yanked open the door. "What are you doing here?"

"Put on your shoes—we've got to go." Apple burst past Joanna and picked up her purse. "Here."

"What?" She obediently fetched her shoes.

"The neighborhood association meeting about the theater starts in five minutes."

"But Eve said—"

"Eve lied to you. I only found out by accident when one of the members stopped by Tallulah's Closet." She stopped suddenly. "Have you been drinking?"

"A little. But apparently not enough."

Apple sped to the old chapel of St Philip Neri. Years before, the congregation had moved into a new brick church and left the smaller original chapel for events and meetings. A cinder block propped open the heavy oak door to let in evening air. The few neighbors who showed up fanned themselves with meeting agendas.

"Ladies, have a seat. We've already started," a heavy woman with a cap of grey-streaked hair said from the pulpit. She leaned on her cane and waved her free hand toward the mostly empty rows of folding metal chairs. Joanna recognized her as a visiting nurse who lived a few blocks away and walked her poodles each afternoon past the store. Eve sat in the front row, hands folded in her lap.

Behind a table on the stage were five chairs, four of them filled with other neighborhood association members. One was Deena, the exuberant redhead and former rock and roll groupee who owned the coffee shop across from the theater. Next to her sat a tattooed man with horn-rimmed glasses. Joanna knew him as a local filmmaker whose girlfriend shopped at Tallulah's Closet. The other two were a thin, bearded man Joanna didn't recognize and a woman sporting dreadlocks and a "Powered by Kale" tee shirt.

"Here, drink this." Apple handed Joanna a styrofoam cup of thin coffee and slid into the chair next to her. Joanna took a sip and put the cup on the floor under her chair. She was plenty sober.

Damn that Eve.

"Now that the meeting minutes have been approved, we'll move on to the business of the evening: permit hearings. These permits have already been approved by the city, conditional on the neighborhood's agreement. We have two items to consider. Item one, conversion of the yard behind Maclay's Barbecue into an outdoor eating area. Mac, would you like to present your case?"

Mac Maclay, his body slow, possibly from a surfeit of brisket, lumbered to the stage. He mopped sweat from his brow, peeked over his notes at the audience, and quickly retreated behind his papers. "I thought it would be nice to take that area where the dumpsters—"

"Speak up," the nurse said.

"Take that area where the dumpsters are," Mac said more loudly, "and put out some picnic tables where folks could eat." He pulled out his handkerchief once more to pat down his forehead.

After a moment of silence, it appeared Mac had concluded his remarks. The bearded man on stage raised his hand. "And what do you propose to do with the dumpsters?"

"Move 'em."

Another long pause followed. The nurse rose from her seat. "If you're finished, you can take your seat now, Mac." He gratefully stepped down. The nurse turned to the other two people on stage. "Any more questions?" They shook their heads. "Anyone in the audience have anything to say?" Other than the rustling of agendas, the room was silent. "Then let's vote."

"I vote aye," said the bearded man.

"Aye," said Deena, the coffee shop owner. Joanna had already mentally removed Deena's overly busy necklace and had dressed her in an early 1970s patchwork sundress. "I have to add I think Maclay's is the best Scottish barbecue in town."

"Aye, although I'd like to see more vegan offerings," the dreadlocked woman said.

"I have a vegan—" Mac pronounced it "vedge-ann" "—coleslaw."

"That cabbage is not organic."

"Save it for later, Lou," said the film maker. "Aye."

"Aye for me, too," said the nurse. "The ayes have it. Next up, change of use of Clinton Street Theater to a retail space. Eve Lancer."

"Look," Apple whispered. Sitting in the back row was Paul. Against Joanna's will her pulse quickened. Paul nodded toward them. "He must have come in while Mac was talking," Apple continued. "How much you want to bet he's here to support you?"

Joanna leaned toward Apple. "Or Eve. She definitely gave him the treatment at the store the other day."

"Stop it," Apple said.

Eve set up a laptop and projector on a small table in the aisle. Her heels clicked as she gracefully mounted the stairs and unfurled a movie screen. She glanced into the audience, and a frown momentarily marred her beauty when she spotted Joanna and Apple. She quickly relaxed again. "Hello everyone. I put together a small presentation — nothing really — to give you an idea of my vision for the new Clinton Street Theater. You see, I don't want to change it, really. I just want to enhance it. I want it to be a credit to this wonderful neighborhood."

Her smile was warm. It said, Trust me. I want the best for all of us. The bearded man looked ready to chuck his wedding ring and go home with her now. No matter how many times she saw her, Joanna still couldn't get over the perfection of Eve's features — the heart-shaped face and dimples when she smiled.

Eve opened the laptop and clicked a few keys. "Making the Clinton Street Theater a Vital Neighborhood Center" the first slide read. She clicked to the next. An interior designer's drawing of a Hollywood Regency room — the audience area of the theater — filled the screen with French blue walls and ivory and gold molding. The old low ceiling seemed to have disappeared, and faux Louis XVI armchairs took the place of the theater's current sprung seats. Golden ropes held abundant silken drapes away from the movie screen.

"My plan is to gut the inside of the theater, then redo it as if it were the private showing room in a Hollywood mogul's house in the 1930s, the time of Carole Lombard and Clark Gable. I'll open for movies some nights, but during the day the movies will be silent—backlit projection—and the space will be retail for high-end vintage clothing."

She clicked to another screen, this one showing a few racks of dresses on wheels. The dresses, drawn in pastels, dripped in marabou and sequins. In the background was a glass-fronted refrigerator filled with orange-labeled champagne bottles. Joanna could practically smell the hothouse roses.

"I'll have private events at the theater from time to time, and the stage will be perfect for fashion shows. My business manager estimates that the theater will attract an additional three hundred people a month, from all around the metro region. These people will shop in local stores, eat in our restaurants—" Joanna groaned silently when she said "our," "—and become ambassadors for the neighborhood as it grows."

"This one is the entrance to the dressing rooms, where the snack bar is now." The screen showed thick velvet draperies tied off with tassels. An ornamental gold hook hung to the side—with the Lanvin coat on it. Joanna gasped. The illustrator's touch had restored the coat to its 1930s pristine condition, but there was no doubt about it. It was Marnie's coat.

Joanna nudged Apple."Look. The coat." As far as Joanna knew, Eve had never seen the Lanvin coat in person. There's no way she could have had an artist draw it from a description. Eve must have the real thing. Anger coursed through her body, and she sat on her hands to keep them from trembling.

Eve looked at the slide and smiled in pure self-satisfaction. "Any questions?"

Joanna stood abruptly. "Where did you get that coat?" The force of her voice surprised even her. She pointed at the screen, still lingering on the dressing room view.

"I have some wonderful items to put out once the store opens. This coat, a Lanvin from the 1930s, is one of them."

"But how did you get it? It was stolen from my store. It has to be the same one—look, the drawing shows a little of the lining. It's a replacement lining, pink and green."

Eve's voice was calm. "Oh, I don't know anything about that. A homeless person sold it to me. I was glad to be able to help him out and acquire something beautiful for the new boutique at the same time." She dismissed Joanna by looking at the audience. "Any other questions?"

Reluctantly, Joanna sat down. She'd have this out with Eve later.

"Do you have a name for it yet?" a nun knitting in the front row asked. She was probably responsible for closing up the chapel after the meeting.

"How about *All about Eve*?" Apple muttered to Joanna.

"Not yet," Eve said, "But I welcome your suggestions. I'll hand out my card at the end of the meeting. Feel free to call any time with ideas."

"What kind of films will you show?" the film maker asked. The Clinton Street Theater traditionally held a few local film festivals, including Filmed by Bike and an annual gay and lesbian series.

"Films from Hollywood's Golden Age, of course," Eve said.

"Such as?"

She smiled again. Joanna realized she probably couldn't identify a single 1940s movie without prompting. "All the classic movies people love," Eve said. "You know, Humphrey Bogart, stars like that."

God, Eve was handling this well. The audience was clearly enraptured. Joanna wanted to get up and wipe the drool from the bearded man's face. How could she possibly compete?

The film maker crossed his arms. "You're not from this neighborhood, are you?"

Joanna's attention sharpened. Maybe she had a chance yet. Eve had a new condo in the Pearl District, the kind built with exposed pipes to look like it was carved from an old warehouse. An old warehouse with granite countertops and travertine tile bathrooms, that is.

"I've loved this neighborhood for years," Eve replied, avoiding the question. "Why, I've even been in touch with the drama teacher at Cleveland High School, and I'm going to help her do the costuming for *Bye Bye Birdie* this year." A few people in the audience murmured their approval.

The dreadlocked vegan raised her hand. "I see a refrigerator and wine bottles. Will you be serving food, too?"

"Only for private events and the occasional glass of champagne for shoppers, of course." Her heels ticked rat-a-tat as she approached the table. The bearded man appeared to have trouble keeping his breathing regular. "One of my best friends runs Earth Goddess catering. Perhaps you've heard of them? Local, sustainable food. Maybe not as tasty as Mac's." Eve's laugh rang like bells. "But tasty nonetheless."

Suddenly Tallulah's Closet felt shabby and small. A store Joanna had once envisioned as a welcoming boudoir with beautiful things to wear now seemed second rate. She didn't have a refrigerator stocked with Veuve Cliquot. She wouldn't be able to lure *Vogue* to feature the store. She was starting to build a little bit of a cross-town clientele, but it was nothing like what Eve would be able to attract with her new boutique.

Still, Tallulah's Closet had been a neighborhood fixture for three years. Joanna helped plant flower baskets for the light poles and held a benefit fashion show for the community garden. She wasn't a business looking to turn a buck and move on. Unlike Eve, she really loved what she did. Joanna had to say something, had to defend Tallulah's Closet. Should she wait for the audience comment period at the end or jump in now?

Deena seemed to read her mind. "What about Tallulah's Closet? We already have a vintage clothing store, and it's just down the block from the theater."

Joanna would find that patchwork sundress and bring it to Deena personally.

"I'm glad you asked," Eve said. "I see Tallulah's Closet's presence as an asset. With two vintage clothing stores in the neighborhood, people will know it as a vintage clothing destination."

Joanna couldn't take any more of this. Heart hammering, she stood. "I don't agree. Eve's store will shut down Tallulah's Closet before the year is through. The neighborhood can't support more than one vintage clothing store. Once Tallulah's Closet closes, where will neighbors buy their vintage clothing? Sure, Eve's store will be around to supply evening dresses, but they won't be cheap. If you doubt me, look at her website. Look at the stock and the prices."

Eve shook her head, "No — "

"When fall comes, where are you going to get your old Pendleton skirts? When you need a cotton sundress for the summer, where are you going to go? Eve won't have them, and if she does they'll be priced to sell to her clients in New York."

"You just proved my point," Eve said, arms akimbo in a victorious stance. "We complement each other, not compete."

"Deena, if a coffee shop opened across the street from you, what would happen to your business? Especially if the owner of that shop had the money to take the losses until you went under? If Eve's store is approved, Tallulah's Closet will cease to exist." Joanna felt as if she were clinging to a log in a rushing river. "I couldn't survive if I didn't sell the occasional wedding dress or high-end cocktail dress. I sell the 1940s sandals and old hostess gowns because I love them, not because they make enough money to keep me afloat. With my high-end sales leached away, I might as well close the store now."

"The focus here should be what's best for the neighborhood." Eve's voice took a steely edge. "Which is ready to take the next step forward."

Joanna's voice raised a notch. "My plan has always been to stay here for the long run. I started Tallulah's Closet not to get rich, but to match beautiful clothes with people who love them." She took a deep breath. "All I ask is that you consider these things before you vote." As Joanna looked around the audience, she knew her argument sounded weak. Clicking from a nun's knitting needles filled the silence.

Apple whispered, "Good work," as Joanna sat down.

The nurse hoisted herself from the table with her cane. "Is that all? Any other comments or questions?"

A chair scraped at the rear of the room. Paul rose. "All this talk is moot if the landlord hasn't agreed to the new lease. That building needs a lot of work. God knows what you'll find once you gut the interior. Is the building owner really ready to go through with this?"

Their eyes met. She tried to telegraph her gratitude.

Eve pulled a lock of hair behind her ear. "Hello, Paul. Those are such good points. I met with the landlord this afternoon and signed the lease. He's having it notarized tomorrow. Assuming the vote goes well, of course."

Joanna's heart dropped.

"I'm fully aware of potential problems with the space, and we've built renovation into the lease agreement." Her hands went to the twisted gold pendant resting low on her chest. "There's a lot of woodwork in the lobby. I'll need a skilled craftsman to restore it, by the way."

So, he was here looking for work. Figures. Joanna dropped her eyes and turned to the stage again.

"Thank you," the nurse said. "Are we ready for the vote?"

Apple clutched Joanna's hand.

"Aye," the bearded man said. "I look forward to having you as a neighbor."

The film maker snorted. "Nay. The theater's too important to the community to be left to a bunch of films you can find on the old movie channel at home."

"I have to say nay, too," Deena said. "I'm thinking of the long run, and in the long run I want to see Tallulah's Closet on our block."

"Aye," the dreadlocked woman said. "It sounds like the new store will be nicely integrated with the neighborhood. I like that."

Two ayes, two nays. Only the nurse's vote was left. "I, too, appreciate having Tallulah's Closet in the neighborhood. Without it, I don't know that we'd have grown as much as we have. We have a flourishing artistic community. Hell, you can't turn over a rock without finding a musician or writer, and Tallulah's Closet has been a natural part of that." She shifted on her feet, leaning on her cane. "But the neighborhood is getting tonier all the same. Eve is right. It's time to move to the next level. My vote is aye."

"The ayes have it."

Chapter 25

Joanna slammed the phone in its cradle. She'd left her third message for Eve about the Lanvin coat. Knowing Eve, she'd make Joanna stew a while. Pepper lay, belly up, in a patch of morning sun near the chaise.

She took a calming breath and dug Don's business card from a stack of papers on her desk. It read simply, "Donald Cayle, Investment Properties" and listed a downtown address. While she waited for his secretary to patch her through, she downed two aspirin and half a glass of water. Her grandmother had always said when you feel bad — and she felt plenty bad — you should do something nice for someone else. At least giving Don the safe deposit box key and so proof of his paternity was a start.

Don's voice was gruff but upbeat. "Hello, Joanna. I want to thank you again for arranging Marnie's memorial service. What can I do for you today? Looking for a new space for your shop?"

Not such a bad idea. "It's funny you say that. I just might be looking for a new space."

He chuckled. "We need to talk before you make any hasty decisions."

"That's why I called, actually. To talk. But not about Tallulah's Closet — at least not today. Before Marnie died, she sold me some clothes. I found something in a coat she brought in, and I was never

able to return it to her. I thought — you know, you were close with
Marnie — that I'd like to give it to you. I think you'll appreciate it."

"That's very thoughtful of you." His chair creaked, and she pictured
him standing up. "Do you want to drop by the office? No, it looks
like I have a meeting at eleven, then I'll be out most of the afternoon.
I'll tell you what. Why don't you come by my house around five and
we'll have a drink? I'll call the housekeeper and have her make up
something to leave in the ice box. She's a terrific cook. Besides, I'm
glad you called. I was planning to give you a call myself — I have
something for you, too. Something I think you'll be glad to see."

Mid-afternoon at Tallulah's Closet, Joanna lifted her head from
mending the lining of the jacket of a Forstmann suit as Nina entered
the store. The scent of Jungle Gardenia wafted across the room.

"I brought some clothing you might be interested in. Where can
I put this?" She held up a thick garment bag.

Joanna tucked the needle into the lining and set down the jacket.
"Let me take it." She hung the garment bag at the edge of clothes
rack. "Thank you, Nina."

"Oh, it's just a few things I don't wear anymore. My waist isn't
what it used to be."

Joanna unzipped the garment bag and drew out a navy blue dinner
suit, two cocktail dresses, and a mink stole. One of the cocktail
dresses, a Lilli Diamond, was of lipstick red fabric shot through with
silver thread. A perfect holiday dress. The other, deeply décolleté,
sported a banner of pink chiffon that crossed the torso diagonally,
then dropped freely down the back from the shoulder to the waist.

She ran her hands inside the dresses, one of which still had its dry cleaning tag attached. They were in top condition. At least she'd have something to sell before Eve ran her out of business.

"These are perfect for the store. I wish I could have seen you wearing them." Nina certainly knew how to dress for her figure and coloring. Elizabeth Taylor might have taken a few pointers. She picked up the suit. "A whole different mood. I love the inside." It was a late 1950s Lilli Ann suit with a tight skirt to below the knee and a jacket with three-quarter length sleeves and a shawl collar. "Tissé à Paris" was woven into the suit's silky lining.

"Gary was in the military and I went to a few functions with him. I didn't see a lot of use in playing up the dancer angle." Nina ran her fingers down the stole's shoulder. "I wasn't sure if you took fur. But it's an Oleg Cassini."

"We don't get many takers for mink stoles, but I like to have one or two on hand."

Nina's gaze roamed the store, then lit on the restroom at the back of the store. "Is that where you found Marnie?"

"No. She was here. Right where I'm standing, actually." As if the ground had turned hot, Joanna stepped away. They both stared at the linoleum.

"I just felt a chill down my neck," Nina said. Then, more quietly, "Poor old girl. At least she was surrounded by things she loved."

"I miss her." If only she'd known about Marnie's connection with her grandmother while she was alive. Joanna sighed and stepped back behind the tiki bar to hang the clothes to be priced later.

"Let's not talk about that. It's too nice out to be depressed. How's business?" Nina asked.

Another sore spot. "Someone's opening a vintage clothing shop on the corner, in the theater. It's supposed to be pretty spectacular."

Nina, a businesswoman, saw the implications immediately. "Retail's a bitch, let me tell you. I guess it's the same if it's old clothes or fish." She reached into her bag for a pack of cigarettes.

"It's nice to see you, though." Joanna meant it, too. "Let's have lunch again sometime. Oh — I saw Congressman Remmick and asked him about Marnie. You know, to see if he might be Troy's father."

Nina slid the cigarette she held back into its pack. "No kidding. What'd he say?"

Remembering the conversation, Joanna's face burned. "At first he pretended like he barely knew her. Then he admitted to an affair."

"Well, then. It's like I thought."

"He can't have kids. Some kind of medical thing," Joanna said. Nina's brows raised. "It was awful."

"Oh dear. Kind of embarrassing." She laughed. "I'm sorry. I'm just imagining it."

"It was horrifying. I think he suspected I was trying to blackmail him."

"Sorry about that." Nina patted her hand. "It seemed like a sure thing. I'm still shocked that Marnie could have had a child and given him up for adoption."

That Troy even existed was the astonishing part. Adoption was less of a surprise. Then she understood. "Do you have children?"

Nina fidgeted with the strap on her purse. "No, I was pregnant once, but, well, at the time it wasn't ideal. For a number of reasons. When Gary and I finally decided to start a family, it was too late." She rested a pink-taloned hand on the tiki bar. "Oh, I'm not complaining. I've had my day, and Gary has been good to me. But I wish I would have thought of it sooner."

"I'm sorry."

Nina nodded. "Don't waste time. You're pretty enough to find someone. If you want a family you need to get started now." She looked into the distance, and the animation left her face, adding years.

Better change subjects. "I saw Troy yesterday. It turns out Marnie left him just about everything in her will."

Nina's eyes snapped to Joanna. "Did she? She got around to writing a will, then."

"Apparently so."

"I guess she knew she was dying, knew she wanted to leave something to her son. At least she had the heart for that." Nina held a pair of milky blue Czech crystal earrings to her ears and put them down. "I don't get it, though. If Chick isn't his father, then who is?"

Best to keep Don's letter to Marnie under wraps for now. "I've wondered the same thing myself. To tell the truth, I had even wondered if Troy is her son at all. He seemed to come out of the blue."

"Oh, I'm not surprised Marnie got herself in trouble. Her life was a land mine of bad decisions, if you ask me. I just wonder..." She stopped short.

Maybe just one little hint wouldn't hurt. "Troy mentioned that Don gave him his card and wanted to get together sometime. Could Don be his father? Troy is about thirty. Was still with Marnie then?"

Nina shook her head. "No, it's impossible. Don would never have let her keep the baby. He knew how to take care of those things."

Joanna picked up her mending. "Why not?" she continued. "He seemed to really care about Marnie. Maybe he would have liked having a son."

Nina's hand slammed down on the tiki bar. Joanna jumped and the needle pricked her index finger. Wide eyed, she stared at Nina. What had got into her?

"I said it's impossible."

"Nina, I'm sorry—"

"You can send a check for the clothes to the Wet Spot. I have to go." The front door's bell jangled violently after her. Joanna stared at the closed door for a moment, then put her finger in her mouth and tasted warm, salty blood.

Chapter 26

At a few minutes after five, Joanna pulled up in front of Don's house. A canopy of chestnut trees sheltered the street, cooling the air and casting a moving pattern of dappled shade on the pavement. As she walked up the steps to the house's wide veranda, she patted the side pocket of her purse. Yes, the key was still there.

Don didn't answer the bell. She stepped to the left of the door to the broad window. The open curtains revealed a large living room with a fireplace and two leather couches. Joanna rang again. Surely he hadn't forgotten their meeting. Maybe he was in the backyard, reading the paper, and couldn't hear the bell.

She walked down the steps and to the right side of the house, where a Cadillac dominated the driveway. At the top of the driveway rose an iron gate. Its heavy latch clanked open. In the backyard, French doors topped a deck shaded by a mimosa tree. She hesitated. It was too quiet back here.

Just then a flutter of fabric ruffled a back window. Or was that a shadow from the tree?

"Don?" she said tentatively, crossing the yard to the far edge of the deck.

An orange and white spaniel pushed open the French doors and ran toward her, nails clattering down the steps. She crouched slightly, ready to run, but the spaniel just wagged his stumpy tail and nudged Joanna's hand with his nose. God, she was jumpy. She scratched the dog's ears and let out her breath.

A sharp crack exploded the quiet. Once, then twice. Gun fire.

Joanna closed the distance to the house in a few steps and flattened her back against the wall, her breath coming in ragged gasps. The dog burrowed under the deck. What the hell was going on?

Silence again. She scanned the backyard but didn't see any bullet holes. To her left the backyard fence joined the house. To her right were the French doors, now ajar, going into the house. To leave, she'd have to pass by them. Too exposed. Above her was the window where she'd seen movement.

Her foot touched a plant in a small pot. She dropped her purse, and, sinking slowly, knelt for the pot. Her hand trembled as she hoisted it to chest level. She steadied herself. Now! She hurled the pot across the back of the house. Bullets pierced the fence where the pot shattered.

Blood chilled in her veins. Don wanted to kill her. He lured her here, and now he would kill her.

A door slammed, and she jerked her head. The front door, maybe. Someone leaving? Or was it a trick? Nearer, a moan escaped the house. The dog, his belly brown with dirt, squeezed out from under the deck and nosed through the French doors. Joanna heard the gasping moan again.

Someone was hurt. Heart thumping, she crept up the steps to the deck and peered in the open doors. A waist-high counter separated a small eating area from the kitchen. The counter was cleared except for a full highball glass in a puddle of condensation.

Joanna stepped around the counter, then backed into the

refrigerator. Lying on the floor, face up, was Don. With a bullet hole in his chest.

She ran for the front door and onto the veranda just as a car peeled into the distance, another car honking at it. The leafy trees obscured her view up the street. Whoever had fired at her, it hadn't been Don.

She returned to the kitchen and stepped around Don to reach the phone on the counter. A bullet had left a hole in a cupboard. She steadied her voice. "Please send an ambulance. Someone has been shot." A sickly sweet smell, almost floral, hung in the stuffy kitchen. After she stuttered Don's address to the dispatcher, she took Don's wrist and felt in vain for a pulse. A stream of blood made fingers down his linen shirt. A ladybug alit on his neck. She brushed it away.

"Don," she whispered. "Who did this to you?"

*
**

Joanna was still in the kitchen holding Don's hand when the police burst in the front door. Her other hand pressed a cloth napkin over his wound.

"Officer Riggs," one of the policemen said. He was large and had a black mustache. In street clothes, he'd still look like a policeman. He took her upper arm and led her to the living room.

Two policemen rushed past them and another lingered on the veranda, front door ajar.

"Why don't you tell me what happened?" Riggs pulled a small notebook from his pocket.

"We need an ambulance." Joanna looked toward the kitchen.

"On its way. Name, please?"

"Joanna Hayworth." Another officer dropped her purse, smudged with dirt, at Riggs's side. "I had an appointment to meet Don — you know?" She gestured toward the kitchen. When Riggs nodded, she continued. "Five o'clock. I rang the doorbell and no one answered. I went around the back, because I thought Don might be out there. It's a — was a — beautiful day, and the dog ran out the back door, so I called inside. I heard gunshots. Two of them." She felt herself getting lightheaded. "That must have been when Don was shot. Why isn't the ambulance here?"

"Easy, easy," Officer Riggs said. "Dugan?" he yelled into the kitchen. "You got a bottle of water? I think there's some in the cruiser."

"Someone shot at me then took off out the front door and sped away. I called you."

"Did you get a look at him?" The other officer had returned with the bottle of water.

She gulped from the bottle before replying. "No. I think the car was gray. Small. That's all I can tell you."

Through a glass panel on the front door stood Detective Crisp — the cop who had come to the store when Marnie died — accompanied by two people with large cases. He knocked twice, then entered. Riggs motioned toward the kitchen, and the new arrivals headed that way. A siren screamed nearby. Finally, an ambulance.

Officer Riggs turned back to Joanna and picked up his pen. "Nice dress," he said quietly. "That vintage?"

She looked at the officer with surprise. Don was shot, maybe dead, and the policeman was commenting on her clothes? "Yes, in fact it is. I have a vintage clothing shop on Clinton."

"It's amazing that so delicate a fabric lasted so long. And with lace-edged ruching on the bodice, too."

Now she understood. She had a few customers like him. Probably none of his buddies in the police force knew about his hobby. On another day she would have hinted at the larger-sized dresses she tried to keep in stock.

A team of paramedics pushed through the front door. A woman in street clothes — a crime scene investigator, maybe — came to the couch and opened her case. "I'm going to swipe your hand for gunpowder, and we'll need your fingerprints, too."

"Yes, yes, of course." Joanna looked down at a crimson stain on the side of her sandal. She must have walked through blood on her way to the front door. Maybe she could she could drive home barefoot. "You don't think I did it, do you?"

"Just eliminating all possibilities, ma'am."

While Joanna was being fingerprinted, Detective Crisp pulled up a chair. He set a large plastic bag containing a manila envelope next to him. "So, it's you again. You and another body." Officer Riggs handed him his notebook, and the detective glanced at the notes. "Why don't you tell me what happened?"

Joanna recounted her story. Again.

"You say you were to meet Mr. Cayle. Was there a particular reason for that? Are you doing business with him?"

"No, I had something I wanted to give him." She looked up at Officer Riggs. "May I have my purse? Thank you." The technician taking her fingerprints handed her a wet wipe. She rubbed the ink off her fingers and reached into her purse's side pocket. "This." She held up the key.

Crisp took the key and examined both sides. "That safe deposit key again."

The paramedics returned through the living room, this time moving more slowly. The detective made eye contact with one of the paramedics, who shook his head. "Riggs, call the M.E.," Crisp said. Joanna's heart sank.

The detective handed the key back to Joanna. "How well did you know Mr. Cayle?"

"He's dead, isn't he?" It was more a statement than a question.

"I'm afraid so."

She played with the key, pressing its ridges against her palm and pinching it between her fingers. Finally she put the the key on the armrest of the chair and looked at Crisp. "I didn't know Don very well. I only met him a week ago."

"Why did he have this for you?" He lifted the bag with the manila envelope. She saw her name on the envelope's side in Don's loose scrawl. As she reached for the bag, the detective pulled it back. "Evidence. When and if it clears, you'll get it."

"I don't know. He said he had something for me. I assumed it was something to remember Marnie by." If he knew what was in the envelope, his expression didn't show it. Joanna picked up the key again. "I think you should take this. Someone wants it, they'll do anything to get it, and I don't know why. I mean, Marnie died in a pretty strange situation — "

"And we're following up on that."

"Well, now someone killed Don and shot at me, too. Don't you think that makes the key important?"

The detective looked to the side and pursued his lips, as if thinking, before turning back to Joanna. "I'm only telling you this because Evans — Marnie — was found at your store. We've linked Cayle and Evans back to some shady business in the 1960s. Cayle used Evans's name on some real estate deals and routed another mob gang that thought it had a stranglehold on local gambling. Frankly, I'm not all that surprised to find out someone caught up with them."

"But that was ages ago. What could it matter now?"

"A few deaths, a few people getting out of prison. Sometimes it takes a while to settle all the scores."

Joanna shook her head. "No. I don't believe it. Why would someone steal the Lanvin coat? Why slit its lining?"

He paused. "The fact that someone moved Evans's body to your store—I haven't figured that out yet. But look. Did anyone know you were coming here with the key?"

"Well, no, but—"

"Did Cayle know you had the key with you, so that he could have told someone?"

"No, he knew I had something for him, but—"

"Even if he did know, why would someone kill him when he didn't yet have the key?"

She couldn't argue with his logic. She returned the key to her purse.

"We're going to process the scene, but we'll need to talk to you again." Crisp examined her. "You have an uncanny knack for turning up when people die."

She raised an eyebrow. What was he getting at?

The detective glanced at the handcuffs dangling from the uniformed policeman's belt, then back at Joanna. "Riggs, the residue test?"

"Negative."

A long moment passed. Finally, the detective tucked the Tallulah's Closet business card Officer Riggs had taken from Joanna's purse into his notebook. "Can we still find you at this number?"

She released her breath. "Yes. I'm at the shop most afternoons." The spaniel at the other side of the living room lay down on the floor. He raised his head when he saw he had Joanna's attention. "What are you going to do with him?"

The dog stood and wagged his stump. "We'll call the county to hold him. The deceased's family can pick him up."

"Do you think I could take him home? At least until you find someone to take him permanently? I hate the thought of a dog going to the pound when he could be with a person. I'm pretty sure Don lived here by himself." Even as she said the words, she knew she was crazy to take on a dog.

The detective looked at Officer Riggs, who raised his eyebrows and shrugged. "We don't normally do this, but I guess, given that we'll be in touch with you, that would be all right. It will save us the hassle of getting animal control out here."

"Are you all right now? Feeling okay?" Riggs asked.

"Yeah, I'm fine. Thanks." She stood up slowly. As she untethered the dog from the armchair where one of the officers had tied him, she looked back through the dining room toward the kitchen. Someone knelt over Don's body. The dog trotted toward the front door the police officer held open for them. A wave of lightheadedness started again, and Joanna put a hand on one of the veranda's cool cement pillars to steady herself until it passed.

She walked down the steps of the porch to her car, and the dog jumped into the seat next to her. She closed her eyes and breathed deeply. She wished she had never seen the safe deposit box key. She was finished with the key now. She didn't care how it got in the coat, what it unlocked, and who wanted it. Elvis Presley could be Troy's father—she didn't give a damn. In the morning she would drop the key off downtown then post a note in the window of Tallulah's Closet to "the person who lost the safe deposit box key" saying the key was now at the bank. Yes, that's what she would do. Her breath steadied.

Looking for attention, the dog dipped his head under her arm. "Some faithful companion you are." Joanna turned the key in the car's ignition, once and then twice before its engine sputtered to life. "I hope you like cats."

*
**

Holding a bag of dog food under one arm and the dog's leash with the other hand, Joanna struggled to fit the house key in her front door. When the key finally slid in, the bolt wouldn't turn. It was already unlocked. Remembering the scene at Don's, Joanna's hand hesitated on the door knob.

Inside, she gasped and dropped the bag of food. Aunt Vanderburgh and the other portraits lay broken and scattered, a butcher's mix of flesh tones on the rug. Her gaze shot to the wall where they'd hung. Crudely carved into the plaster were the words LEAVE THE PAPERS ALONE.

The blood rushed from her head. She grabbed the door frame for balance.

The dog shot down the basement stairs after Pepper, dragging his leash behind him.

"God damn it." She picked up her phone and for the second time that day called 911.

Hours later, after the police left, Apple smeared plaster on the words carved into the wall, blending a white trail over the cream paint. Joanna swept up bits of glass from the broken portraits. The spaniel was in the backyard. He had dug a bed in the pea gravel and basked in the waning sun.

Apple dampened a rag and feathered the plaster's edge. "You won't be able to sand it until tomorrow, but when it's done and painted, no one will ever know what happened."

"I'll know." Joanna leaned the broom against the wall and picked up the dust pan. "Who would do this? I feel so—violated."

"I do sense a lot of anger here."

"Duh." She tipped a dustpan of glass shards into the garbage pail.

"Not yours. I mean angry energy. In the air." Apple stepped down from the ladder. "And you're not staying here, that's for sure. You're coming with me tonight and for as long as you need."

"Oh Apple, thank you." Detective Crisp had said the same thing—she shouldn't be alone until she could get a security system installed.

"I wonder where they are with the investigation?"

"I don't know." Joanna sighed. "They didn't get any fingerprints here, and whoever broke in apparently used the front door." For a few minutes, Joanna had even wondered if the detective thought she defaced her own walls. Her terror was too real for him to suspect her for long. "With Don's death, though, I'm sure they'll step it up." She ripped a fresh garbage bag from its roll. "The message on the wall, it said to leave the papers alone. I wonder what papers they mean? A birth certificate is just one sheet, not papers."

"What's this?" Apple was holding the silk rose Joanna had taken the night she and Paul were at the Reel M'Inn. "Isn't it from the *Carmen* costumes? What's it doing on your mantel?"

"That's—nothing."

Apple's eyes narrowed. "Uh huh. It would be nice if you had someone around to watch out for you, you know."

"Apple, please…"

"Paul came by the store today and asked how you were."

She ignored Apple and tied the top of the garbage bag. Glass shards clinked as she lifted it from the pail. "I was so sure it was Don who wanted the key. Who else could it have been? He found out he was Troy's father, and he wanted proof. Somehow he'd discovered where Marnie hid the safe deposit box key. I thought for sure I had it all figured out."

"Could someone have killed Don for other reasons? I mean, he's been around a long time. Marnie's obit mentioned mob connections."

"The police did, too." Joanna lifted the bag to carry outside. Its sides bulged with jagged angles.

"Jo, be careful—"

"Ouch!" Joanna dropped the bag on the rug and pressed a hand to her calf. "It's okay. I'll get a wash cloth."

Apple followed her into the bathroom. "The cut doesn't look too bad. Here—let me get that." She took the wet cloth from Joanna's hands and pressed it against her leg. "Really, it's just a scratch."

Joanna's voice was quiet. "When I left Don's, I was ready to give up. Not now. I need to find whoever did this."

Apple shook her head and rummaged in a cupboard for a bandage. "But what about the love child? Shouldn't he be able to get in the safe deposit box? You told me he was named in her will."

"He can't. Marnie's lawyer doesn't know anything about a safe deposit box, either. I asked him. It doesn't matter now, though. The police finally agreed to get a letter from the lawyer to open it tomorrow. I'm meeting Detective Crisp first thing in the morning."

Apple leaned against the bathroom door frame and hugged her shoulders. "I don't know, Jo. I don't feel good about this. I get a really bad vibe here."

"You already said that." Joanna tossed the bandaid's wrapper in the wicker trash can. "Look. Maybe whatever's in the safe deposit box will put the whole thing to rest, or at least give the police a reason to follow up. If these mysterious papers are there, the police should have them." She wasn't going to let Apple talk her out of it.

Both women turned at the sound of scratching at the back door. Joanna opened it, and the dog rushed in, then stopped short at the sight of Pepper reclining on an armchair.

"They had it out in the basement while I was talking to the police," Joanna said. "See that?" She pointed to a thin line of dried blood on the dog's nose. "Pepper's work."

"What's the dog's name?"

"Don't know. I only have him until the police track down Don's relatives. In the meantime, what should we call him?" She scratched the spaniel's head. The silky fur on his ears wound loosely around her fingers. "How about Curly? He has a little bit of the Three Stooges thing going on. Plus, it has 'cur' in it."

Apple scratched the dog above his tail. "We're done here. Why don't you get a few things to take to my place?"

Joanna led the way to the bedroom. She clicked the switch on the swirled white Murano lamp on the bureau. "I guess I should feel lucky. I mean—Don." The gun shots. Don's bleeding chest. Such an unreal afternoon. "At least here no one was hurt."

"You weren't here to hurt. Maybe that's the lucky part of it."

"Maybe. Or maybe they waited until I was gone." Joanna pressed her palms to her eyes and rubbed. Would this ever be over? "There's an overnight satchel in the closet. Will you grab it?" She pulled out a dresser drawer and gathered a handful of underwear.

"Joanna."

Something about Apple's voice stopped her cold. Ice gripped her intestines.

"The inside of the closet door," Apple said. "Look."

Dread washed over Joanna. Reluctantly, she turned toward the closet. "Oh my God." Dangling from a boning knife like a dead hare was an ash blond wig. Marnie's wig.

Joanna clapped a hand over her mouth to quell the rising nausea.

Chapter 28

Detective Crisp was late. Still shaken from the discovery of Marnie's wig, Joanna leaned against one of the massive Corinthian columns adorning the bank's facade. Customers stepped through the wide, bronze-trimmed revolving doors, releasing wafts of cool air.

She held a large cup of coffee from a cafe down the block. Apple drank mostly tea. No matter how strong she made it, it still wasn't coffee. Tea didn't cut it after sleeping on Apple's lumpy sofa bed with a dog. Especially a dog who snored.

Finally, the detective strode across the street. A large sterling arrowhead anchored his bolo tie today.

"Did you bring the key?" he asked without even greeting her.

Joanna handed it to him. "You've got the letter from Marnie's attorney?"

He nodded. "Let's go."

The detective led her into the bank and across a broad expanse of marble floor toward an information desk at the back of the lobby. No one was at the desk. Crisp rang the bell. As Joanna studied the deco chandeliers hanging two stories above, the detective tapped his fingers on the desk's broad oak surface.

A bank officer emerged from one of the side offices. "How may I help you?" She wore a gray rayon suit with cheap black heels. Joanna fought the urge to suggest she try a 1940s suit in a warm color, maybe cocoa. With an ivory and navy polka dot blouse.

"I'm Detective Foster Crisp, Portland Police, and I'd like access to a safe deposit box rented to a Margaret Evans." He showed his badge, then opened his briefcase and produced a few sheets of paper Joanna assumed was the testamentary letter from Marnie's attorney.

The woman looked at the papers then at the detective. "Has there been a crime?"

"That doesn't matter, does it?"

The bank officer's eyes widened. "Let me see what I can do." She led Joanna and Detective Crisp to a desk with a computer and sat down. After a minute, the bank officer said, "Margaret Evans doesn't have an account with us."

Crisp shot Joanna an "I told you so" look.

"Maybe Marnie Evans?" the detective asked.

She clicked a few keys. "No, nothing."

Joanna's heart sank. How could this be? She was doomed to live with Apple forever. Maybe she'd better start drinking tea now.

The detective placed the key on the desk. "This is a key to a safe deposit box at this bank, correct?"

"Well, yes," she said after a glance.

"Who, then, is registered for this box?"

The bank officer wrote the number from the key on a post-it, then returned to her computer. "Someone named, let's see, Pursell. Yes, Franklin Pursell. He was last in less than a month ago."

Franklin. Ray's brother and Marnie's first love. Why would Marnie be carrying around the key to his safe deposit box? Joanna turned to the detective. "An old lover of Marnie's. Died in a construction accident a few weeks ago."

The bank officer looked up from the computer, puzzled. "Pursell is the only person listed on this account. There should have been only one key. How did he get in the box without this key?" The bank officer tapped the key against the desk.

The key was a tiny brass shape on the faux veneer. Franklin was in construction. It couldn't have been that difficult to make a copy if he knew a machinist. Had he hid the key in the coat, or had Marnie? When Marnie brought the coat, Joanna hadn't seen any newly repaired cuts in its lining. Whoever hid the key did it years ago.

The detective's expression was unchanged. "We'd still like to see the box."

She held her breath. If this didn't work, she doubted Crisp would go to the trouble to get permission from Franklin's family, too.

The bank officer paused. "I'm not sure. I mean, if he's dead, you're supposed to have a testamentary letter." Crisp continued to stare impassively. The bank officer sighed. "I guess, I mean, you are the police. Just a moment." She stood up and walked across the bank, her heels clicking on the marble floor.

"Do you think she's asking her boss?" Joanna said.

"Beats me. She doesn't have to show it to us, you know." He tapped a boot-clad foot.

Minutes passed. "Marnie's wig," Joanna said. "Did you find anything on it?"

"Don't know yet."

The bank officer returned. "I guess it's okay. Being that you're the police and all. Harry will show you down to the safe deposit boxes."

Joanna started to smile, then stopped after a glance at the detective. An elderly security guard strolled across the lobby toward them. He led them to a bank of elevators and descended a floor. They passed through a dim, low-ceilinged room.

"Before they rewired everything, I used to have to come down here to turn on lights for the whole bank. I hated it. Back there," the guard gestured toward a hall by the elevators, "are rows of smaller vaults. Years ago a lady had a heart attack in one and died. They say some nights you can still hear her working her adding machine."

He led them to a hall that let into a vault the size of a small house. A round steel door at least two feet thick stood open at its entrance. Inside the vault, photographs of past Rose Parades hung on bare patches of wall between rows of numbered boxes. "We used to keep the Rose Queen's crown here. Now the Rosarians have it."

The security guard stopped by one of the rows of numbered steel drawers, checked the key, then strode partway down the aisle. Joanna and Detective Crisp followed. The guard ran his finger down a column of bronze-fronted boxes, each with two key holes. He inserted a key chained to his belt into one of the locks midway down the column. It wouldn't turn. Joanna held her breath. The guard looked up and laughed nervously. "Just a minute. Sometimes they get stuck."

After a few more jiggles, the key completed its rotation. He inserted the key that had fallen from the Lanvin coat into the adjoining lock. This one turned easily. Harry drew out a steel drawer. "That's it. You can look at it here," he gestured to a table at the end of one of the rows of safe deposit boxes. "Or we have a room just outside."

Detective Crisp turned to the door. "Let's take this to the room."

Outside the vault, opposite the hall they first entered, was a windowless cubicle with a table, two beat up office chairs, and a dusty plastic plant. "Just let Diane upstairs know when you're finished." The security guard left.

The detective tapped the the box on the table between them. "Well, go ahead."

She touched its metal surface. The lid was cool and heavy in her hand. Someone was willing to kill for what was in this box. What would it be? Jewelry, maybe? Some kind of incriminating evidence? She looked up at the detective.

"What are you waiting for?"

She lifted the lid. Scattered across the roomy compartment were envelopes with handwritten addresses. She lifted them — maybe ten in all — onto the table. Mixed in with the envelopes were a piece of paper, some photos, a pair of cuff links with "F M P" engraved on them, and a yellowed stub from an airline ticket.

She picked up the photocopy first. A birth certificate. "Franklin was Troy's father. That's what this says." The detective didn't respond to the incredulity in her voice. So Don was wrong — he wasn't Troy's father at all. The private detective he hired must have come to the wrong conclusion.

But if Franklin was the father and knew it, what was the secret? Why was someone so eager to get into the safe deposit box? Franklin was dead now, so he wouldn't have any reason to hide his paternity. She started to speak, then hesitated. The letters in the box were addressed to Franklin with Marnie's name in the upper left corner. The detective picked up a few of them, glanced at their contents, and tossed them on the table.

"Are you satisfied? Is this what someone killed Marnie and Don and broke into your store and house for — a birth certificate and some love letters?"

"I'm sorry. I — I just don't understand it."

The detective shook his head, but his voice softened. "I've got to get back to the station. If you want to look at the letters, fine. I'll get in touch with Pursell's family." He pushed himself back from the table. "Don't let the ghosts get you." The sound of his footsteps on the linoleum floor echoed through the vault then muffled as they hit the carpet.

Joanna sat alone with the letters spread on the table. The busy streets of downtown rumbled with traffic above her, but here it was quiet but for the steady vibration of the massive building's ventilation system. The distant hum of the elevator's motor started, then stopped. She sorted the letters by the postmarked dates on their envelopes and began to read.

Marnie's first letter, to Franklin at a post office box on Sauvie Island, was from Oysterville. Her handwriting was proper and careful, and she formed her letters as Joanna imagined she learned in school. The paper was pale yellow with a bottom border of blue and pink tulips. It was a teenaged girl's love letter written to a boy who had moved to the city. She must have missed Franklin terribly. She had enclosed a photograph of herself in shorts and a cotton sleeveless blouse holding a tabby kitten. Behind her was a lush hedge of rose bushes.

Similar letters followed. Marnie's childlike language, straightforward and unashamed, told that she was crazy in love. She wrote of people and places—Roberta, the Clam Digger, Mr. Dee, Uncle Tony—that must have once been the everyday fabric of Franklin's life, too. She wrote about moving to Portland as soon as she graduated from high school, although her mother didn't approve. She missed Franklin and worried he would forget her.

The last of the older letters was dated June 1956. That must have been when Marnie moved to Portland to be with Franklin. Soon after, she began working at Mary's Club. A gap of twenty years passed before the next letter. In the meantime, Marnie would have broken up with Franklin and begun seeing Don, although she must have continued her affair with Franklin even after his marriage.

In this letter, Marnie wrote Franklin she had left Don, and she was pregnant with Franklin's child. Her writing was now more stiff, angular. She said she couldn't bear the infrequent meetings they'd had since he'd married. She wrote she wanted to be with Franklin for good, or never see him again. Joanna could almost hear Marnie's voice reading the words.

The next letter was in a manila envelope which must have also contained the copy of the birth certificate. The timing, six months later, was about right. The letter was more of a note, really, asking for help with medical bills. It also said that she'd given the baby, a boy, up for adoption and that she didn't know, and couldn't find out, who the baby's new family was.

From the fresh ink and crisp white paper of the last letter, Joanna knew without looking at the postmark that it was recent. She drew the letter to her nose. Cigarette smoke.

She read. "Dear Franklin. I don't know where to send this letter, so I'm mailing it to your old office address. Maybe they'll forward it. I know it's been a long time since we've been in touch, but I'm writing because I've met our son. He's a good kid. He's studying to be a lawyer." Well, what she didn't know couldn't hurt her. "I'm giving him a little money to help him get by. He doesn't know that you're his father. Also, I wanted to tell you that I have ovarian cancer and the doctors say it's terminal. They want to do all sorts of things to me to make me live longer, but I say, why bother? We've all got to go sometime, and I've had a decent run of it. I may live years, who knows? After all this time, Frankie, I think of you every day, and

I wish you well. Love, Marnie."

Joanna put the last letter back in the safe deposit box. Each of these letters, so flat in the hand were full of emotion — hope, love, and, eventually, loss. How strange what love makes you do. Marnie wanted to be with Franklin, and Franklin chose his wife instead. But he couldn't give Marnie up completely, and he kept these letters locked away, all told over fifty years. Marnie wanted stability and chose Don, then repaid his care with an on-again, off-again affair with Franklin.

Joanna stood up and stretched. She'd been reading for over an hour. The letters told a sad story, but as engrossing as they were, they didn't explain how the key to Franklin's safe deposit box ended up in Marnie's coat. Or why someone wanted it so badly.

Chapter 29

On her way back to the store, Joanna stopped by her house to check on the cat. He was sleeping on the newly-straightened couch, and after a few sniffs Joanna recognized Fleurs de Rocailles on his fur. He must have been hiding in the vanity cabinet when the intruder broke in. The living room felt bare without the portraits above the couch. Instead of camouflaging the warning, broad smears of glaring plaster drew her memory back to it.

She dumped some kibble into Pepper's bowl, kissed him on the head, and quickly left. The dog was at Apple's house, probably digging a hole in her goddess garden. He didn't seem worried to have lost Don — his appetite was good, and he had pulled at the leash on his morning walk. If only people were as resilient as dogs.

Before unlocking the door at Tallulah's Closet, Joanna peered through the plate glass window. Mannequins hulked in the dark. But that was normal. She probably shouldn't be alone here, either, but she found comfort in the thought that a yell would draw someone from Dot's in seconds.

Inside the store, she dawdled as she flipped the light switches and clicked on the lamps on the shelves at the room's perimeter. The morning's revelations had left her feeling pensive. Sometime today Franklin's widow would find out her husband had a child with

Marnie. Her heart sank as she imagined a police cruiser showing up unexpectedly at Franklin's house and the creak of the policeman's leather holster as he sat down to tell the widow about the safe deposit box. It wasn't that long ago Franklin died. And now this.

She picked up the phone. She'd call Ray and fill him in on the details. Maybe if he knew about Franklin and Marnie's affair, he could help break the news to Franklin's wife.

The call bounced to voicemail. "Hi, Ray. This is Joanna Hayworth. Do you have a few minutes? I want to talk to you about Marnie." It was eleven o'clock in the morning. She figured Ray had been awake for hours. Maybe he was working in his garden, or turning a harvest of tomatoes into sauce for the winter. She hung up and reached for the price gun.

Her body jerked as the doorbell rang.

"Jumpy today, aren't you?" It was Eve, with a garment bag slung over her shoulder.

She would have to show up now. "Look, if you've come to talk to me about your store, I'm not—"

"Relax." Eve hung the garment bag on a rack near the tiki bar. "I've come with a peace offering." She unzipped the bag. It was the Lanvin coat.

Joanna's hands leapt to the coat. She peeled back the garment bag and ran her fingers over its shoulders. Marnie's coat, home at last. Had she been alone, she would have hugged it. It didn't change the fact that Eve would do her damnedest to run Tallulah's Closet out of business, but it was a decent start.

"Thank you. I—I should have known you'd never keep a coat you knew had been stolen from someone else. I'm sorry about what I said at the hearing." She eased the coat completely from the bag and returned the bag to Eve.

"Well…" Eve shifted feet.

"Yes?" Joanna hung the coat behind the counter.

"When I got the coat, the lining was kind of messed up, so I had to have it fixed. Plus, I had to pay the homeless guy who sold it to me."

She should have known. Eve wanted money. "Of course." She reached for her checkbook. "How much?"

"About two hundred dollars should do it."

"Two hundred dollars?" Joanna's jaw dropped. "I paid less than a hundred when I got it."

Eve shrugged. "It costs what it costs. That is, unless you don't want it."

Joanna capped her pen and pushed the check across the bar. "Here."

Eve smiled, producing the dimples that had broken so many hearts. "I'll be getting over to my new space, then. The interior designer's coming to take some measurements." She trotted to the front door, then turned. "Good luck selling that thing. None of my clients wanted it."

With effort, Joanna resisted the urge to run after Eve and chuck a mannequin's arm at her.

Eve gone, Joanna leaned on the tiki bar and examined the Lanvin once again. So much drama around the coat. Such a beautiful coat, too. She had trouble envisioning Marnie's tiny body inside it. She buried her fingers in a strip of silver fox, then opened the coat to inspect the mended slash near the bottom of its lining. She sighed. What a lot of pain that coat had caused. Well, the coat was hers now, and she wouldn't let it go, no matter how much money it could bring the store.

She turned at the sound of the front door's bell to see one of the women from the Remmick fundraiser hesitating at the doorway. Joanna summoned her most welcoming smile.

"Come on in." She hung the Lanvin coat aside. "It's nice to see you. I have a suit that would look terrific on you — it's almost exactly the color of your eyes."

Later that afternoon, Joanna sorted through the day's credit card receipts. The timber executive's wife had left with two of the store's best cocktail dresses, and to her surprise, an Astrakhan vest. Next to the stack of receipts was a half-eaten tuna melt — no mayonnaise, provolone instead of cheddar — from the bar next door. At the rear of the store, a teenaged customer tried on 1980s pumps. She sat surrounded by shoes on the zebra-striped chair. The soundtrack to *Funny Girl* played in the background.

From the corner of her eye, Joanna caught sight of a dark, stocky man entering the door. She dropped the receipts, and one hand flew to the phone. She returned the receiver to its cradle and relaxed. It was only Ray.

"Hi there." Joanna flattened her hands on the tiki bar to calm them. "You must have got my message."

"Yeah, I saw you were calling from your store, and I thought I'd stop by. Nice place," he said without looking around. He wore jeans and a tee shirt with the Rolling Stones' trademark lips across its chest.

"Thanks. Just a minute and I'll catch you up."

The teenaged girl carried two pairs of pumps to the tiki bar. "These will look perfect with the zipper-leg jeans I got last week."

Joanna wrote up a receipt for a pair of white Nina pumps and a pair of sequined Stuart Weitzmans. She had seen enough episodes of *Dynasty* in her childhood not to want to wear 1980s clothes herself, but they were too popular not to stock at Tallulah's Closet. Plus, they were a whole lot easier to find at thrift stores than 1940s house dresses. "Enjoy those." The teenager left.

When she turned to Ray, he was staring at the Lanvin coat.

Joanna shot him a questioning look. "Do you want to see it closer?" She lifted it from behind the counter and handed it to him.

"Marnie sold you this coat, didn't she?" He touched its red leather waist gently and held it out in front of him as if to imagine someone inside it.

"Yes. She did."

"This coat used to belong to my aunt. She was wearing it when she died." He hung the coat on the edge of a rack of dresses and continued to gaze.

"Your aunt wore Lanvin?"

"Great aunt, actually. Her husband was a soldier in World War II in Europe. He brought it home for her." He tore his glance away from the coat. "It wasn't new when he got it. I think he bartered with a French family somewhere outside Paris. My aunt wore it everywhere, all the time, no matter how hot it was outside. Bowling, church, whatever. It became a little bit of a town joke."

"Do you want the coat? Sounds like it's important to your family. I'd be happy to give it to you." What the hell, the coat seemed destined to travel the city. She vowed she'd never give the coat up again, but it was different with Ray.

"No, no. It brings back memories, but it's not my aunt. She's not with the coat anymore."

"You must have really loved her."

"Yes, I did. We all did. She was a community fixture—was even chair of the tribal council when she died."

"I'm sorry."

"One night Auntie came home, fell down, and hit her head on a bookcase. There was blood everywhere. Franklin found her. She was getting up there in years, and she must have lost her balance. It was a bad omen."

They both stared at the coat. Joanna broke the silence. "Funny you say 'bad omen.' It's had a tough history even since I've had it. I found Marnie's body under the coat, for one thing. And it was stolen a couple of days later. I just got it back this morning."

"Marnie's body. You said you found her here, but under the coat?" He shook his head. "Too awful. And yet—I have to wonder if the coat was cursed by Auntie's death. Since my brother died…"

Joanna waited, but he didn't finish his thought.

He started again. "Not long after Auntie died we had to give up the tribe's application for recognition. Franklin took the coat."

"And gave it to Marnie."

He nodded. "He and Marnie were very close, you know. I'm surprised they never married. For a while Franklin had the idea that he was too good to go with a dancer. His business was doing all right, and I guess he thought he was hot stuff. So he married Leona. But I know he never forgot Marnie."

Joanna remembered the gorgeous beaded chiffon dress Marnie had bequeathed to her. "I used to wonder if Marnie would have married anyone. Maybe she didn't want to lose her independence, or she was just too removed from people. But now I think she never got over Franklin." She pushed aside the plate with the sandwich and leaned her forearms on the tiki bar. "This brings me to why

I wanted to talk to you. Remember Troy, Marnie's son, the one who came to her memorial service?"

"The kid who was going to law school? Sure, of course I remember him."

"Well, Franklin was his father." It made sense now. The family resemblance was clear in Ray's face and coloring.

He stood up straighter. "Can't be. They broke up years before."

"I've seen the birth certificate. The coat—your aunt's coat—just after Marnie brought it in, a key to a safe deposit box fell from its lining. Naturally I thought it was Marnie's. When my store and house were broken into—"

"Your house was broken into?"

"Just yesterday." She shivered at the memory. "Anyway, to make a long story short, I figured someone wanted the key. The police agreed to open the safe deposit box, and we found out that the key—and the box—didn't belong to Marnie at all. The box was Franklin's. Your sister-in-law should be hearing about it soon."

"And the birth certificate was in the box."

"A copy of it was, along with some letters from Marnie to Franklin. I wanted to tell you to see if—well—if you'd let his wife know before the police do."

Ray strode to the front of the store and looked out the window. He returned to Joanna. "I suppose that was all that was in the box. No other papers?"

There it was again. The mention of "papers." "No, that was it. The birth certificate and the letters. Oh, and a pair of cuff links, plus a few ticket stubs and photos. Things like that. The police said they'd notify Franklin's next of kin."

"Yes." He seemed to be thinking.

"There's something else." He needed to know about Don. She looked at her tuna melt, cold now, and lost her appetite. "I went to see Don yesterday at his house. No one answered the door, so I walked around back and heard shots. I found him lying on the kitchen floor. He'd been killed." She felt for the stool behind her and sat down.

"What?" He backed into a rack of dresses and grabbed them to steady himself.

"It should be in the papers soon."

"Joanna, you need to stay out of this. Are you done with this now?"

"Stay out of what? Besides, I don't know what else I could do if I wanted to. I just have to hope that the police get to the bottom of it." Don's body, one arm stretched out on the kitchen floor. The wig, dangling from a knife. The police had better be busy.

"Something is going on that doesn't concern you."

"What are you talking about?" She leaned forward. "You know something about that key, don't you? And what is this about 'papers'?"

"Look." Ray's voice was low but forceful. He locked eyes with Joanna. She pulled back. "Just stay safe and keep out of the way. Do you hear me?"

This was not the gentle Ray who gardened and made cinnamon rolls. "If you know something, you need to tell me. Don's been killed. I can't sleep in my own house, and I'm terrified even being alone in the store. For God's sake, Ray."

"Stay out of it, and you'll be fine." The words cut cold and sharp. "If you don't, no guarantees."

She swallowed.

He took a last glance at the coat, then left.

Chapter

30

Joanna regained her breath. The threat in Ray's eyes stayed with her. She was at a dead end. But she had to admit she wasn't, as he demanded, "done with it."

He'd mentioned the mysterious papers again, too. She knelt by the shelf under the tiki bar to find the price gun to tag some blouses and stopped mid-reach. The bank officer had said Franklin recently visited the safe deposit box. Could he have removed something? The box was plenty big and less than a third full.

The store was quiet but for the hum of the fan and Rosemary Clooney's honeyed voice on the stereo. A few tattooed women in cut-offs wandered into the bar next door. A bus lumbered by. Maybe the shoes the teenager got earlier and the clothes the timber executive's wife bought would be her only sales of the afternoon. She found that people often didn't want to try on clothes when it was hot outside, and, frankly, if they weren't liberal with their antiperspirant, she didn't want them trying them on either. Body odor on 1940s rayon was almost impossible to get out.

Her thoughts returned to Franklin. Too bad she couldn't talk to Ray about him. She'd like to know more about how he died. Time to call her friends at Central Library. After a short chat about her cats and a few helpful tips on flea prevention, the reference librarian confirmed the story she heard at the Remmick fundraiser: Franklin Pursell, owner of Pursell Plumbing, had fallen from an open wall in a condo complex under construction above 23rd Street. He had died on impact. Joanna pictured Marnie in her living room, smoking a cigarette, learning about the accident on television.

What the hell. She dragged in the sandwich board with "Tallulah's Closet" painted on it in Deco script and locked up the store. She wanted to see, firsthand, where Franklin had died.

*
**

Joanna pulled the Corolla into a rare open parking space in the Uptown neighborhood in front of a spa with a pseudo-French name. Just up the hill loomed the half-finished condo complex.

She stepped out of the car and held her hand above her eyes to shield them from the sun. The complex took up two city blocks. It was a mass of steel and concrete with about half of its windows installed. Five stories of balconies jutted from the building's face, but the railings weren't yet attached. It would be all too easy to fall.

Partway up the block yielded a better view. A few hundred yards of gravel stretched in front of the condo's skeleton, and a scissor lift raised a man to a third story opening where he helped two workers inside the structure install a window.

"Can I help you?" came a voice behind her.

Startled, she turned to see a tall man wearing a hard hat. With the noise of the construction, she hadn't heard him approach. "Oh, I knew Franklin Pursell, the man who died here, and I was thinking about him today." Maybe she'd never met Franklin, but it wasn't a complete lie. She was beginning to feel she did know him.

"I see. I thought you might be from the City. A building like this, we get a lot of inspections. Of course, you don't look much like an inspector." He eyed her 1950s ivory cotton dress bordered with orange and blue flowers.

A few construction workers had stopped working and were staring at her and the man with the clipboard. Was the one on the right Paul? Her fingers went to her grandmother's ring. The man in the crew turned. No, someone else. Her grip relaxed. The man caught her glance and smiled.

"I wonder—would it be too much trouble to see where he worked?" Joanna asked.

The man in the hardhat pointed at her red 1940s platform sandals. "Those shoes aren't exactly regulation. You're not one of those crime scene fiends are you? Get a thrill out of seeing where people died?"

"No, believe me. If anything, the opposite is true." If anything, she'd trade every Bakelite bangle in the store never to encounter a dead body again. "I saw Franklin's brother this morning, and, well, I thought it would, you know, bring closure to know where Franklin spent his last days."

"All right. I guess it will be okay just this once." He held out his hand. "Dan. Foreman. Come with me into the office and we'll get you a hardhat."

She followed him into the side of the structure through an opening that looked like it would become the entrance to a multi-level parking garage. Inside was cool and dark. They mounted a stairway lit by lamps strung on orange extension cords and entered an office framed and sheet-rocked into a corner of the third floor.

Three men sat around a long folding table in the middle of the room. Two of them seemed to be arguing about wooden flooring with another man with a Russian accent. Beyond the table, a coffee pot put out an acrid odor. A large whiteboard scribbled with notes covered one wall, and a grid of dirty file holders spanned another. Dust powdered the floor.

"Hey boss," one of the men at the table said to Dan, but his eyes were on Joanna.

"This is a friend of Franklin's. I'm going to show her his office."

"Family?" He turned to Joanna.

"No, but a friend of the family."

"She knows Ray." The walkie talkie on Dan's belt erupted in staticky voices, and he lifted it to his mouth as he wandered to a desk in the corner of the office.

"Ray?" a man at the table said, his fingers gripping a Styrofoam coffee cup. When Joanna nodded, he said, "That couldn't be easy." He looked at his coworkers and raised his eyebrows.

"Yeah, those two could barely stand to be in the same room."

This was interesting. Nothing she could remember that Ray did or said led her to think he had a problem with his brother. "I'm sure Ray feels awful about it now." She gave what she hoped was a knowing look.

"Put this on and follow me." Dan had returned and handed her a pink hardhat. "Visitor's hat. Smaller size for the ladies. I'll show you his office." He led her into the parking garage again, then to a smaller office framed in nearby. He opened the door to reveal boxes of equipment leaning against a wall and a man in jeans, a tee shirt, and dirty work boots hunched over a well-used desk.

"Roberto, I'd like you to meet Joanna, a friend of Franklin's. She's interested in seeing his office. You taking a break?"

"Sure, I have a minute." Roberto stood and shook Joanna's hand as the other man left. Roberto was short and muscular, and his curly hair was flattened around the edges where his hardhat normally sat. He leaned on the desk and folded his arms, studying her. "I don't remember seeing you before."

"I haven't been here before." She shifted on her feet.

Roberto stared at her for a minute. "What do you want to see?"

Good question. What was she here for? What did she think she'd find? She sneezed from the building's dust. "Oh, I don't know—I—I guess I just wanted to get a feel for what his life was like here."

"You don't know Franklin, do you?"

Damn it. She brushed a speck of plaster from her skirt before meeting his eyes. At this point she didn't have anything to lose by being honest. "You're right. I'd never met him. But I've heard so much about him over the past few weeks, and I know his brother, Ray."

Roberto continued to stare without speaking.

She drew a breath. "And I knew someone who was very important to Franklin, at least at one time. She recently died. I guess it's for her sake I'm here."

"The girl from Oysterville?"

She nodded.

Roberto relaxed. "Franklin used to talk about her sometimes." A glimmer of a smile appeared on his lips then disappeared. "So she died, huh?"

"Yes, a heart attack." He clearly knew Franklin well. She cocked her head and decided to throw out a line. "It's a shame about Ray. I wish he and Franklin had gotten along better."

He nodded. "Really is a shame. I knew Franklin a long time. We worked together for twenty years. All that time he talked about Ray like a brother would, but lately whenever I saw them together they were fighting."

"That's too bad." She tried to think of tactful way to get him to elaborate. "Family, too."

Roberto grabbed his hardhat and walked toward the door. "Yes, definitely a shame. In fact, they had a fight the day Franklin died. Right here." He pointed toward the desk. "I walked in on them. I don't know Ray that well—he helps out from time to time with some of the scheduling—but I can't imagine he feels very good about it now."

"I wonder what they were fighting about."

"Couldn't tell."

"Did Franklin mention anything recently about some papers? Or maybe you found some strange papers in the office?" The place was a mess, although as far as she could tell, most of it was assorted bits of tubing.

He turned by the door and raised an eyebrow. "Papers? No. Why?" He held the door open for her.

"Just something Ray mentioned once. Where are we going?"

Roberto turned around to look at her. "You want to see where he died, don't you?"

She followed him to the edge of the parking garage where the outside wall hadn't yet been constructed. A waist-high wooden barrier ran along the opening. A few men with cigarettes loitered by its edge.

"Get back to work," Roberto told them. "You're not supposed to be smoking here, anyway." The men wandered back into the garage.

Joanna peered over the gaping edge of the garage. Fifty feet or so straight below was a dumpster filled with wood scraps, broken sheetrock, and sharp-edged, cut steel girders. Beyond the dumpster was a row of port-a-potties, then a chain link fence with a wide gate.

"He fell down there." Roberto pointed to the dumpster.

"Off the edge. Awful."

"We didn't have the barrier up then. Put that up after he fell. Eventually the whole thing'll be walled up. It's open now to load in materials."

They both looked over the edge for a moment, silent. Joanna pulled back. "It's hard for me to believe that he would have just fallen like that."

"Exactly," Roberto said, as if he had been waiting for her observation. "He was used to working in big, open structures. I don't get it."

"What a horrible way to go."

"He died when he hit some scrap metal. Probably a girder. He must have come back, late, to finish something up. One of the day laborers found him the next morning."

"Sounds like you're not so sure it was an accident."

"I don't figure he would la-di-da walk over to the edge of the garage and fall in. None of us went close to the edge except to throw garbage off, and even then we were careful."

"So you think someone pushed him?" She watched him.

"I didn't say that. I just don't think he fell."

What is he getting at? "Well, if he didn't fall by himself, then he must have been helped by someone. Or—" She looked up "—was he a drinker?"

"Nope. Well, maybe a beer here and there, but I've never seen him drunk. The company will tell you he'd been drinking when he died, though." Roberto gestured toward the main office then leaned forward and lowered his voice. "Because that's what the insurance company wanted to hear. They found a couple of old beer cans in our office, a little alcohol in his blood, and they weren't too interested in looking into it further."

"Is there a particular reason you don't think his death was an accident?"

He walked back toward the plumber's office without replying. She followed him, and when they were inside he shut the door. He sat in the beat-up chair and leaned back. "Something was up with Franklin. I'm not sure what, but something was."

"Do you mean between him and Ray?" She lifted the hard hat from her head and pulled free a curl caught in its frame.

"Maybe. He'd been really distracted over the week before he died—I had to redo the gas stack for building one. Then, a few hours after his fight with Ray, he was yelling at someone on the phone. Not like Franklin. 'You can't get away with this,' he kept saying."

"Is that all he said?"

"It sounded like he made a plan to meet someone later that day."

"Ray again?"

"Don't know. No idea. And it's not like we can ask him."

His voice slowed. Joanna understood. This makeshift office and scores of offices like it had been his and Franklin's safe world for years, just as Tallulah's Closet was to her. It was the place they could leave their personal drama behind and escape through work. Until one of them couldn't. "I'm really sorry about Franklin. You two must have been close."

Roberto nodded. "He was a good man. He came a long way from his roots, you know, in building up the company. Sometimes, after we'd been working a long stretch and the both of us were up late, he'd talk about home and how he thought about moving back to the peninsula and living in a little house on the beach. Fishing for a living. He still had a boat at Sauvie Island. He'd talk about your friend, too, and about the other people where he lived. He was even writing a history of his tribe, spent years on it."

She remembered the bundle of papers at Ray's house.

"And yet," Roberto continued, "At the end of the day he'd drive home in his brand new truck to his nice little house and his family, and that was that."

"I'm surprised he didn't retire. Especially if money wasn't a problem."

"He liked working. He was good, too—twice as fast as some of the younger men on the crew. You can't work your demons away, though."

Someone rapped at the door. Roberto quickly picked up a stack of papers on the desk and reached for a pair of reading glasses before shouting, "Come in."

Dan, the foreman, stood in the doorway. "Finished here?"

Joanna glanced at Roberto, who was ostentatiously flipping through the papers. "Uh, yes. Thank you, Roberto."

"Come on. I'll walk you offsite." Dan took Joanna's elbow. They crossed the garage and descended the cement stairs, passing the dumpster she had seen from above. "I bet Roberto talked your ear off."

"He was very friendly. He told me a little about working with Franklin."

"He didn't tell you his theory that Franklin's death wasn't an accident?"

She was wary. "He did say something, but not much."

"I wouldn't pay him much attention. That's Roberto for you. It was an accident, caused by drinking and carelessness. Maybe age had something to do with it, too. It's unfortunate, but that's that."

They reached the chain link fence.

She glanced back up at the open edge of the parking garage. Standing in the shadows was Roberto, hands on his hips, watching.

Chapter 31

Apple reached across the table and set down a bowl of pasta with a cruda tomato sauce.

"Is there mint in this? It smells delicious." Joanna lifted forkfuls of linguine to her plate.

"Mint, oregano, basil, parsley, garlic, olive oil, and a little vinegar. Parmesan cheese is in the green bowl."

"Thanks." The dog had lodged himself under Joanna's chair, where he sighed loudly, clearly hoping a few noodles might slither off someone's plate. "Has Curly been any trouble?"

"I'm getting to like the guy," Gavin, Apple's husband, said. He had dark hair and a closely-trimmed beard. An earring shaped like a crescent moon dangled from one ear. He must have stood out in his office of engineers.

"If you keep giving him table scraps, you'll make him sick," Apple said.

"Did you look at the dog biscuits you bought him? The cheese and peanut butter flavors, I get that. But charcoal? Do dogs really like charcoal?" Gavin snorted.

"This one does. I don't know what he wouldn't eat."

"Hopefully you won't have to keep him—or me—much longer. Thanks for putting up with us for a few days," Joanna said.

"Oh, don't even think about it." Apple passed around a plate stacked with slices of baguette.

Apple and Gavin's house was built at the turn of the century for the railroad workers. Friends ignored the front door and entered the house through the kitchen, passing an enameled stove and shelves lined with teapots, cookbooks, and tins of tea. A brightly patterned Indian cloth covered the dining room table. In each of the windows dangled a crystal like the one Apple hung at Tallulah's Closet to ward off bad energy.

"How were things at the store today?" Apple handed her the bread plate.

"Slow." Joanna drew out the word. "Not much happened." She'd filled Apple in on the contents of the safe deposit box when she came to relieve her at the store after visiting the bank. Apple had been firm it was time to leave the case to the police. Instinct told Joanna it would be better to keep her in the dark about Ray's visit and her trip to Franklin's job site.

Apple put both hands on the table and looked Joanna in the eyes. "I stopped by this afternoon. I didn't like to think of you there alone, but Tallulah's Closet was closed."

Damn it. "Oh, that. Well, it was so slow I thought I'd drive out to some thrift stores, you know, try to find some things for the store." Joanna shoveled pasta in her mouth and avoided Apple's gaze. Curly got up from under her chair and walked the few steps to Gavin, where he lay down again.

"You did, huh? I'd love to see what you found."

The clock on Apple's bookshelf ticked in the silence. Joanna set down her fork. "Okay. I didn't go to thrift stores. I closed up early and went to see where Marnie's old boyfriend died. I'm not sure what

I was after, but after reading Marnie's letters to Franklin — that was his name," she addressed this part to Gavin, "I just felt like I wanted to see where he spent his last days."

Apple shot Gavin an "I told you so" look and returned her gaze to Joanna. "You've got to leave this alone. It's too dangerous. Remember the wig?" She paused to let that sink in. "Besides, the police are investigating Don's death. They know what they're doing."

Curly shuffled around the table to Apple and looked up. Not getting a response, he continued to Joanna and nudged her hand with his pink nose. She ran her finger up the bridge of his nose to the creamy fur sprinkled with spots on his forehead. "I don't think they do. Know what they're doing, that is. Someone is after whatever was in the safe deposit box. I think it might be some kind of documents. The police don't understand. Until the papers are found, I'm not safe." Didn't she get it?

"Apple's right, Jo. One person has already been killed. Maybe two, if you count Marnie."

Three, counting Franklin, Joanna thought, but she'd keep quiet about that. Irritation simmered. It was easy for Apple and Gavin to preach about leaving things alone — their lives were peaceful. They could go about their days without wondering if someone with a gun was waiting for them somewhere. What did they know about how she felt?

She filled her wine glass, silently bemoaning the lack of something stronger to drink, and replaced the wine bottle on the table with a clunk. "You don't have to tell me. I found Don's body, remember?" Frustration rose in her voice. "I can't even sleep in my own house. What am I going to do? Sit around and wait until someone runs me down on the street?"

"It's not just about you," Apple said. "If you keep poking around about the safe deposit box, and the murderer finds out you're here, none of us is safe."

Gavin's hand, holding a scrap of bread, dropped off the table. Joanna set down her wine glass. She fought to slow her breathing. "I'm sorry." A pang of guilt shot through her. It hadn't occurred to her she might be putting other people at risk. "You're right. Tomorrow I'll move back home."

"That's not what Apple means. You're welcome to stay here as long as you like. But we don't want to see you taking any foolish risks. The police have a homicide bureau to get to the bottom of this. Let them do their job and stay out of the way."

She bit her lip. The police were on the wrong trail, she was sure of it, if they were on any trail at all.

The three sat for a moment without speaking. Curly slinked out from under the table and crawled to the corner of the kitchen. Joanna looked at Apple then Gavin. "I think he's going to be sick."

Gavin had converted the basement into a large master bedroom and bathroom. Off the living room was the house's original bedroom, which Apple used as a painting studio. While Joanna pulled out the studio's sofabed, Apple came in with a cup of herbal tea. She set it on a side table.

"How are you feeling?" she asked.

"Oh, all right." Joanna sat on the edge of the sofa bed.

"I'm sorry about dinner. I'm worried about you, that's all."

Joanna touched her hand. "I know. I appreciate it. I just feel so wound

up, but so helpless at the same time. Marnie, the store, my house…"
She slid off her sandals. "I think I'll take a bath, if you don't mind."

"You could use the relaxation. I brought you a vintage *True Ro-
mances* to read. I know how you love old magazines. Look—Lana
Turner's on the cover. She can't be more than sixteen."

"Thanks, Apple. That's so sweet of you." She ran a finger over the
magazine's gold and red hand-tinted cover then reached for the tea.
"It's been such a strange few weeks."

"The police are following up on Don's death. You know that. He
was too important. Assuming whoever killed Don was the same
person responsible for everything else—well, then, mystery solved.
As for Eve's store, we'll deal with that once it happens."

"Oh, Apple. I want to be home. I want everything to go back to
normal. Everything has gone haywire and all at once." If she were
home now, she'd be wearing her 1950s turquoise quilted robe with
the black ribbon trim and finishing up a Preston Sturges movie.
Maybe she'd spray on a little Habanita before bed.

Apple rose. "I'll draw the bath. Bring in your tea, and we'll talk.
There are some bath salts on the counter. Try the lavender. It'll help
calm you down."

The tub full, Joanna stepped into the bathroom and left the door
ajar. Apple had lit a candle and set it next to the mirror above the
sink. Its flame reflected back into the otherwise dark bathroom.
A soft shaft of light from the lamp on the nightstand fell across the
bathroom floor.

"Apple?"

"Hmm?"

She was in the bath now, the water up around her neck, and her
hair twisted and knotted loosely on top of her head. The warm water

felt so good. "Do you, you know, are you getting any messages about this whole situation?"

Apple laughed quietly. "I wondered if you'd ask."

"I'm asking. Any guidance is welcome."

"Over the past few days I've heard one voice, your grandmother's. I'm not sure you want to hear what she has to say."

Her grandmother. Joanna bit the inside of her lip.

Apple seemed to read her mind. "Don't worry—I've told you before, she doesn't blame you. You were just a kid."

"I can't stop thinking about her. Ever since Marnie died."

Apple nodded. "She's been trying to get through to you, but you haven't been listening."

"Cut to the chase, please."

"She thinks it's time you've settled down. She's worried that you're not leaving yourself open to love. And she wants you to pay more attention to Paul, the guy who installed the locks."

"Apple!" The bathwater sloshed around her as she sat up. "There's some crazy guy out there killing people, and my store is getting run out of business, and the best my spirit guides can do is try to jump start my dating life?"

"Fine. Look, I call them like I see them. You want advice from the other side, ask them yourself."

Joanna slid back into the water. "Sorry. It's just that..." Apple seemed so happy with Gavin. What could she understand about her reluctance to get involved with anyone? She wasn't sure she understood it herself.

"What?" Apple's voice was soft.

"I'd like to meet someone. I would. But I don't see how—I mean—it couldn't turn out well. Besides, I do so well on my own."

"What are you afraid will happen? I know you had a, well, let's just say a rough time of it before you went to live with your grandmother, and then after the accident—"

"I don't want to talk about it."

"I know, I know. We won't talk about it. But you can't escape it, Jo. You've got to face your feelings head on. Why are you so afraid of getting involved with someone?"

She looked at her toes resting on the far end of the tub. "I don't know. I really don't." Paul's hand under her chin had been strong but so gentle as he cleaned the scrape on her head. Her throat constricted. "When I think about getting close to someone, I freeze up. I almost can't bear to know what might happen next." Apple didn't reply, so Joanna continued. "I know it sounds strange. I almost—well, I almost wonder if I'm meant to live alone." She'd never said these words aloud before. They hurt. "You know, some people are born blind or without an arm or something. Maybe this is my affliction, and I just have to deal with it."

To her credit, Apple didn't dismiss her words out of hand. "You might choose the wrong guy. Or he might leave you." She took a breath. "Or die. Bad things can happen. But wonderful things can happen, too." Springs creaked as she shifted on the sofa bed. "I know you're afraid, and I know it's easier to be alone or choose someone you don't really respect. Take the chance, Jo. Do it. Not everyone will let you down."

The bathwater was beginning to cool. A lump had settled in her throat, and she didn't want to speak. *I'm such a mess,* she thought. In the distance a train sounded its whistle.

"All right. I'm leaving you with Curly. Don't forget to blow out the candle when you're done."

*
**

Joanna shifted on the sofa bed to avoid a spring lodged in her back. Something was different. No Curly, that was it. She'd become used to his furry body pressed against her as she slept. She sat up and let her eyes adjust to the dark. A low growl came from near the bathroom door.

"Curly?" Joanna whispered.

She made out his body, his head pointed to the window just to the sofa's right. Fur bristled in a ridge along his back. His growl grew louder. She pulled up the sheet and turned quickly toward the window. A black shape moved away. Fear prickled through her body.

Curly's growl became a sharp bark.

"Hush, hush." Her heart rattled in her chest. Should she wake Apple and Gavin?

Curly, still focused on the window, stopped growling. Except for the murmur of crickets, the night was silent.

After a long moment, Curly looked at Joanna, wagged his hind end, and jumped back in bed. Whatever it was, the threat was gone. But it was hours before she got back to sleep.

Chapter 32

"Sleep well?" Apple asked as she struggled to open a box of coffee filters. "Gavin bought you some coffee."

"Here, let me get that," Joanna said, reaching for the box. "I slept all right, I guess. Did Curly's barking wake you up?" She heard the shower downstairs turn on. The dog loped down to the basement.

"I figured he must have heard something outside, maybe a stray cat."

Maybe. She thought of the dark shape in the window. Could it have been a tree moving in the wind? "How would you feel about swapping work days with me this week? I have an errand I really need to do."

"What is it? I already dropped the checks at the bank, if you're worried about that." The kettle boiled, and Apple poured water into her teapot and the cone holding Joanna's coffee. "Soy milk?"

"No half and half?" Apple shook her head. "Soy milk would be great." As Apple reached for the refrigerator, Joanna took advantage of her turned back to deliver her carefully prepared excuse. The last thing she wanted to do was spark a fight like last night's. "I thought I'd look into getting a security system for my house. You're right. I need to protect myself."

Apple set the soy milk on the counter and looked straight at Joanna. "Security system?"

"Yes, I — " She pretended to straighten her skirt. "I want to be safe. The police recommended it."

"I don't believe you. A security system has a number pad, you know. It has a computer. Not exactly your style." Her voice began to rise. "You're up to something, aren't you? You lied to me yesterday, and you're doing it again."

Joanna's face burned. She'd never lied to Apple before everything started with Marnie. They'd never argued like this before, either. "Okay, okay, you're right. I kept dreaming about the key and thinking about how you said sometimes you just have to face your troubles head on instead of avoid them."

"You know I wasn't talking about Marnie and Don when I told you that." She put a lid on the teapot and pushed it back on the counter to steep.

"Still, you had a good point. The police don't seem interested at all in the safe deposit box. Sure, they're going to investigate Don's murder, but I really think they're headed in the wrong direction. What's going to happen next? Franklin's wife ends up dead?" She splashed soy milk into her coffee, turning it cement gray instead of the cocoa charmeuse color half and half made.

Apple examined her thoughtfully. "This is about the accident, isn't it? It's not about Marnie or Don at all. You were just a kid, Jo. You weren't the one driving. I know it was…horrible, but you have to stop blaming yourself."

Joanna looked away. "I need to do this. I want to visit Franklin's wife and try to find something out about the papers. If I know what they are, or at least where they are, I can tell the police, and they can figure out what to do next. I'm not going to confront anyone, honest. This is my best bet for getting everything back to normal."

Apple poured tea into a porcelain cup painted with four-leaved clovers. "Those papers could be anywhere. Even if you knew what and where they were, how would you get your hands on them?"

"I don't have every detail worked out yet. Franklin didn't seem to have kept them in his office. He might have hid them at his house, but maybe not—after all, he kept them from his wife in the safe deposit box all those years. At home, she might find them. But maybe he has another apartment or a vacation house."

"And how are you going to find that out?"

"I'm not exactly sure yet. Could you bring your laptop to the shop?"

"Why don't you ask Franklin's brother?"

No, she couldn't do that. Ray's warning had been final. "I can't. If he found out I was digging around in Franklin's business—well, I hate to think about it. He was adamant that I stay out of it," she admitted.

"He warned you away, too?" Apple sighed. "Oh, Joanna. I don't like this. I don't like it at all. But it doesn't look like you're going to quit." She drew her robe closer and took a sip of her tea. "All right, I'll bring the laptop. Wait a minute." She went to the basement then came back with a thin, silver pendant suspended on a leather cord. "Wear this for protection."

"What is it?"

"It's the Hand of Fatima. See?" She held it up. The pendant had the shape of a stylized hand with fingers extended. Silver swirls covered its front. "Don't do anything stupid. Promise me."

Joanna draped it around her neck and hugged Apple. The necklace glinted against her black cotton blouse. "If it will make you feel better. I'll meet you down at the store. It's about time to open."

She called goodbye down the stairs to Gavin and Curly and made her way to the car. The leaves on the maple in Apple's parking strip ruffled in the summer breeze. From up the block, she saw something stuck under her windshield wiper. It didn't look like a ticket.

She approached the car and started to tremble. It was lilac fabric. Torn from her Ceil Chapman dress.

*
**

Apple closed the laptop perched on the tiki bar at Tallulah's Closet. "Nothing," she said to Joanna. "I can't find anything on Franklin in the city's database except that he has a house out on Yamhill, on the other side of Mount Tabor. From the internet photos, it looks like a family home. I doubt he'd hide anything there."

The dog lounged at the back of the store in an armchair normally used by men waiting while their wives or girlfriends shopped. He was charming two suburban women looking for dresses to wear to a friend's wedding. On the stereo, Julie London exhorted some man to cry her a river.

Joanna got up and wandered to a clothes rack. Deep in thought, she methodically straightened the dresses, spacing the padded satin hangers evenly along the rod. She couldn't stay at Apple's. Not now. And home was out of the question. She had to get to the bottom of this, find those papers.

A truck from Zapped Electric rumbled up Clinton and stopped in front of the theater. Apple groaned from the front window. "Eve's already getting bids on the new wiring. When do you think she plans to open?"

A pang shot through Joanna. Eve. No time to think about that today, but soon. After she figured out who had killed Marnie and

Don and broken into her house. Very soon. "Don't know." She continued spacing the hangers.

Apple returned to the tiki bar. "We're going to need another lint roller to get the dog's hair off the upholstery." She stopped and turned around. "Hey, are you listening?"

Joanna's hand reached an apricot chiffon negligee with a matching robe. "I have an idea." She held up the peignoir. Yes, this would do just fine. With any luck, she wouldn't have to use it.

Franklin's house was a split-level ranch on Mount Tabor, an extinct volcano on the east side of town. Joanna parked on the steep hill below the house, praying the Corolla's emergency brake could take the strain. She climbed the steps and paused at the landing to look behind her. In the distance, the crags of Mount Hood rose from the summer haze. The roofs and fenced gardens of modest houses cascaded down the hill to the far away facades of the Chinese restaurants and used auto dealerships of 82nd Avenue.

All she had to do at Franklin's was explain the situation and ask his widow if there was any place — a cabin, or maybe somewhere around the house — he might have hidden some papers. It shouldn't be too hard, she tried to convince herself. She pressed the doorbell.

An elderly woman wearing stylish glasses opened the door. Silver streaked her long black hair, which was wrapped on top of her head and fastened with an ivory comb. Frantic barking came from the backyard. "May I help you?"

"Ms. Pursell?"

"Yes." She looked friendly, but wary.

"My name is Joanna Hayworth. I'd like to talk to you about Franklin."
The widow's expression began to harden.

"I know things have been difficult for you lately, and I'm so sorry
for your loss. It's just—I think Franklin may have been mixed up
in something dangerous, and people's lives are at risk. I know that
sounds dramatic, and it's a little complicated, but I need your help."

Franklin's wife made no move to invite her in. Through the thin
slice of open door Joanna saw a Native American basket hanging
on a wood-paneled wall.

"May I come in? It shouldn't take long to explain. You can call
Ray and ask about me if you want." On second thought, maybe that
wasn't such a good suggestion, but too late now.

The widow paused. "All right. For a minute." She opened the door,
and Joanna entered a sun-bathed room smelling gently of lemon wax
and cedar. A low couch upholstered in beige linen anchored one side.
Modernist wooden chairs with leather seats flanked the fireplace.
They'd fetch a few month's mortgage payments at a downtown boutique. Shelves of books and Native American artifacts lined one wall.

"This room, it's so—"

"I know. I was an anthropology professor. Married to a plumber,
you don't have to say it, I heard enough about it from my colleagues."
She turned to the sliding screen door to the backyard, where a large
black and white mongrel bared its teeth and growled with lapses
into frantic barking. "Blackie, shut up!" She turned back to Joanna.
"My husband's dog. I've had it with her. Never wanted her in the first
place." She pushed the sliding glass door shut, muffling the barking,
and lowered herself to the couch.

Casting around for a way to ease their conversation, Joanna remembered her talk with Roberto, Franklin's partner. "Anthropology, huh?

You and your husband must have shared that interest. I understand he was writing a history of his tribe."

The widow shook her head and snorted. "Franklin was a plumber. I'm sure he had some nice stories, but I wouldn't call that anthropology. Anyway, he never asked for my help. But that's not why you're here. Tell me, what's so important that I know?"

"Well…" She realized to tell the story, she'd have to talk about Franklin and Marnie's relationship. She didn't want to be the first to tell her, and if the widow already knew, she didn't want to reopen old wounds. She took a breath. "Have you seen Ray lately?"

"Yes. Just this morning, in fact. He—"

A toilet flushed down the hall. Troy sauntered into the living room and stopped short at seeing Joanna. "Hello."

Her jaw dropped.

The widow's glance passed from Joanna to Troy. "You two know each other?"

"Yeah, I know Joanna. She used to be friends with my mother. My birth mother, that is."

Franklin's wife's eyes narrowed. She stood up. "Get out." The dog began to bark again at a higher pitch, this time punctuated with snarls.

"I—"

"I said get out. No friend of that, that woman is welcome here." She moved to the sliding glass door and placed her hand on its handle, poised to open it. Foam gathered at the corner of the dog's mouth. "Leave."

Joanna backed toward the front door. On the landing again, she heard Troy's cheerful voice inside. "Bye, Joanna. Give me a call." She took the steps in twos to the street, her heart racing faster than her feet on the flagstone.

Chapter 33

What the hell was Troy doing at Franklin's house? She started the car. Sure, he'd want to get to know about his father, and it's possible another letter in Marnie's glove box, one she hadn't seen, divulged that Franklin was his father. Or maybe Ray had talked to Troy. In any case, Franklin's wife hadn't been keen on Marnie, but she seemed to have taken to Troy. That figured. Something about him brought out the mothering instinct in women. As her grandmother would have said, Troy could charm snakes.

A few minutes later with Troy still on her mind, Joanna eased the Corolla into a parking space in front of the police department's southeast precinct. Plan A hadn't worked so well. Apple was right. She doubted Franklin had hidden the papers in his house — the house was clearly his wife's domain. She hoped Franklin had carved out a space for himself and his dog in the basement, at least. Funny how a man who'd deserted a woman because she was a dancer would find himself looked down on by his wife because he was a plumber.

Time for Plan B. A blast of air conditioning hit her as she pulled open the police precinct's heavy front door. "I'd like to see Officer Riggs, please. It's about the Don Cayle homicide."

The receptionist picked up the phone. A row of institutional chairs crowded the waiting area. Why offices felt compelled to buy special "office" furniture instead of using regular, comfortable furniture she never understood.

"Go through the door to the left then take the first door to the right. Riggs is at his desk."

Joanna entered a large, open room with two rows of desks. At the front of the room, hand-scrawled notes covered a white board. The window air conditioner unit vibrated noisily. Officer Riggs, his large body crammed behind the small desk, sat toward the back. Two other officers looked up as she came in. One returned to his paperwork while the other grabbed his hat and left.

"Hello, Ms. Hayworth." Riggs said. Then, more quietly, "Nice bracelet, by the way. Is that a Judy Lee?"

Joanna sat down at Riggs's desk and touched the green and coral charms on her Chinese-themed bracelet. "Good eye. It's from the early 1960s."

"The quality on a Judy Lee is so much higher than its given credit for."

"I always look for them, especially the necklaces and bracelets." She set her bag on the floor next to his desk. "But I came here to ask you something."

"About the Cayle case? Are you sure you don't want to talk to Crisp?"

The police officer toward the front of the room looked back at Riggs and Joanna. Joanna leaned closer to Riggs. "I feel more comfortable with you."

Riggs blushed. "Well, all right. Did you remember anything about that afternoon that you wanted to tell us?"

"It's complicated, but—" She looked him straight in the eye. "I hoped you might be able to tell me if someone named Franklin Pursell, who died not long ago, had a vacation house. Maybe something at the coast. You must have a computer database that gives that sort of information."

"We do, but that's for official business only. Why?"

"Oh, but this is official. I've figured out that Don's killer was looking for papers—papers that Franklin may have hidden before he died." She gave a beseeching smile. Apple would be so much better at this.

"Franklin Pursell? Never heard that name. Besides, Crisp already has a suspect and is out following up on it right now. And it doesn't have anything to do with anyone named Pursell or his vacation house. I think you've got it wrong."

A suspect? This was new. "Who?"

"I can't say."

She hesitated at the news, but felt firm about her hunch. "This would mean so much to me. Just one little address. I don't want to know anything personal, just an address. Besides, Franklin's not even alive."

She opened the top of her large handbag, and a fluff of chiffon burst out. "It's probably public information anyway, I just don't know where to get it."

Riggs's hand reached to touch the chiffon nightie, but his eyes were on the officer at the front of the room, absorbed in paperwork.

"Apricot looks so lovely on someone with dark hair. If your, uh, wife is a brunette, it will really flatter her. Plus, it's plenty large, so if she's a plus size—" Joanna looked meaningfully at Riggs "—it will fit, no problem."

"Put it in here," Riggs said in a husky voice and opened a deep bottom drawer. Joanna transferred the negligee to the drawer in one swoop. "What was that name?"

"Franklin Pursell."

Riggs clicked a few keys and scrolled down the screen. A minute later he said, "No vacation house. But there's a boat registered in his name at Sauvie Island."

Of course, Franklin's boat. She should have remembered. She thought of the photos she'd seen of Marnie and Franklin lounging in his boat more than forty years ago. The boat was probably Franklin's private refuge, somewhere his wife rarely if ever visited. It would be the perfect place to hide something important.

"The boat's name?"

"Nope. I've got a registration number, but that's it. That's all I can tell you." He touched his desk drawer to make sure it was shut. "Now you'll have to leave. I'll walk you out." He rose. "Wait—Crisp has an envelope for you. Something that was left at the victim's house with your name on it."

Yes, the envelope from Don. He never did tell her what it was. Photos of Marnie, maybe.

Riggs led her down the hall to another locked room with shelves. He pulled down an envelope large enough to hold a modest document. "We checked the papers out and don't need to keep them as evidence."

Papers? Joanna drew in her breath. Maybe Franklin's papers? Then she wouldn't have to find this boat after all. Adrenalin shot through her as she turned the envelope in her hands. It was new and didn't look like it had spent years languishing in a safe deposit box, but Don could have simply transferred the papers to a sturdier envelope. This could be it. Of course, how could he have broken into Franklin's safe deposit box?

Back in the hall, Riggs asked quietly, "Is apricot really good for brunettes? I always thought it could make a person's skin look ruddy."

"Oh no." Joanna lifted her purse to her shoulder. "It brings out peaches and cream."

In the car, Joanna tossed her purse on the passenger seat and cranked opened the sun roof to let out the late August heat. The roof stuck partway open. Probably wouldn't close again, either, damn it. She abandoned the sun roof and rolled down her window before pulling the envelope closer. With trembling fingers she used a key to slice through the tape the police had used to seal the envelope, and slid out a paper-clipped sheaf of legal-sized documents. She quickly flipped through the pages. It was a lease agreement with a black slash across each page. "Void" stamped the front. A note with "Don Cayle Investments" engraved on the top fell when she unclipped the pages. She recognized Don's handwriting right away.

"Dear Joanna," it said, "I thought you'd like a copy of a voided lease I'm putting in the mail today to Eve Lancer. When she came to the office this morning to sign it, she didn't have much nice to say about the vintage clothing store down the street—your store, Tallulah's Closet. Marnie wouldn't have appreciated it. Best, Don."

Joanna's hand flew to her mouth. So, Don had owned the Clinton Street Theater. When she'd called to meet him and give him the safe deposit box key, he'd mentioned he had something for her, even told her not to be "hasty" about finding another storefront to rent. As relief washed over her, she started to laugh. Almost immediately, tears pricked at the back of her eyes, and she swallowed a sob. She dabbed her eyes with the hem of her skirt and took a few calming breaths. "Thank you, Marnie. Thank you, Don." No need to worry about Eve moving up the block. At least for the moment. Knowing Eve, she wouldn't give up easily.

She slid the lease back in its envelope. Thank God for Don. She had to admit Eve did have some good ideas about how to sell vintage clothing. Joanna had been too complacent with Tallulah's Closet. Maybe it was time to find some big auctions and go after higher end clothing and clientele, although she'd always stock casual wear and lower-priced items for neighborhood regulars. It wouldn't hurt, either, to shore up her savings so that money wouldn't be so tight during the slower, post-holiday months.

A crow cawed from a young tree in the parking lot, and Joanna's smile turned somber. She put the lease on the passenger seat and started the car. With one hand she pushed back hair stuck to her forehead. Marnie and Don, both dead. The voided lease was heaven sent, but it wasn't the papers she sought. Which meant she still had to find Franklin's boat.

It was late afternoon now. It couldn't be too hard to get into a boat, especially once it was darker. That is, if she could find which boat at the marina was his. And if she could figure out how to break in.

Chapter 34

Joanna considered her options as she drove home. She had little idea how boats were laid out or even how they might be locked. She'd passed her teens reading through Nancy Drew instead of hanging out with Apple's brothers and taking part in stunts like breaking into the tool shed, and she wasn't sure the reference librarians downtown could help her with this one. Still, a lock was a lock, right? Surely, if you could pick one lock, you could pick another. All she needed was a little instruction.

The house was stuffy. Her errand here would only take a few minutes. Pepper ran out from the bedroom and wound himself through her legs, looking for a scratch behind the ears. She longed to put on music, fill the vases with dahlias from the garden, and cook dinner, but it wasn't safe yet.

After feeding the cat, she clicked on the light to the basement and descended into its damp cool. She found an empty suitcase with a pink ribbon looping the suitcase's key to its handle. She brought the suitcase upstairs and opened it on the couch. Pepper jumped in. She lifted him out, shut and locked the suitcase, then cut the key off the handle and left it on the coffee table.

"I hope this isn't a bad idea, Aunt Vanderburgh. I know you—" Joanna's speech to the portrait stopped short when she glanced up at the wall, bare but for the broad smear of fresh plaster. Damn. Well, she'd better get on with it.

Next to the phone was the scrap of paper with Paul's number on it. Her breath quickened as she lifted the receiver.

Paul picked up on the second ring. The sound of his voice momentarily flustered her. "Hello?" he prompted again.

"It's Joanna. How are you?"

"Good. I'm working on some trim for a Queen Anne house up the street. A little tricky, but it's coming along."

"I have a suitcase that's locked, and I can't find the key. I wonder, if I brought it to you do you think you could open it? I know you have tools." All she'd need to do is watch and ask a few questions. A quick trip to the hardware store for a file or whatever would complete her mission.

"I guess I could try."

"Would you have time to try today—like maybe this afternoon?"

"Sure, bring it in. It shouldn't take too long." He gave her directions to his shop.

She hung up the phone and paused for a minute. Then she picked it up again and called the Reel M'Inn to order chicken and jojos to go. It was getting close to dinner time, and she was hungry. She was willing to bet Paul hadn't eaten either.

She changed into a slender black cotton, sleeveless dress. If she was going to break into a boat, she'd best not attract too much attention. For good luck, she sprayed Tabac Blond behind her ears and tucked the tiny atomizer into her bag. Finally, she traced sheer red lipstick on her mouth and checked herself in the mirror. Too tousled to be Audrey Hepburn, but acceptable. As an afterthought, she draped Apple's Hand of Fatima pendant around her neck. Couldn't hurt.

*
**

A blast of smoky, barely cooled air hit Joanna as she pushed open the padded naugahyde door to the Reel M'Inn. The bartender recognized her right away. "Well, if it isn't Princess Martini. All these jojos for you? Or maybe you're saving some for Paul?"

She felt her face getting warm. "I need his help with something—"

"I bet you do."

"—And I thought he might be hungry."

"Then take an extra tub of dressing. The boy likes his ranch."

Paul's shop was not far. She parked on the street, then carried the suitcase and the warm bag of chicken and jojos up the alley and rang the bell. Next to a sky blue door was a large roll-up metal door raised about three feet off the ground. A dog barked, then squeezed under the roll-up door and ran towards Joanna, wagging its tail.

The blue door opened. "Gemma!" Paul said. "Come here." He patted his thigh, and the dog, a shaggy German shepherd mix, trotted back to him. "Sorry about that. She's really friendly. He took the bag Joanna handed him and looked inside. "This is great—thanks. Come on in."

He held open the door, and she passed close enough to him to smell the mix of wood and soap that clung to his skin. Inside, the shop's ceiling soared two stories high. Stairs to her right followed the wall up to a small loft, and she glimpsed a lamp and the edge of a bed through the railing. The main floor housed a woodworking shop with two thick workbenches pushed against a wall hung with hand tools. A small stove, a refrigerator, and a kitchen table were grouped in the back corner under the loft.

She hesitated. Being there, where he worked and ate and slept felt so — well, intimate. But she'd come here for a reason. Focus.

Paul set the bag of food on the counter next to a French press and handmade coffee mug with a wide, deep bowl. "Not a palace, but it works for me," he said.

Gemma had finished sniffing Joanna's suitcase and hopped into a worn armchair near the work table. From tall wooden speakers, Ray Charles sang one of Joanna's favorite songs, the one where his "baby" serves him "coffee in my favorite cup." Paul pulled the dust mask that rested on his neck over his head and set it on a workbench. A speck of sawdust stuck in the hair near his ear.

"I like it. It looks — comfortable," Joanna said. "Where are all the tools? You know, the saws and all that?"

"I do most of my work with those." He pointed to a row of chisels hanging above a workbench. Hand planes lined the back of the workbench beneath them. "There aren't a lot of us left, woodworkers who stick with hand tools, that is."

She understood the appeal of handmade trim. Just like a hand-woven rug or a blown glass goblet, the almost imperceptible imperfections woke the eye to its beauty.

"This must be the suitcase." He lifted it onto the kitchen table and tested its latch. "It's locked all right. How about if we eat first and then deal with it?" He set the suitcase on the floor and pulled two hand-thrown plates from a freestanding cupboard. He placed one in front of Joanna.

The intimacy of the gesture both warmed and rattled her. "These are wonderful." Joanna felt the cool heft of the ceramic plate.

"My sister made them."

"Nice. Does she live around here?"

He didn't respond for a moment. "No," he said at last.

Neither talked as Paul opened the box of food and using a fork lifted jojos and chicken to each plate.

Feeling as if she'd somehow misstepped, Joanna changed the subject. "How did you get into woodwork?"

He seemed to relax slightly. "When I was a kid, I used to get into trouble a lot. I was always fooling around with things, taking them apart to see how they worked. Once my mom found me with a screwdriver in my hand and the TV set in a dozen pieces." He sat down. Gemma sighed from her armchair. "She didn't know what to do with me with my dad gone and all, but my uncle took me under his wing. Remember? I told you about him."

She nodded. The uncle in prison.

"I don't think my mom knew about his — activities." The break-ins. "After the TV incident I spent most of my time after school with him in his wood shop, his 'straight' career. School didn't really do much for me, but I loved the shop." He went to the refrigerator for an O'Douls. "You want one?"

"No thanks." She touched the edge of her plate. "These really are gorgeous. The sheen almost looks like the glaze on a donut. Tell me about your sister."

He set the bottle on the table and sat down. "Well, she was my little sister — "

Was?

" — She died. A car accident."

Joanna felt a flush rising from her neck. "I'm sorry. I didn't know." She thought of her grandmother. She knew what he must be feeling.

"No. It's all right. It was a while ago. She was in high school."

He hesitated as he spoke, and Joanna caught a hint of something familiar. Yes. She understood.

"You blamed yourself, didn't you?" she asked.

He looked up in surprise. "I guess I did. How did you know?"

"It's natural. But I bet you weren't anywhere near."

"Not near, but I should have been. I was supposed to be keeping an eye on her while my mom was at work, but instead I was at my uncle's shop." He fidgeted with the bottle cap. "She shouldn't have been alone."

Her throat began to close. She wanted to tell him. Take a risk, came Apple's voice. You've got to do it. "I know how you feel. My grandmother died in a car accident, too. When I was a girl."

"Tell me about it."

"I don't know, I —"

"It's hard to talk about, isn't it?"

A hundred images flashed in her brain. "Yes," she said finally. "The accident was my fault." There. Now it was out.

"Your fault," he repeated. "But you said you were little."

"I was. But she wouldn't have died if not for me."

"Tell me," he said. Just as he had that night at the Reel M'Inn, he leaned forward and focused his gaze on her. He was listening.

But where to begin? She remembered weeks when her mother would lay in bed, staring, unseeing, at the ceiling. Her father was long gone. When the county social worker drove her to her grandmother's, Joanna hadn't said a word. She sat in the backseat and focused on tracing a perfect circle in the fog left by her breath on the window.

"When I was a kid, I went to live with my grandparents." Everything was different there. After a while, she had come out of her shell. She made up funny songs and sang them while she and her grandmother picked blackberries early in the morning, before the summer heat set.

"One day…one day I was in the backseat of my grandmother's car." An old orange Datsun, tiny compared to most of the cars on the road then. "We were driving into town, and I was chattering nonstop about something. We were on a winding, two-lane highway. You couldn't always see well coming through the canyon." Her throat tightened. "My grandmother was concentrating on driving, but I wanted her to see something I'd drawn. She kept saying, 'Just a minute, honey,' but I didn't listen. Finally I pulled her shoulder back."

The logging truck had struck the driver's side of the car, hurling the Datsun against the shale embankment, where it flipped on its back in the road. Her grandmother's scream against crunching metal haunted her sleep for years. It was half an hour before an ambulance arrived. The logging truck's driver had pulled her from the wreckage and set her in the cab of his barely damaged truck. She was bruised and had a lump on the side of her head, but was otherwise unhurt. "Close your eyes," he'd said again and again. "Close your eyes. Don't open them."

"It was my fault," she repeated. "She died."

Paul slid his hand across the table, palm up. "I'm sorry," he said simply.

Surprised even as she did it, she rested her hand in his. His callused thumb touched the side of her palm. His dog jumped down from her chair and stared up at them — or more likely, their plates. Feeling self conscious, she withdrew her hand and picked up a jojo.

"Did you hear about Don Cayle from Mary's Club?" Paul asked.

"Uh huh." She took unusual pains arranging the chicken on her plate.

"He was murdered."

"That's what I heard."

He picked up his fork and set it down again. "What aren't you telling me?"

She avoided his eyes. "I don't know what you're talking about."

"I just asked you about Don Cayle's murder, and you don't want to talk about it. What's up?"

The emotional energy in the room had taken yet another turn. The chicken in her mouth turned to cardboard, but she continued chewing, then swallowed. "I told you that I'd heard about it. I'm not sure what else there is to say."

He started nodding, but ended by shaking his head. "You're not satisfied, are you, about Marnie's death? And now Don." He nodded toward the locked, empty suitcase now sitting next to the table. "What's the deal with the suitcase? And I see that you're dressed with a little more restraint than usual. All black."

Joanna continued to avoid looking straight at him. "It's not exactly the time for cheerful dress, is it? As for the suitcase, I just happened to notice when I was taking a few things to Apple's that it was locked shut. I thought maybe you could pick the lock for me."

He pushed his chair back and folded his arms. "Why are you taking things to Apple's?"

Uh oh. She was getting in deeper. "Well, my house was broken into the day before yesterday."

"Your house was broken into." He tapped his finger on the table a few times. "You're up to something, aren't you? You're not a very good liar. You want to pick a lock, and you hoped maybe I could show you. You don't need the suitcase at all. That's the truth, isn't it?"

Frustration piled on top of the emotion of the last few weeks set off a wave of anger. "What if it is true?" Her voice rose. "What's it to you?"

"Joanna, your store and house were broken into, Marnie was found dead, and Don was shot and killed. I don't know what's going on, but this isn't anything you should be messing around in."

First Apple, now him. Trying to stop her. She stood up. "I want my life back." The force of her voice startled her. The dog sat up, alert.

"Where's your boyfriend, anyway? Why doesn't he talk some sense into you? I didn't see him at the neighborhood hearing, either."

"I don't know what you're talking about." This wasn't going at all the way she'd planned.

Paul barely paused. "Besides, what makes you think you know something the homicide bureau doesn't?"

"Listen. I'm almost positive this whole thing centers on some papers hidden on a boat at Sauvie Island."

"A boat?" He shook his head. "So you thought you would sneak down there tonight. In a dress, no less." Then, more emphatically, "Don't do it. It isn't worth it."

She refused to look at him. She was too upset to talk. What was she thinking, telling him about her grandmother? She sat down again, but turned her head away.

He leaned back and took a breath. "Look, I'm sorry. None of this is any of my business. I guess, well, with my sister and everything I didn't want to see someone else get hurt." His voice had softened, and he pushed aside his plate. "Remember how I told you about my uncle, the one in prison for burglary?"

She nodded but still wouldn't raise her head.

"He and Don did a job together in the early 1960s. When all this came up—Marnie, your store—I went to talk to him." He paused. "Are you listening?"

She nodded again.

"In the old days, Mary's Club had a gambling room in the back. Not legal. Don worked with some local mobsters to get things set up, and I'm sure he paid a few policemen to look the other way, too. One night he arranged to have Uncle Gene break in and steal a couple of days' haul. My uncle got his cut, and the rest went into Marnie's bank account—at least, temporarily. Don told his partner in the mob that the money was stolen. I'm not sure if they believed him, but they couldn't prove otherwise." Paul rose and carried his plate to the sink. "I think it finally caught up with him."

He had Joanna's complete attention now. "But why wait so long? That was over forty years ago."

"I can't say, unless it has to do with Marnie. She knew she was dying. She might have put pressure on Don for some of the payout. When he refused, she told his old partners."

Joanna's brow furrowed. "It's a good story, but it doesn't make sense. No. Someone warned me off of looking for 'papers.' Some kind of papers were in Franklin's safe deposit box, and he took them out and hid them. Someone wants them." She looked straight at Paul. "Really badly."

"What do you mean by 'papers'?"

"I'm not sure. Not yet."

"Did you try telling Crisp? He'd be the one to care. If there's something on this boat you're talking about, let the detective deal with it."

Paul's dog got down from the chair and sat next to Joanna, eyeing her plate.

Joanna took a deep breath and released it slowly. "I know you're right. I've been trying to get out of this mess since it started, and it seems like I just keep getting in deeper."

"Call the police. Call them now. It's still early evening, you should be able to get someone on the phone. Tell them about your suspicions and let them look into it."

"I really don't think it would do any good. Every time I've tried to talk to the detective about the key, he shoots holes through my theories. He doesn't care what I have to say. Besides, I can't call right now, I don't have a cell phone."

Paul picked up his cell phone from the kitchen counter and put it on the table next to her. "It's just one call. The worst he can do is hang up on you. They should be following up on this, not you."

She sighed. She didn't like being bullied, and was tempted to tell Paul to shut up. At the same time, he had a point. She wiped her fingers and reached for the phone. He watched her. She took the phone to the corner of the shop, away from him, and punched in the detective's phone number from his business card. He never seemed to answer his phone anyway. Just when she was mentally preparing a message for his voice mail he picked up.

"Detective Crisp."

"Uh, yes, this is Joanna Hayworth."

"Yes." The detective certainly didn't encourage a lot of conversation.

"I didn't think you'd answer."

"I'm here now."

Well, okay. "Yes, remember when we went to the safe deposit box?"

"I do."

"Remember how the bank officer said that Franklin Pursell had visited the box not long ago? I think he took some important papers from the box before he died. I think the papers are on his boat, and—"

The detective cut her off. "Ms. Hayworth, we found Cayle's murderer."

"You did?" She turned to face Paul's direction. He was feeding a jojo to his dog.

"A few hours ago we brought in Nina Kim, and she's confessed."

Joanna gasped. "What? Nina?"

"That's what I said. She's downtown right now. So, if you don't mind, I have work to do." The detective hung up.

Stunned, Joanna continued to hold the phone to her ear. She finally pressed "end" and crossed the room to Paul. "They found out who killed Don. It was Nina, an old friend of Marnie's. Nina killed Don. She confessed." She sat down.

"So you don't have anything to worry about. You're safe now."

"Yes," she said uncertainly. She remembered the sickly odor at Don's house and now recognized it as Nina's Jungle Gardenia mixed with heat and blood. Nina had done it. Nina killed Don. She should have known. And yet...

"Yes, but what?"

"She couldn't have broken into my place. Even if she killed Don then burned rubber on the way to my house, she wouldn't have had time to break in and search it. I had seen her at the store less than an hour before I went to Don's. She couldn't have done it then. It doesn't make sense."

Paul stood up. "Joanna, listen to me. It's over."

"I don't know, something doesn't seem right." She rose and paced the workshop floor, leaving a trail of footprints in the sawdust.

He lifted his hands. "It's over. Let it alone."

His fingers encircled each of her shoulders. She reached up and put her hands against his chest in reflex. His skin was warm under the tee shirt. He looked down at her, and she caught her breath. She grabbed a fistful of his tee shirt and pulled him toward her until their mouths met.

The kiss was long and full, and his mouth tasted like champagne. The electricity she'd felt earlier now trembled through her to the bone. She slid her arms around his back and pulled him closer. Then stopped.

It was too much all at once.

She pushed him away. "Let go of me." Her voice came out more loudly than she'd expected. Tears burned at her eyes as she reached for her purse. "Goodbye."

The suitcase lay, forgotten, on the workbench.

Chapter 35

Joanna sat in the car in front of her house and forced herself to breathe more slowly.

The detective said Nina killed Don. But that didn't necessarily mean she killed Marnie. And what about carving the threat in her wall? Nina wouldn't break into her house, arrive smiling at Tallulah's Closet to sell clothes, then head off to shoot Don. No. And what about Franklin? What could Franklin's papers have to do with her?

Nina had once admitted to Joanna that lots of people thought she wanted Marnie dead. Joanna gritted her teeth in frustration. If only she could talk to Nina, she'd know for sure. She looked at the house. Pepper stared at her from the front window. It would be so nice to walk in, drop her purse on a chair, and settle in for the evening, but she couldn't. Not yet, anyway. She started the car. The detective had said they were holding Nina downtown.

The streets near the police station were quiet this early Saturday evening, and for once parking was easy. Central Precinct was in a new, six-floor office building with the jail's gym at the top. Rumor had it that women would sit in the park across the street and gaze at the top of the police building in the hopes of seeing a loved one on the treadmills.

In contrast to the more lax neighborhood precinct where Joanna had visited Officer Riggs, reception at Central was forbidding. Joanna passed through a metal detector and had her purse searched before reaching a uniformed policeman at a desk.

"I'd like to see Nina Kim, please. She was just brought in."

"Nope." The officer scratched his buzz cut with a pen. "Visiting hours are over."

"It's not to visit. It has to do with her case. It's important," Joanna pleaded.

The officer raised an eyebrow. "Detective send you?"

"Yes. Detective Crisp." A white lie. But if he knew how important this was, he would have asked her to come.

The officer picked up the phone. Sun-faded photos of the mayor and the police chief hung above the plastic ficus next to his desk.

"He's not answering. You say he asked you to come?"

She nodded.

"All right. Go up to the fifth floor." He waved her to the bank of elevators.

Upstairs, the elevator opened into a small foyer with a few chairs. She went to the counter. On the other side of a sheet of bulletproof glass, a harried-looking woman rose from her desk. Behind her lay a warren of cubicles, and offices lined the perimeter. Joanna wondered if they were interrogation rooms, or if that only happened on TV.

"Joanna Hayworth. I'd like to see Detective Crisp, please."

The woman rolled her eyes. "He never tells me when people are coming. He's expecting you?"

The fewer lies she told the better. Rather than say yes or no, she smiled.

"Have a seat."

She turned to the plastic chairs near the elevator. She was almost in to see Nina. Maybe Nina had already confessed to the other murders and explained about the key. If not—if she weren't responsible—she'd tell Joanna. She knew it. Just a few minutes of conversation and her questions would be answered.

The elevator opened, and two uniformed policemen got out. "You Hayworth?" the meatier one asked. She nodded. He hooked an elbow under her arm and lifted. The other officer hooked her other arm.

"What are you doing?" She flailed for her purse, and the meaty officer stuffed it under his arm.

"You're outta here. No one's expecting you—Crisp's busy. And don't think you can try it again next shift. We have your face on the computer downstairs." In the elevator, they kept a firm hold on her arms.

"I just wanted to ask one thing, that's all. It has to do with a murder," she said. "Don't you care?"

"Not so much," one of the policemen answered. "And we have telephones here, you know."

"I tried to call, but he wouldn't let me finish."

"There you go," the policeman said.

"Can I at least have my purse back?"

The elevator dinged to the lobby. The policemen handed over her purse and pushed her out. The door closed. Joanna rubbed her upper arms and turned to see the guard she'd talked to when she arrived standing, arms folded in front of his chest. He nodded toward the front door, and Joanna took the hint.

On the street, she leaned against the cement wall separating the sidewalk from the plaza above and sighed. Great. Now what was she going to do?

A hummingbird zipped down from the plantings on the plaza to the park across the street and disappeared into the shrubbery. There on a park bench next to that shrubbery sat Nina's husband, Gary.

"Gary!" She ran across the street, narrowly missing being hit by a bus pulling away from the curb. She caught her breath as she neared his bench. "Remember me? From Marnie's memorial service?"

He turned his head away. "I don't want to talk now."

She sat down next to him. Her voice was gentle. "I heard about Nina. That's why I'm here. I came to see her."

He didn't respond for a moment, then asked, "They let you in?"

"No."

"Me neither. Her own husband. They said they'd talk to me later."

Her eyes softened with compassion. Her problems were nothing compared to Gary's. "Do you — do you know why she did it?"

"Nina is a good person." He looked small. Joanna waited for him to add more. "She loved Don. I thought that was over, but I guess not. She told me she'd heard something about Don and went to see him. He wouldn't talk to her, then someone else came, a woman. She knew Don kept a gun. So she…" His voice faded.

A woman. That would be her. "But how —"

"I thought it was over a long time ago. Why did she go see him? She told me it was over after the baby, after she…" This time anguish choked off his voice.

The story began to gel. "Did Nina get pregnant by Don? Then have a — a procedure?"

Gary nodded without looking up.

Shit. "And she wasn't able to get pregnant again?" Abortion wouldn't have been legal that many years ago. Lord knew where or how it was carried out.

He nodded again. When Joanna had hinted that Don might be

Troy's father, Nina had been furious. She must have thought Marnie had kept Don's baby, a baby she could never have. Joanna glanced at the impassive facade of the police headquarters. For all her pain, Nina didn't kill Marnie or Franklin. She didn't care about the safe deposit box.

Gary's body wracked with sobs next to her. It was all Joanna's fault. Don had died for nothing. She remembered him lying on the kitchen floor, his shirt soaked with blood. If she hadn't said anything to Nina, maybe he'd still be alive, and Nina would be home.

"Gary." His gaze met hers briefly then dropped to his hands. "I'm more sorry than you can know."

Whatever the hell was going on, it had to stop. She would get those papers and find the murderer if it were the last thing she did.

Chapter 36

The sun lowered in the sky. Sauvie Island was only seven miles from downtown Portland but felt much further. Farms and pasture dotted the island, and a few well-to-do Portlanders had built custom mansions with views of the river. She drove with her windows open. Now that summer was near its end, the evening air was cool. The Corolla's engine knocked and hissed every few minutes, but seemed to be driving all right. She'd call the mechanic in the morning.

She crossed the bridge onto the island and drove west along the canal separating the mainland from the island. She pulled into the parking lot of a convenience store to ask where to find the marina.

Standing near the cashier with a box of breath mints was Andrew. He wore the black, Italian-cut suit she knew he kept for special events.

"Joanna. What are you doing here? Are you all right?"

"Sure, I'm fine." Odd that he'd ask. "I'm going to visit a friend, that's all."

"I didn't know you had friends out here."

"Well, I do. I just wanted to check where his houseboat is moored." She emphasized the "his." "Anyway, what are you doing here?"

"Another fundraiser for Remmick. You know the founder of Yoga Heart dotcom? He has a spread just down the road past the marina. Should be an interesting crowd. Vegan hors d'oeuvres."

She made a face. "Well, I'd better go." She turned toward the cashier. "I don't want to be late."

"All right. Well, have fun."

She heard the purr of his BMW a minute later as it left the lot. The cashier drew a crude map to the marina. She took it back to the car and set it on the passenger's seat. Old Blue's starter whined once and then twice but wouldn't turn over. The third time she turned the key, she heard nothing at all. Damn. She was so close. The marina wasn't far by car, but at least half an hour by foot. It was getting dark, too. She tried the ignition once more, and this time the Corolla reluctantly sputtered to life.

She crept down the road atop the dike. Whenever she tried to shift above second gear, the car jolted in protest. After an excruciating few miles, she saw a line of boats — mostly houseboats but some fishing and cruising boats — moored on the canal below the road as the cashier had said. The outlet road to the marina led down to a small, unlit gravel parking lot. As she shut off the engine, it emitted an ominously final bang, shaking the entire car. She smelled burning oil and groaned. After she checked out the marina, she'd find a pay phone and call a tow truck. Old Blue wouldn't make it back to town under her own power.

A mercury light affixed to a power pole partway down the marina buzzed to life as night fell. Traffic hummed faintly along the two-lane St. Helens highway on the mainland. Otherwise, it was quiet.

She strode across the parking lot and stepped gingerly onto the wooden pier. The water flowed deep and heavy below her. Windows glowed pale yellow in a few of the houseboats, and one man sat on his deck facing the canal, the tip of his cigarette a bright speck of orange. She moved confidently, as if she belonged.

If Franklin still had the boat she'd seen in Nina's photos, it would be wooden and big enough for a bed, but not too large. She wished she'd thought to bring a flashlight. The canal was almost black now, reflecting waves of fuzzy light from the lamp down the pier.

About two-thirds of the way up the marina was moored a wooden boat that fit the bill. She knelt to read its prow. "Goldilocks," it said in chipped black paint on a green background. Bingo.

Was that a car slowing on the road above the dike? No, nothing but the lapping of water against the pier. She stood up, then stepped gently onto the boat. She paused and again looked toward the parking lot. No one could see her.

At the front of the boat, pointed toward the canal, was a windowed cabin. A coil of rope sat on the deck next to a bucket, but otherwise the deck was clear. She pulled down the door handle. Locked, of course. She looked around the perimeter of the cabin. This was the only way in. Too bad she hadn't got that lock picking lesson.

One of the windows toward the rear of the cabin didn't close as tightly as the others. She pried her fingernails under the window, which was designed to open out, and it gave a fraction of an inch before the latch stopped it. A nail file would have been perfect to slip in the crack to open the window's latch, but she didn't have one. Apple's necklace clanked against the boat as she leaned forward. Yes. She lifted the Hand of Fatima pendant over her head then slid its thin edge through the window. It easily flipped the latch, and the window opened.

Although she could now reach inside, it was too small to crawl through and too far from the door to reach the inside handle. She could, however, reach through and unlatch the window closest to the door. Once that window was open — its latch stuck for a moment—she slid her arm into the cabin up to her shoulder and unlocked and opened the cabin door.

Inside the cabin she stood listening. Besides faraway sounds—something dropping in the water, maybe, and the honking of an early flock of geese headed south—the night was still. She shut the windows.

At the front of the cabin was a steering wheel and a swivel seat. The smell of damp canvas and mildew permeated the cabin. In the thin moonlight she made out a wooden dash dotted with chromium-rimmed gauges, some of the chrome flaked off and the gauges cloudy. On the far side was a bench whose padded lid looked like it might lift for storage underneath. It didn't have a lock. Joanna raised it. Nothing but a pair of rubber boots, a rain slicker, and a gas can. Nothing else in the main cabin would hold papers.

At the rear of the cabin, a door led down into the boat's hold. She paused a moment, her fingers on its handle. It wasn't too late to go back to her car. She could call a tow truck, and within an hour she'd be sitting in Apple's living room drinking chamomile tea. Joanna remembered the torn piece of dress left under her windshield. She couldn't return to Apple's. She had to find the papers.

She opened the door. Again, she regretted not bringing a flashlight. From the scant light shining through two portholes she made out a bed, larger than a single but not quite a double, straight ahead. A bed where Marnie had spent time so many years ago. On both sides of the small hold were storage benches like the one in the cabin above. She ducked her head and felt her way down the stairs. To the right, next to the bottom of the stairs was a bathroom, its door ajar. It was barely large enough to hold a person. To the left of the stairs was a door to what looked like a storage area under the cabin.

One of the benches was fastened with a small padlock running through a metal latch. Her necklace wasn't going to be able to open this one. She set her purse at the foot of the bench, then lifted the seat and tugged. The metal latch gave a little in the old wood it was screwed to. Maybe the necklace would work after all.

She slid the edge of the pendant into the cross-hatched head of one of the screws attaching the latch to the top of the bench and turned. The pendant's soft silver bent, but with a few minute's work she had removed the latch's first screw. She swiftly undid the other and lifted the bench's seat.

Inside was a worn manila envelope with its flap open. Her breath quickened as she slid out the papers. It was too dark to make out what they said, but the papers were yellowed at the top and had been fingered through many times. This must be what Franklin had taken from the safe deposit box. Had to be. Relief flooded over her. Now to get out of there.

Just then, the boat rocked slightly. A wave on the canal? Maybe a boat was passing by. The deck above her creaked. No, someone was definitely on the boat. She hadn't thought to lock the cabin behind her. Heart racing, she placed the envelope back into the bench and silently closed the lid. She moved lightly across the room and flattened her back against the wall next to the stairs.

The cabin's outside door opened above her, and a man's shadow fell across the entrance to the hold. Her body vibrated with adrenalin. The person came down the stairs and stood inches from her at the entrance to the hold, the only way out of the boat. Screaming would do no good, but if the stranger took one more step, she could throw her body forward and maybe knock him down.

"Joanna?" a voice said tentatively from the stairs.

Paul. "What are you doing here?" She almost cried with relief.

He stepped into the hold. "I tried to call you. I felt bad about the way we left things. You weren't answering your phone, then I remembered you were staying with Apple. I had a hunch you might come here."

"So you followed me?" Her voice was louder than she'd intended.

"Hush. Come on, we'll talk about it later. Let's get out of here."

"Wait, though. Look what I found." She lifted the bench's seat. "Remember how I told you Franklin had hidden some papers? This must be them." She held the envelope and slid out its contents. "They don't look like any legal documents I've ever seen, but they're old, and obviously some sort of record." She held it closer to the porthole's light and flipped through the pages. "They're covered with handwriting. Strange. Mostly names and dates."

"Great. We'll look at them later. Let's leave."

The boat rocked again. They looked at each other. Joanna dropped the papers back in the bench, and Paul grabbed her arm. He opened the door to the bathroom and pulled her in, closing it behind them. The room was barely large enough for both of them. He bent over her, his arms around her waist, leaning against the wall separating the bathroom from the stairs to the cabin above. Neither of them could stand straight. Her arms hung at her sides, but her face was pressed against his neck. His pulse throbbed.

She wondered if someone had seen Paul come on to the boat. A security officer, maybe. Her breath was ragged. If that was so, why didn't he say so? Her back began to ache from the strain of bending. As if reading her mind, Paul slid his other arm behind the small of her back, letting her lean against him. His mouth was near her ear. She smelled skin and sawdust.

Footsteps descended the stairs from the cabin. Despite the lack of light, whoever it was moved quickly, if unevenly. The stranger paused at the bottom of the stairs, and a thin beam of light passed under the edge of the bathroom door. The steps moved forward and paused again. A man's voice said, "What?" and the lid to the bench creaked as it lifted.

Then came the sharp sound of the door to the storage area under the cabin as it was thrust open. He knew someone was on the boat and was looking for her. Paul reached over to hold the door handle just as the stranger tried the door. She closed her eyes.

As suddenly as it started, the pressure on the door handle stopped and the boat rocked side to side. Could someone else, again, have come on the boat?

"Who's there?" the man in the hull with them called out. The uneven steps she'd heard made sense now. It was Ray. He clearly hadn't expected this last visitor.

Quick, sure footsteps descended the stairs. "Hello Ray. It's been a long time, hey?"

With a start, she recognized the congressman's voice. She looked up at Paul but couldn't see his face in the dark.

"What do you want?" Ray asked.

"Something Franklin left for me. Something I was supposed to have a long time ago. Well, well. This, right here." Paper rustled. "I see you were looking for the same thing. I suppose you think you're going to save the tribe."

Remmick's voice was closer now. He must be standing in front of the stairs going up to the cabin. Ray would be toward the bed. Did Remmick have a gun?

"Did you kill my brother?"

The question hung in the air for a few seconds.

"He fell. Didn't you read the papers? It's dangerous to be walking around a half-finished building at night. Too easy to slip on something and take a tumble. But, if I did, I would have had reason to. He was blackmailing me."

She was convinced Ray knew she was on the boat. He couldn't know Paul was there. Would Ray give her away? Paul's neck muffled her gasp. Her purse. She had left the Cordé wrist clutch on the floor next to the bench. It was dark in the boat. It's possible that no one would see it. Paul turned his head down to her and she mouthed the word "purse" into his shirt.

"I know what happened that day," Ray said. His voice was calm. "When you and Franklin came home to take the tribal rolls. Franklin wrote it all in his tribal history. He left it to me when he died. He said Auntie came in and found you on your way out. She tried to get the rolls away from you."

Feet shifted and wood creaked as someone sat on the padded bench.

"So she fell," Remmick said. "She'd been drinking—nothing new there. She was old. When I wouldn't hand the papers over to her she hit me with a lamp. I bled like a son of a bitch. Did your brother put that in his book? Of course I was going to push her away. You'd have thought that damned coat would have softened the fall. We laid her out on the coat and tried to revive her. It's not my fault she didn't make it."

The congressman's voice had been as calm as Ray's. Now it leapt in pitch. "I don't see why you would complain. How many members of the tribe are left, anyway? A couple dozen? It's not like Franklin didn't get his cut."

"But you broke your promise. Franklin said the land would stay untouched, that the tribe could still use it. And now you're letting them turn it into some kind of golf resort."

Remmick's voice took on an actor's quality, like he was giving a speech. "What you don't understand is that sometimes the good of a few people has to be sacrificed for the good of others. It's my job to make sure people in this country have work and that the economy continues to grow, not to see that a few Indians get their hands on land that they haven't properly owned in years."

The bench creaked again. "Franklin didn't appreciate that, and I see that you don't either," Remmick continued. "He was supposed to have destroyed the papers. That was our deal. He gets the documents from your aunt showing continual tribal governance, he gets rid of them, and we get a little compensation from Bowman Timber to make things easier for everyone. I didn't think he'd keep them and try to blackmail me later. For the good of everyone, these papers need to be destroyed. I think you understand that, Ray."

Remmick must have the envelope now. Would he leave?

"What about Marnie? What did she have to do with all this?" Ray asked.

"Marnie's death was damned inconvenient, but it wasn't my fault. Franklin told me the rolls were in a safe deposit box and that he'd hidden the key somewhere I'd never find it. It didn't take too much persuading for the sentimental bastard to tell me where it was, once he thought I was on board with him. A few days later, I paid Marnie a visit. She didn't have the key. Didn't even know what I was talking about. She told me she sold the coat to some old clothing store, and we were on our way there when she had a heart attack."

Clever Franklin, Joanna thought. He had moved the papers by then. And he left the whole story in his tribal history for Ray to discover.

"You could have just left her, then called 911."

"Couldn't do that. Couldn't be found with an ex-stripper. Anyway, it was easy enough to wait until I could get to the store myself and kill two birds with one stone. So to speak."

With disgust, Joanna wondered how long he sat with Marnie's body in the car next to him. She tried to twist her head to ease the strain on her neck, but there wasn't room. Paul, at least four inches taller and much broader shouldered, had to feel it worse.

"And now you're here," Ray said.

"It didn't take me too long to figure out — as you did — he'd taken the papers somewhere else. Thanks to a chance encounter and the loyalty of one of my staff, I figured out they were here. Which reminds me, I don't have time to stand around forever."

Too many seconds seemed to pass. If Andrew had told Remmick she was on the island, he might have guessed her story about visiting a friend was a lie. She prayed Ray wouldn't even cast a glance at the bathroom door. She clung to Paul with a crazy hope a squad of police would arrive or Ray would break out some jujitsu moves.

The congressman's voice cut the silence. "You haven't started carrying a purse, have you?"

The door to the latrine abruptly flung open from the outside. She looked up to see Remmick's face contorted in fury. He slammed the door shut just as Paul was reaching out. The door clicked with a chilling finality. Of course the boat would have doors that locked from the outside to keep them closed on choppy water.

"Goodbye, Ray." A gunshot exploded the silence, and Joanna's whole body jumped. Footsteps flew up the stairs behind her to the cabin, paused, then came partly down the stairs, then back up to the deck again. She smelled diesel. They were trapped.

Without speaking, Paul felt in her hair and extracted two bobby pins. In the cramped space of the latrine he bent forward, crushing her head against the wall. She felt his hands doing something with the bobby pins in the scant space behind her thighs. The keys in his front pocket pressed into her hip. He stood slightly, and the doorknob rattled as he used the bent bobby pins on the lock.

The door popped open. Thank God. The smell of smoke and boat fuel filled the room, and Joanna struggled to breathe.

"The boat's on fire—get out. I'll take care of this guy," Paul said. "I'll help."

Ray lay unconscious against the bench. Her foot touched her purse, and she slid it over her wrist, then grabbed his feet. Paul took his shoulders. They pulled him to the fuel-slicked stairs to the cabin. She coughed and pushed open the door to the sight of fire snaking across the deck.

"Come on." Paul dragged Ray up the stairs to the cabin. The fire caught the cabin's wood trim and raced around it, igniting the door frame. "Hurry!"

She coughed and pushed Ray through the door, catching her shoulder on the door jamb and searing her upper arm. The biting smoke burned her eyes, but on the dock at last she gulped fresh air.

Paul knelt over Ray. "He's breathing." He took off his tee shirt and pressed it against the wound on Ray's chest. "The bastard was going to leave us to die."

She felt the heat as orange flames tipped with black smoke enveloped the boat, leaping higher by the second. People from the surrounding houseboats surged onto the dock. One was on his phone. There was no sign of Remmick, and thanks to the Corolla's demise, no way to go after him.

She paced anxiously. "He's going to destroy those papers. I have to go find him." The roar of the fire nearly obscured her words.

"No. You're crazy. You're staying here." Paul's voice was firm. He bent over Ray's body, one hand on the blood-soaked tee shirt, and another on the wooden pier.

Joanna stood behind him. She looked up toward the parking lot through the black smoke of the burning boat, then again at Paul. "Give me your keys."

"No way."

It was her only chance. She kicked the back of his calf, and when he straightened to grab it, she plunged her hand into his front pocket, looped her fingers through his key ring, and pulled. A siren sounded in the distance.

"I have to go." She stumbled backwards, then righted herself and ran up the dock.

"Joanna, wait," Paul yelled, but she kept running.

Chapter 37

Paul's truck was parked next to her Corolla. Joanna fumbled with the keys in the door, then hoisted herself onto the truck's solid bench seat. The seat was pushed back to accommodate Paul's height, and she had to stretch her legs to reach the pedals. The truck lurched forward and kicked up gravel as she accelerated out of the parking lot.

The congressman would almost certainly have returned to the Yoga Heart fundraiser. Andrew said the mansion was beyond the marina. She peered up darkened driveways she passed looking for a mass of cars. A few miles up was a side road marked by a large yin-yang sign. She slowed the truck — its clutch was stiff — and turned. The house appeared around a bend. Fully lit windows illuminated the night, and sitar music wafted across the parking area. A security guard in a black uniform stopped her as she pulled up.

"Are you on the guest list, ma'am?" He looked doubtful. She realized her hair was falling down and she smelled of smoke. The raw pink burn on her shoulder was starting to swell.

"It's an emergency. Will you call Andrew, the congressman's chief of staff?"

While the guard radioed the house, Joanna descended from the truck and checked her face in her compact. Not pretty. She fished in her purse for a tissue to wipe her forehead. Reflected in the mirror she saw Andrew stroll toward her from the house past the congress-man's black Lincoln.

"What are you doing here? You have a black mark on your face. A couple of them, actually. Where's your friend? The one you were visiting?"

The security guard, satisfied Joanna was legit, walked away. "I'll tell you later. Right now there's someone I need to see." She strode to the house with Andrew following.

A six-foot statue of Buddha faced her as she entered the front hall. A mixture of sandalwood incense and fruity alcohol permeated the room.

"Lotus Martini?" a waiter asked.

"No, thank you." To the right a hall led to what she suspected were bedrooms. Straight ahead, beyond the Buddha, was the entrance to the kitchen — at least, that's where the waiter came from. To her left spread a spacious, high-ceilinged room where guests gath-ered. Hundreds of votive candles lit the room — they flickered from tables, shelves, and even the floor. Large cushions covered in pink and orange raw silk were strewn next to low tables holding vases of orchids and the dead ends of cocktails. A woman in a lurex leotard demonstrated the warrior pose on a platform in the room's center. The room opened onto a patio with a fire pit, its flames through the plate glass windows reminding her of the fire she just left. Inky forest spread beyond the patio.

Andrew came up behind her. "Joanna, what are you doing here?"

She ignored his question. "Where's Remmick?"

"He has business in Washington he's had to deal with off and on all evening. I think he's in the library." Andrew nodded toward a door across the main room. "Why?" He moved in front of her. "Look,

Jo, don't go in there."

She pushed him aside and started across the room.

Hand on the doorknob, she took a calming breath. She twisted the handle and pushed. The library could have been pulled straight from a Manhattan high rise. Instead of the bright Indian colors of the main room, this room was all polished steel and black leather. A plasma screen television stretched along one wall across from a leather sectional. An image of Gandhi floated, twisted, and dispersed across the screen of a computer on another wall. Despite being called a library, only a few books rested on the glass coffee table in front of the couch. A closed French door connected to the patio. Muffled sitar music and voices drifted in from outside.

Remmick sat in a high-backed chair at the desk with the tribal papers scattered in front of him and an open scotch bottle and half-empty tumbler at his side. His reading glasses perched on his nose. When he heard the door open he swiveled to face Joanna. He looked at her for a full five seconds, surprise turning to fury. God, how the burn on her shoulder throbbed. She pressed her palm against it.

Remmick said, "Get out."

"No. I came to get the papers."

"I don't have anything that belongs to you. Leave. Now."

If she didn't get those papers, where would she be? It would be her word against Remmick's—a trusted congressman—that he killed anyone. And Ray might never regain consciousness.

The library door opened and the security guard she had talked to outside entered. "Is everything all right in here, congressman?"

The guard was here. A witness.

"I have important phone calls to make, and this woman is harassing me. Escort her to her car and make sure she leaves."

"Wait," Joanna said. Flattery. Talk to his ego. "I understand. I heard you back there. You want to save jobs, do something good for the economy. Your record shows that. That's why you'll be our senator."

Remmick's gaze stayed fastened on Joanna, but it softened slightly. The desk lamp cast dark shadows under his eyes. The guard backed off from Joanna but hovered near the door.

"I just wanted to tell you that you can have it both ways, Mr. Remmick. Why not toss the tribe a bone? Make them partners with Bowman Industries? You've done so much good for the state. You can't help what happened. You were just unlucky."

He slumped into the chair. "Unlucky," he muttered. "If that damned Indian didn't keep his end of the deal, I'd never have had to — " He pushed the whiskey glass away and gathered the papers in one sweep. Rage returned. "None of this has anything to do with you. Get out now."

The congressman's wife, Laura, appeared at the door. "There you are, Charles." Puzzled, she looked at Joanna then again at the congressman. "Have you been drinking?"

"Hold on," Joanna said as the guard took her arm. "Ask him why his pants are torn." After years of working in vintage clothing, she could spot a moth hole or a ripped seam from across the room. The tear must have come from the sharp-edged latch on the bench in the boat.

"Ask him about those papers," she said. "He's been down at the marina, that's where he got them. He's killed for them. He murdered Franklin Pursell and hid the death of Marnie Evans." She was running out of breath. She suspected that she sounded like a lunatic. The guard's hand on her arm tightened to a bruising grip.

Remmick shook his head. "Look at you." His confidence regained, he spoke calmly. "You need help, but I'm afraid you won't find it here. And I've been in the library mostly all evening, haven't I?" He looked at Laura, then put his arm around her.

Laura drew back.

"Haven't I?" he repeated.

"Marnie," Laura said, almost to herself. She backed up a few steps and looked at the floor. "No, Charles. I tried to find you an hour ago, and you weren't here. The car wasn't here, either." Her voice quavered.

He looked at Laura as if she were a stranger. His voice took on a cold edge. "I had something I needed to do. It didn't concern you."

"You didn't kill her, did you? Tell me you didn't kill Marnie," Laura said.

"She doesn't know what she's saying."

Bewildered, the guard loosened his grip. Remmick, still holding the tribal papers, strode to the patio door and opened it. Joanna tore free of the guard and ran after him. The people around the fire pit smiled and a few rose to meet Remmick, but he ignored them and tossed the papers into the flames. The blowing heat caught some and torched them orange and then brown and scattered others over the patio. She grabbed frantically at the loose papers.

The congressman lifted a poker resting in the fire. "Put them down." He pointed the poker at Joanna. "Give them to me."

"Someone stop him!" she said.

"They don't let us carry guns," the guard whimpered.

The tip of the poker was white hot fading to orange. She retreated until her back flattened against the cool glass of the main room's window. A reflection off the windows of the dining room showed the woman demonstrating yoga poses now in downward dog.

"Give me the papers. Now." The congressman spoke so quietly only she could hear. She smelled the whiskey on his breath.

Probably ten people stood and watched, but no one moved. "Chill, dude," one of the guests said.

"Stay put," Remmick told the wide-eyed guests. "I've got this under control."

Joanna's breath was shallow and ragged. He's lost it, she thought. He's completely lost it. Andrew stood at the edge of the crowd. She looked at him beseechingly. Surely he would help her.

He looked troubled, but kept his distance. "I can't."

Remmick smirked. "Who do you think broke into your house? He knows where you hide your spare key. And how do you think I found you at the marina? Nice lead on the tribal rolls."

She shivered at the chill in his voice. The fingers of one of her hands slipped toward the zipper on her wrist clutch behind her. In her other hand, she held tight to the papers she had saved, fearing her sweaty palms had obliterated their writing.

"Now give me the papers."

She needed just a few more seconds. "You know you can't get away with this. Ray is still alive." She hoped this was true. "He'll tell everything." Digging past the lipstick, past her coin purse, her fingers found what they sought. Now, if she could get it in the right position. "It's too late. You may as well just give up."

"It's too late for you, you mean." Remmick raised the poker to her neck. Her hand, clutching the vial of Tabac Blond, shot to his face and pressed the atomizer.

Remmick dropped the poker and staggered back, holding his eyes. The leather and vanilla perfume mingled with the scent of wood smoke. She slid from the wall. Poised to run, with the forest at her back, she darted from the congressman.

A motion in the living room caught her attention. Two policemen stood in the window.

Chapter 38

Joanna and Paul leaned over a table at Tallulah's Closet. The Lanvin coat lay splayed open between them. Joanna took a pair of scissors and sliced up the middle of the lining.

"If I'm right, we should see the stain," she said as she cut. "The lining is definitely newer than the coat, and it makes sense Franklin would have had the old one replaced, especially if it was bled on."

She peeled the lining back on both sides. A large, dark brown mark shaped like Australia spread across the top half of the coat.

"Sure enough, you're right," Paul said.

"It's got to be Remmick's blood. And the aunt's. Isn't it funny that evidence against Remmick was here all along?"

Paul leaned back and pulled from the bottle of non-alcoholic beer he'd brought. "Marnie probably never even knew the key was in the coat the whole time she had it."

"When Franklin gave her the coat, he must have thought he and Marnie would always be together, and he'd always be able to get to it. Even after he married someone else, they still saw each other. Witness Troy." She pointed to his bottle. "Hey, do you have another of those?"

"Right here." Paul handed her a bottle from his bag.

She twisted off the cap and drew a swig. "Ugh. Foul." She pressed the cold bottle against the bandage on her shoulder.

"Yep."

"Anyway, I doubt Marnie wore the coat at all. It's too big for her and not really her style. She kept it only because of Franklin, I'm sure."

The bell at the door jangled. A woman stuck her head in. "Are you open?"

"Not officially, but come in," Joanna said.

The woman went to a rack with a few pairs of 1980s boots hanging from it and looked at the tags. "These are so Studio 51," she said.

"Studio 54?" Joanna said.

"Or Area 51," Paul said.

Joanna sipped again from the O'Douls and grimaced. When she got home, she'd have a proper Martini.

"I went to see Ray today at the hospital," Paul said. "He has a nasty lump on the side of his head, and he broke a rib when he fell, but he should be all right. I don't think we did him any favors by dragging him out of the boat the way we did."

"It was better than leaving him in there."

"Marnie's son was at the hospital, too, calling him 'Uncle Ray' and asking a lot of questions about the tribe. He really seems to be into getting to know his new family. He even wants to help Ray reopen the tribe's case for recognition."

"It must have been Ray who broke into the store the second time and stole the coat. Had to have been."

"He said he wants to tell you he's sorry in person."

"He doesn't have to. I'm just glad to hear he's going to be all right." She'd bring Ray something decent to eat tomorrow. He must be hating that hospital food.

The woman who was shopping had moved to a circular display of skirts and was flipping through them.

"He asked about Nina," Paul said.

"It's not looking good for her." Nina was out on bail but ordered not to leave her house until her trial.

Paul set his drained bottle on the display table next to the coat. "Joanna, when everything settles down, do you want to, you know, have dinner or something? I won't ask again. I just thought that after everything—"

She felt heat spread over her face. She couldn't look up at him. "I don't know."

"All right." He stood up and turned to walk to the door.

"I mean, yes."

Their eyes met. She drew in a breath. He said, "You know how to get in touch with me." He walked by the front window and out of sight.

The shopper, who by now was near the back of the store, held up a blue slip. "How much is this? I don't see a price on it."

Joanna turned her head toward the shopper. "Hmm?" She absently drew the tip of Paul's bottle across her lips.

Acknowledgements

Many of the places in *The Lanvin Murders* are real, but what happens in the novel is entirely fictional. At the top of these locations is the model for Tallulah's Closet, Portland's The Xtabay, a top-drawer vintage boutique where I've spent many hours as both an employee and a shopper. With a bedroll and a camp stove, I could happily move in full time.

Although I avoided naming the tribe in the novel, it could stand in for a number of Native American tribes in the Pacific Northwest which go without federal recognition as legitimate nations. They have rich histories and have endured discrimination and indignity we might think never takes place in the United States. Think again.

Crafting good, smart, trashy reading isn't a solitary venture. I have many, many people to thank for helping me smack *The Lanvin Murders* into shape. Chiefly, I'd like to thank my writing group: Christine Finlayson, Doug Levin, Dave Lewis, Ann Littlewood, and Marilyn McFarlane. I'm grateful for your patience, advice, and tolerance for descriptions of vintage accessories.

Thank you, too, to the dozen or so readers of early drafts. You were all invaluable in helping me bring the novel from idea to finished manuscript, and I couldn't have done it without you.

Yet more thanks to Wes Youssi at M80 Branding for the cover and interior designer Eric Lancaster.

For monthly updates on vintage living à la Tallulah's Closet and information on the series, subscribe to my newsletter at www.angelamsanders.com.

CPSIA information can be obtained
at www.ICGtesting.com
Printed in the USA
FSOW01n1753271215
14753FS